THE GUARDIAN'S GAMBIT

JR Konkol

The author grants the final approval for this literary material.

Second printing

This is a work of fiction. Names, characters, businesses, places, events, and incidents are either the products of the author's imagination or used in a fictitious manner. Any resemblance to actual persons, living or dead, or actual events is purely coincidental.

Printed in the United States of America
Suggested Retail Price (SRP) $22.95

The Guardian's Gambit is printed in Baskerville

Kelly,

It isn't enough. How can it ever be? Not a day passes where I don't think of the trials you faced... the horrible cards you were dealt. You worked so damn hard, but at every turn, you faced nothing but hurdles and complications. Eventually, you got too exhausted to keep jumping those hurdles, but you never stopped trying.

Hopefully, you can live on here.

In this fantasy world, with the cats you loved so dearly.

Watching from afar as they explore new worlds, and appreciating how they remember you.

Love, Jeff

THE GUARDIAN'S GAMBIT

1.
EIGHT LIVES

The nameless kitten wove in and out of the wooden railing. Both hoomans seemed angry with him for doing so, but it was fun. Besides, neither was paying attention. One was in the other room, looking at a screen, massaging her fingers against the thin rectangle that felt so good to sit on. The other was downstairs, making loud, but pleasant noises on the giant wooden box with the black and white teeth.

None of the other cats were watching either. The only one that didn't hate him was the big brown one. The other two hissed and growled whenever they saw him. The nameless kitten wasn't used to big cats. He got to spend a little time with his mom, but he spent the rest of his time with other nameless kittens.

Why didn't his mommy name him?

The nameless kitten's back paw slipped against the polished wood. He swished his tail to recover his balance, but it wasn't enough. His heart sank as first one paw, and then another lost contact with the railing. He desperately tried to sink his front claws into the wood, but it was too tough to dig into.

The nameless kitten purred as he fell. He didn't know what else to do. He didn't know how long a fall it was. There were too many stairs to count, and he needed to leap to climb each one. It was probably a long way down.

He coughed as his tiny ribs shattered. The wind left his little lungs, and his vision faded to darkness.

• • • • •

"Oh, no!" shouted the man playing the wooden box. "Please be okay," he said from much closer. A moment later, rough hands gently stroked the nameless kitten's fur. Deft fingers carefully pressed beneath his chin, slowly raising his head.

The hooman peered down at the kitten and asked, "Are you alright, little guy?"

The nameless kitten wasn't sure. He felt funny. He was resting on his belly, right where he landed. His paws felt numb, but he was still purring. Nothing hurt. In fact, the hooman's hands felt nice against his fur.

"I told you to be careful, Chairman!" said the man sternly. "Don't walk on the outside of the railing."

"Is everything alright?" called the other hooman from the top of the stairs.

"I think so. He fell, but he seems alright."

"Oh my god," she cried. "Don't scare me like that, Chairman!"

They kept using that word, 'Chairman'. The nameless kitten didn't know what it meant. Were they trying to name him? Only cats could name other cats, everyone knew that, but why else were they constantly using that strange word when talking to him?

"I'm going to give him some time," said the man. He leaned in and kissed the kitten on the forehead. "He seems fine, but I want to be sure. We'll take him to the vet if we need to."

And then the man returned to his loud wooden box, with the wide row of black and white teeth. The nameless kitten rested on the carpeted landing as sound rang out from the wooden box. He glanced up the stairs and sighed. Climbing back upstairs would be exhausting.

He smelled the approaching brown cat before he saw him. The brown cat's golden eyes seemed to flash blue for a moment as he climbed the short set of stairs and joined the kitten on the landing. "You need to be more careful with your lives if you want to stay here," said the enormous cat with a shake of his head.

The nameless kitten's whiskers drooped, and he sighed. "I'm sorry," he whispered.

"It's okay, little guy," said the big brown cat. "It happens to all of us. You still have eight left. Just be more careful with the rest."

"Okay," breathed the kitten.

"My name is Ajax. What's your name, little guy?"

The kitten placed his chin on his paws. "I don't have a name."

"Your momma never named you?"

"No."

"You came from a Kitanja farm, didn't you?"

The nameless kitten looked up at the enormous brown cat, appreciating the darker sections of fur stretching out from his muzzle. "I don't know what that means."

"It's a place where hoomans make little Kitanja, like you. Most Truepaws come from Kitanja farms. It's nothing to be ashamed of. Most cats come out of those places without a name," said Ajax.

"What about you?" asked the kitten. "Did your momma give you a name?"

Ajax shook his head.

"How did you get your name then?" asked the kitten. He pushed his paws into the carpet and flexed his claws. The numbness was fading.

"A Cah'ten Ra named me."

The nameless kitten cocked his head to the side. "What does that mean?"

Ajax flattened out on his belly so that he was face to face with the kitten. "One thing at a time, little Kitanja. This family of cats has a leader… a Cah'ten Ra. His name is Gaius. He can name you."

"The hoomans keep calling me Chairman," said the kitten. "Will that be my name?"

Ajax shook his head. "We avoid using hooman names. They can't stick to one. One day, you'll be Chairman. The next day, you'll be kitten-monster, or stinker, or cutie-pie."

"Which one is Gaius?" asked the kitten. "The one with the stripe on his nose, or the scary one."

"The scary one, I guess," said Ajax. "But don't worry about him. He can be difficult, but he's a good cat. You need to understand, he's under a lot of pressure. This place… it's important."

"But he hisses at me," said the kitten. "So does the other one."

"Loki's just shy," said Ajax. "He'd never hurt you, but Gaius will throw paws if you catch him at the wrong time. He's a Spiritchaser, He sees into many worlds. Sometimes, it sets him on edge."

The kitten climbed to his feet and stretched. He didn't know what any of it meant, but he appreciated Ajax making the effort. "Thanks, Ajax. Thanks for talking to me."

The big brown cat leaned in and nuzzled him. "I remember what it was like when I was just a Kitanja. It was weeks before any of the cats accepted me. Actually, Gaius was the one who finally took me in and guided me by the paw. He taught me what it meant to be a Cah'ten, how to enter the Dreaming, and so much more."

"Will you teach me?" asked the kitten, a glimmer of hope in his voice.

Ajax nodded. "Of course, little Kitanja."

The nameless kitten couldn't contain his purring. "When do we start?"

Ajax climbed to his feet, towering over the kitten. "Follow me into the kitchen, little guy," he said as he deftly padded past the kitten, descending the handful of stairs, before entering a bright room with a cool wooden floor.

The nameless kitten followed, tumbling down the stairs to keep up with the large brown cat. Once he was on the floor, it was easier. He followed Ajax until they approached several plates of food.

"Our hoomans are pretty good at keeping these full," said Ajax, nodding toward the plates. "The dry stuff stays good for a while, but the wet stuff dries out after a day or so. Sometimes you have to meow a few times at the hoomans before they figure it out."

The kitten nodded. He sampled some food from each plate earlier in the day. He preferred the special plates the hoomans set out just for him, but maybe that would stop now that they released him from the small room.

"But the good stuff is in that big silver box over there," said Ajax. "That's where the hoomans keep their food. Some of it is horrible, but a lot of it is amazing." Ajax licked his chops. "And seeing as you're a cute little Kitanja, it's time we teach you how to beg for treats. Hoomans are suckers for Kitanja."

"But how do I get their attention?" asked the kitten.

Ajax briefly wiggled his butt before leaping up onto the counter. How did a cat that big jump so high? The counter must have been at least ten kittens tall! Ajax looked down at the kitten and winked. A moment later, he began meowing at the top of his lungs.

The hooman stopped banging on the large wooden box. "What is it now, Alex?" he grumbled. "I already fed you."

Between meows, Ajax tossed a conspiratorial glace down at the kitten.

"Alright, alright, I'm coming," said the hooman as he approached. He glanced down at the nameless kitten and shook his head. "Alex…are you teaching the Chairman how to beg?"

"Damn straight," said Ajax.

"Can he understand you?" asked the kitten.

Ajax shook his head.

The hooman pulled a handle, and the front of the big metal box swung open, revealing bottles, containers, and a large plate of meat. "You seemed to like this last night," said the hooman as he retrieved the plate of meat and set it on the counter next to Ajax. He ripped off a piece of meat and placed it next to the big brown cat. "You want some too?" asked the hooman as he tossed a piece on the floor.

"Score!" cheered Ajax. "This is the good stuff, little guy."

The nameless kitten sniffed the meat. It smelled like heaven. The kitten quickly wolfed it down, savoring the strips of dark meat and endless pockets of fat. "Wow," breathed the kitten in between frantic purrs. He stood on his back paws and tugged at the hooman's pants.

"Looks like you like brisket, Chairman," he said as he tossed a couple of pieces of delicious meat onto the floor.

Ajax leapt down from the counter, landing a few inches from the kitten. "What did I tell you?" he purred. "Sometimes, hooman food is simply glorious."

The kitten tore into the pieces of meat, barely pausing to chew or even breathe. When he was done, he faced the hooman and meowed, "More brisket! I summon brisket," but his voice was too soft. Desperate to get more meat, he forced his purrs from his body, almost like tiny coughs.

"Okay, Chairman, okay," said the hooman as he dropped several large pieces on the ground. "You keep eating like this and you'll fill your kitten growth battery in no time."

The kitten shot Ajax a quizzical look before tucking into his food.

"Both hoomans here know more about cats than most," said Ajax. "He's talking about your belly, and he's not wrong. Once that tummy of yours swells to the size of a ball of yarn, you'll grow. It happens while you sleep. When you wake up, your belly shrinks back to normal, but the rest of you grows."

The kitten looked at the brown cat and licked his chops. "Really?"

"Kitanja are magical creatures. All Cah'ten are, really," said Ajax with a nod. "It takes a lot of magic to grow a little Kitanja like you into a giant Cah'ten like me. The kitten growth battery is one piece of the puzzle."

"Will I grow up to be as big as you?" asked the kitten.

Ajax flopped over on his side and smiled. "Hard to say, little guy, but it's possible. You have big paws and a really long tail."

The nameless kitten swished his tail back and forth. He slowly spun in a circle, trying to catch it.

"Speaking of long tails, don't flaunt your tail in front of Loki."

"He's the one with the stripe on his nose, right?"

Ajax nodded. "Poor guy has a short tail. He's sensitive about it."

The kitten spun faster. He was so close to catching his tail, but it always seemed one step ahead of him. Tired and dizzy, he flopped down onto the cool wooden floor. "I ate too much. I think I'm going to be sick."

"That'll happen," said Ajax. "But probably not for a few months. As a Kitanja, you can eat all the time. Don't worry, though, we'll teach you about throwing up. There is definitely a right and wrong way to do it."

The nameless kitten smiled at his new best friend. There was so much to learn, but as long as he was careful with his eight remaining lives, there was plenty of time to learn it.

2.
CAH'TEN COURT

The nameless kitten looked at the assembled cats and shuddered. Ajax was the only cat with an upright tail. Loki's tail was twisted behind his legs, displaying his discomfort. Gaius' tail was swishing behind him. He was annoyed, or worse.

"You asked for this Court, Ajax, so get on with it," said Gaius from his chair. The cats sat on chairs with bright red pillows. The kitten was the only one on the floor. "I fear you're wasting my time."

Ajax shot the kitten a reassuring glance. "I know we were all mad the day the hoomans brought this new Kitanja into our house, but I think it's time we recognize this for the blessing it is."

"How can you call that thing a blessing?" grumbled Loki. "The hoomans let him out of the napping room just yesterday, and he's already lost a life."

"We all make mistakes," said Ajax.

The nameless kitten sighed. He hoped the other cats wouldn't find out about his fall.

Loki snorted. "If you ask me, I think the hoomans made a mistake buying this Kitanja."

"Maybe, maybe not, but he's here now," said Ajax. "Besides, ever since losing Thor, we've struggled to keep up. Another Cah'ten will do us good."

"Are you questioning my leadership?" snapped Gaius.

"No, Cah'ten Ra," said Ajax, bowing his head slightly. "Thor was a Truepaw Norsk Skogkatt, descended from Freya's own. His loss would cripple any clowder, even a great one such as this."

Gaius nodded. "While I won't deny our need, I doubt this Kitanja is the answer. Truth be told, I was planning to petition for aid at the next Cah'ten Moot."

"That's more than a month away," said Ajax. "Why don't we work with the Kitanja in the meantime? He is a Truepaw Ragdoll, the same as the rest of us. The great spirits of the far east flow through his veins."

"You mean he is a Truepaw like me and Loki," said Gaius. "I'm not so sure about you, golden eyes."

"Yeah, really," mumbled Loki. "I've never heard of a Truepaw Ragdoll with golden eyes."

Ajax climbed to his feet and rolled his neck, his tail twitching side to side. "Say what you want about my lineage, but don't question the Kitanja's. His markings are as clear as yours, Cah'ten Ra, and the blue in his eyes runs deep."

"Very well, Ajax." Gaius lazily licked his paw and brushed it across the side of his face. "How do you propose we… work with this little Kitanja?"

Ajax sat back down on the red pillow. He was so large, his tail and back paws spilled out over the side of the black wooden chair. "He's too young to have heard his Calling yet, but nothing is stopping us from teaching him about our Callings."

"Do you seriously expect me to teach him the ways of a Spiritchaser?" hissed Gaius. "He's already lost one life. Most Spiritchasers sacrifice several to the Endless Tide while learning to swim."

The nameless kitten rested his head against the wooden floor. He wanted to be as small as possible. He didn't understand what the other cats were talking about, but he didn't like the sound of it.

"The Kitanja can start his training with me," said Ajax. "Whatever his calling, paw-to-paw combat skills will come in handy."

"He's a little small to be a Guardian, don't you think?" said Loki.

Ajax regarded the cat with the striped nose. "The Kitanja has a glorious tail. There's a chance he may grow to be as large as me one day."

Loki tucked his tail between his legs and sighed. "He does have a long tail, doesn't he?"

Loki's tail was certainly short, but the kitten thought Loki's color patterns made his tail seem shorter than it actually was. His fur grew noticeably darker a few inches down his tail. From a distance, it was easy to mistake the lighter section of Loki's tail for part of his body.

"Alright, Ajax," said Gaius after a long pause. "You may start training the Kitanja, if that's what you want to do, but are you sure it's in his best interests? Not every Cah'ten is meant for the Dreaming. Maybe he'd be better off living as Housen."

"He's a Truepaw," said Ajax. "His tail is long, and his eyes shine like sapphires." Ajax swished his tail in agitation. "He's no house cat."

Gaius yawned. "Very well, Ajax. You are charged with introducing this Kitanja to the Dreaming. Teach him how to fight while you're at it."

The big brown cat bowed his head. "Thank you, Cah'ten Ra."

"When he understands the ways of the Guardian, and after you're satisfied with his ability to enter and leave the Dreaming, Loki can begin teaching him the ways of the Wildseeker."

"Oh, come on, you know I work alone," whined Loki. He flashed the kitten an angry glance. "Besides, I don't trust him. He looks shifty. Dangerous, even."

The unnamed kitten covered his eyes with his paws. He was a good kitty. Why was Loki saying bad things about him?

"That's going too far!" growled Ajax. The kitten shifted one paw so he could watch. Ajax leapt from his chair, landing a foot from Loki's. He rose up on his back paws, towering over the smaller cat, despite the chair. "I remember when you were just a clueless Kitanja. Did I ever say mean things about you? No, I didn't!" Ajax swatted Loki's striped nose. "I thought I raised you better than that."

"Ajax!" snapped Gaius. "Stand down!"

"Fine," huffed the big brown cat as he backed away from Loki. "But I'm telling you… this is some foul litter."

Gaius sighed. "When Ajax is satisfied with the Kitanja's ability to enter and leave the Dreaming, the little one will be taught the ways of a Wildseeker. Am I making myself perfectly clear, Loki?"

"Yeah, fine… whatever," said Loki. "So, what happens after that? Are you going to teach him about being a Spiritchaser?"

"I haven't decided yet."

"Oh, I see how it is," said Loki. "Me and Ajax have to teach the little Kitanja, but you're not willing to get your paws dirty."

"You don't understand," said Gaius.

"Oh, I understand plenty. You're okay telling us what to do, as long as it doesn't apply to you." Loki shook his head. "That's some fine leadership."

"Silence!" hissed Gaius.

The kitten slowly climbed to his feet. "Excuse me," he said softly. "I'm not trying to cause trouble. If Loki doesn't want to teach me, I understand."

Gaius jumped from his chair and padded over to the kitten. He took a deep breath before speaking. "Try to understand, little Kitanja, that this conflict… It really isn't about you."

"It sounds like it's about me."

"You'll understand in time," said Gaius. "For now, your job is to learn what the other Cah'ten teach you. There is so much you don't know." Gaius leaned down and licked the kitten's nose. "I don't envy you, little one."

"What about giving him a name?" asked Ajax.

Gaius shook his head. "It's too soon. We should wait until after he's heard his Calling, but I'm curious. What do the hoomans call him?"

"Chairman," said the kitten. "They call me Chairman Meow."

"Interesting," said Gaius. "They probably named you after Mao Tse Tung."

"Meow say what?" asked Loki.

"Mao Tse Tung was a famous dictator," explained Gaius. "These hoomans seem to enjoy naming cats after dictators. They named me Genghis Khan, and our big brown friend is Alexander the Great."

"Yeah, well, they didn't name me after a dictator," said Loki.

"I'm not so sure," said Gaius. "I think they named you Justin as a tribute to the current leader of the frozen county, north of here."

Ajax padded over to the kitten and nuzzled him. "Sorry, little guy, but you're going to have to wait for your name."

"It's okay. I understand," sighed the kitten.

Gaius looked up at the ceiling and meowed an alarm.

"What is it?" asked Loki.

"The hooman is returning from her run. She'll be here soon," said Gaius. "Scatter. Find places to nap. Loki, I want you to sit next to the least satisfactory plate of food. As soon as the hooman sees you, push it away and stare at her."

"Alright, I'm on it."

"How do you know the hooman is coming?" asked the kitten.

"The spirits told me."

"He's a Spiritchaser," said Ajax. "He can do a lot of things. I'll tell you all about it, but for now, come with me. There is a nice patch of sun in the other room. We'll share it."

"Okay," chirped the kitten. Everything was so overwhelming, but it intrigued him. He didn't understand Spiritchasers, Wildseekers, Guardians, or the Dreaming, but he wanted to learn.

3.
BATTLE AND BRISKET

The nameless kitten sprang at the big brown cat. If he stretched his arms as wide as possible, he could just barely get them around Ajax's neck. The trick was timing things right. This time, like most of the times before, he failed to grab a hold of the massive cat. A moment later, he crashed to the soft carpet.

"That was pretty good," said Ajax. "You almost got me, little guy."

The kitten suspected Ajax was humoring him, but he liked the encouragement. Climbing to his feet, he turned sideways, arched his back, and hopped at the enormous brown cat.

Ajax laughed. "Oh no, not the kitten war dance!"

The kitten didn't like being teased. He'd show Ajax! Hopping to get into range, he tried to swat the giant cat, but with his legs rigid and locked, all he managed to do was flail and fall. Hoping to save face, the kitten rolled to his back and reached up, trying to grab Ajax's whiskers.

"Oh, no, you don't, little guy," said the big brown cat as he thrust his face against the kitten's belly. Instead of biting, Ajax frantically licked the kitten.

"Stop," giggled the kitten. "Stop, that tickles!"

Ajax pressed his muzzle against the kitten's belly and blew before pulling back. "If you keep kitten-hopping and rolling to your back, I'll keep zerberting you. How else are you going to learn?"

"But you're so much bigger than me," pouted the kitten. "How am I supposed to attack you?"

"How about climbing on my back?" said Ajax as he flattened himself out against the carpet. "Give it a try."

The nameless kitten jumped up onto the brown cat's back. He placed a paw on either side of Ajax's neck and gently extended his claws.

"There you go!" cheered Ajax.

The kitten considered biting Ajax, but his mouth was too small to bite anything other than the ears. Instead, he licked the back of Ajax's neck. Turnabout was fair play! If Ajax insisted on cleaning him, the kitten planned to return the favor.

Ajax purred and turned his head. "Get that patch of fur on the left side… Yeah, right there. That's what I'm talking about."

The kitten cleaned Ajax for a few moments before leaping from his back. "How much longer do I have to practice today?" he asked. It felt like he trained with Ajax for hours already.

"We can take a break, but not a long one," said the big brown cat. "You have a lot to learn."

"Why do I need to learn this, anyway?" asked the kitten. He understood the value of honing his hunting skills, but he planned to hunt mice, chipmunks, birds, and other small prey. The thought of attacking something larger than himself, like Ajax, made little sense.

"You need to learn how to defend yourself," said Ajax.

"What, from chipmunks?"

"There are things a lot worse than chipmunks out there, little guy." Ajax looked away for a moment. When he looked back, his expression was serious. "Gaius tasked me with teaching you about the Dreaming. Now seems like as good a time as any to talk about it."

The nameless kitten curled up in a ball, yawned, and faced Ajax. The kitten's legs were sore from all the hopping and pouncing, but as much as he wanted to nap, he knew now wasn't the time. Ajax's ears and whiskers were pricked forward, and his eyes were wide. What he was about to say was important.

"I'm not sure where to start, so I guess I'll just come out and say it," said the big brown cat. "This place we're in… this house, with all its rooms. The back yard, with the giant trees. Even the lands that Loki patrols, the endless woods beyond the fence…" Ajax brought his muzzle close to the kitten. "It's only a part of what's really here. There is another world that shares the same space, and for the most part, the same shape."

The kitten cocked his head to the side. What was Ajax talking about? The kitten's hearing was sharp. Surely, he would have heard this other world by now. Even if he didn't hear it, he certainly would have smelled it.

"It's a special place. We call it the Dreaming," said Ajax. "Everything you see here exists in the Dreaming, but it's all different. The Dreaming is a place of spirits, magic, and horrible nightmares. It's a beautiful place, but it can be terribly dangerous."

"Then why go there?"

"I'll get to that part later," said the Ajax.

"How do you get to the Dreaming?" asked the kitten. He wasn't sure he believed Ajax, but he was enjoying the story.

"By napping," said Ajax. "Most cats never learn to enter the Dreaming, but those that do, enter it when they nap. That's why it's called the Dreaming."

The kitten often wondered why all the cats in this house slept so much. Perhaps they were off chasing chipmunks in the Dreaming. The thought of chasing tiny furry vermin in a magical land excited him so much his tail twitched. "Will I be able to go there? You said most cats never learn how."

Ajax nodded. "Most cats live in pampered places. The Dreaming is barely strong enough to tickle a whisker in those areas, but in some places… like this house, the Dreaming is vibrant and strong."

"So, how do I get there?"

"Relax, little Kitanja," said Ajax. "I'll teach you how to go there, but not until you're ready. Like I said before, the Dreaming can be a dangerous place, even if you're just visiting. We need to work on your moves a bit before we go. Maybe after you improve your pouncing."

The nameless kitten sighed. He was too tired for more pouncing practice. "Do you think we can get something to eat first?"

"Sure," said Ajax, climbing to his feet. "Meet me in the kitchen. I'll summon the hooman. You can beg him for brisket, like you did the other day."

The kitten sprung to his feet with newfound energy. He loved brisket. He dreamed of how the salty meat and creamy fat tickled his tongue. Wasting no time, he raced into the kitchen, passing Ajax along the way.

The big brown cat shouted and meowed in the hallway, and it wasn't long before the hooman man came stomping down the stairs. The woman seemed to nap during the day, while the man napped at night. The kitten didn't understand why they slept at different times. It was probably some stupid hooman custom.

"What is it now, Alex?" grumbled the man. "There's plenty of food on your plates." The big brown cat strolled into the kitchen and the man followed. "Oh, I get it. You and the Chairman are begging for brisket again."

"Summon brisket!" chirped the kitten between a cacophony of purrs. "I cast, Summon Brisket!"

"Whoa," breathed Ajax. "What just happened?"

The man opened the front of the big metal box. He reached inside, retrieved the plate carrying the precious brisket, and set it on the counter. "Not a lot left, but you cats can have it," said the man. Curiously, he pressed a button, and another silver door opened, this time beneath the counter. There was an empty white box behind the door. He placed the plate in the strange box before slamming the door shut.

"What's he doing?" asked the kitten. "I want my brisket!"

"Don't worry about it, little guy," said Ajax. "You're going to like this."

The hooman pressed a few buttons, and the box hummed. It beeped several seconds later, and the man removed the plate of brisket. It smelled so much better now. The nameless kitten curled around the man's feet. "Give me a moment to cut it," said the man.

After what felt like an eternity, the man placed several large hunks of steaming meat on the floor. The strange humming box must have somehow heated the meat, which was really cool, but the kitten didn't have time to dwell on the mysteries of the magical box. There was brisket to eat!

The first few bites were like heaven. Cold brisket was good, but this was simply amazing. The temperature was just right, and the juices exploded against the kitten's tongue with each bite. He wolfed down the first two pieces without even breathing. When he finally took a break, he noticed Ajax sitting a few feet away from him with a smile on his muzzle.

"I had a few bites, but I saved the rest of mine for you, little guy," said the big brown cat. "But do that again."

"Do what?"

"That summon brisket thing," said Ajax. "Whatever you did, right before the hooman opened the big silver box."

The kitten licked his chops and quieted his frantic purring long enough to blurt out, "I cast, Summon Brisket!"

"Here, have mine," said Ajax.

The nameless kitten peered at the big brown cat. "But you already said I could have yours."

Ajax cocked his head to the side. "You're right," he said. "That's strange."

The hooman scraped a few more scraps of meat from the plate and dropped them on the ground next to the kitten. "That's all I've got, Chairman, but you know what?" he said, running a hand through his long hair. "Brisket is still on sale over at Woodies, and it sure seems like a hit around here. I'll go out and buy another. Might be a day before I manage to smoke it, but there'll be more brisket, soon enough."

"Did that just happen?" asked Ajax as he watched the hooman leave the kitchen. "Maybe I've been hitting the catnip too hard lately."

"What's catnip?"

"Nip is a lot of fun, little guy," said the big brown cat. "In fact, we'll use some to help you get into the Dreaming." Ajax nodded his head toward a squat glass table on the far side of the dining room. "The hoomans are pretty good about putting fresh catnip out on that table, every day or so."

"But what is it?"

"Don't worry. I'll show you," said Ajax. "But right now, I'm trying to understand what just happened."

"You told me to do what I did before, and I did it," said the kitten. "I summoned brisket."

"Right, I get that, but something happened here." Ajax paused to clean his paw. "This wasn't ordinary begging. The hooman said he was going to go out and buy another brisket for you. That's not normal, little guy."

The kitten grinned. "It should be. I really like brisket. Now there'll be more tasty meats. What's the problem?"

"I don't know if there's a problem or not. I'm just pointing out that it's strange. I think I need to talk to Gaius about it."

"You do that," said the kitten as he padded over to the pile of meat next to Ajax. "I'm going to eat more brisket!"

4.
A PURRPLEXING QUESTION

Ajax aimlessly climbed the carpeted stairs. Something about what happened in the kitchen wasn't adding up. Most hoomans were easy enough to control. All it took was a combination of cuddling and meows, but what the Kitanja did seemed special.

There was a sense of power behind the Kitanja's command. It even affected Ajax. He was planning to give his share to the Kitanja all along, but he felt strangely compelled to respond to the little kitten's demand.

The implications confused Ajax. Cats expressed a wide variety of powers, depending on their Calling. His tremendous size, for instance, was linked to him being a Guardian. Both Gaius and Loki demonstrated a variety of powers, but none of their abilities came even close to directly manipulating a hooman, let alone another cat.

Cats were about consent, after all. Whatever the Kitanja did back there, it didn't feel consensual.

Reaching the top of the stairs, Ajax padded down the long hallway leading to the main bedroom. Along the way, he ducked his head into the primary bathroom, with the oh-so-comfortable tile floor that never seemed to cool. Neither Gaius nor Loki were there, so he continued into the bedroom.

Loki was resting on a pillow at the head of the bed, with Gaius curled up near the foot of the bed. Maureen, the hooman, slept in between the two cats. Loki was gently cradling one of Maureen's hands between his paws. Ajax often found them sleeping in similar positions when they weren't within the Dreaming. It was one way they protected their hoomans.

In truth, Gaius was the one providing real protection. As a Spiritchaser, he frequently interacted with the spirit world, the place he called the Endless Tide. Evil spirits constantly tried to possess the hoomans in this house. Gaius spent much of his time chasing the evil spirits away.

Ajax didn't really understand how it worked, but he didn't think he needed to. Every Cah'ten that entered the Dreaming played an important role. Gaius certainly excelled in his role. Loki, for his part, patrolled the wilds, both in the real world and in the Dreaming. He monitored all animal and spiritual activities in the region, and as far as Ajax could tell, he was good at it.

Ajax was a Guardian, and he was tasked with defending the area. He spent much of his time napping in the backyard. He liked to enter the Dreaming as close to the twin giants as possible. In the Dreaming, their branches connected, high above, forming a gateway of sorts. Spirits seemed drawn to that gateway, and not all of them were friendly.

By sleeping outside, Ajax could respond quickly and aggressively to threats. He was one of the strongest Guardians in the Catsland, but he was by no means powerful enough to best every enemy. Some entities were simply too powerful to tangle with.

Cah'ten needed to enter and exit the Dreaming where their physical bodies slept. By napping outside, beneath the trees, Ajax could quickly escape the Dreaming, should it become necessary. From time to time, one of the hoomans picked him up and moved his sleeping body while he was in the Dreaming. Fortunately, it rarely happened.

Loki yawned. "Hey Ajax, what's going on? Shouldn't you be watching the Kitanja?"

"He's downstairs, eating brisket," said Ajax. "He'll probably nap when he's done. He'll be alright."

"If you say so," said the cat with the striped nose. "The last time we left him on his own, he jumped off a balcony and lost a life."

Ajax didn't need the reminder. "Look, I came up here to talk about the Kitanja. Do you think it's safe to wake the Cah'ten Ra?"

Gaius slowly opened one eye. "I'm awake."

The whole Spiritchaser thing creeped Ajax out. Gaius often slept with one eye open and seemed able to pay attention to the real world and the Endless Tide simultaneously. Occasionally, Ajax even found Gaius sleeping inside the Dreaming. Apparently, a Spiritchaser could enter the Dreaming, and then somehow go to sleep, letting him watch both the Dreaming and the Endless Tide. Just thinking about it made Ajax's head hurt. Two worlds were more than enough for the big brown cat.

"Why have you interrupted my vigilant watch?" asked Gaius.

"Yeah, can't you see I'm holding paws here?" added Loki.

Ajax sighed. The other cats were so damn melodramatic. "I'm concerned about the Kitanja. I think he just expressed one of his powers, and I can't figure out what his Calling is."

"What did he do?" asked Gaius, as he rolled to a sitting position and opened his other eye.

"That's just it," said Ajax. "He didn't really do anything. He said, I cast summon brisket, and the hooman said he'd go out and buy another brisket."

"Jeff loves brisket and other smoked meats," said Gaius. "I fail to see this as an expression of power."

"But it was more than that," said Ajax, shaking his head. "I felt it. I was already planning on sharing my portion with him, but hearing him say those words compelled me to share."

"But what you're describing… that's not something that cats do," said Gaius.

"What about a Conjurepurr?" said Loki. "I'm pretty sure they can do fancy things like that. Conjurepurrs can do just about anything."

"Conjurepurrs are a myth," hissed Gaius.

"Nuh-uh," said Loki.

Gaius rolled his eyes.

"Okay, hypothetically… let's pretend Conjurepurrs exist," said Ajax, observing the Cah'ten Ra for a reaction. "How can we be certain it's our Kitanja's Calling?"

"Fine, I'll play along," sighed Gaius. "We'd need to wait for clearer expressions of his Calling. Convincing a fat hooman to buy another brisket is hardly confirmation. Some of a Conjurepurr's other mythical abilities are more obvious."

"Such as?"

"Purrtection," said Gaius. "I've heard it described as a magical barrier or protective field within the Dreaming."

"Like my Spirit Armor?" asked Ajax.

Gaius shook his head. "No, this is different. Your armor appears around you and only interacts with spirits. As I understand it, Purrtection creates a solid barrier."

"What about Telepurrtation?" asked Loki. "That power sounds neat."

"You see, this is why I know Conjurepurrs are a myth," snapped Gaius. "All of their abilities are based on stupid purr-puns!"

Ajax chuckled. "I have to admit, the little Kitanja was quite… Purrsuasive."

"Oh, good one, Ajax!" cheered Loki.

"Silence!" hissed Gaius.

"Sorry, I couldn't help it."

Gaius leapt from the bed, landing next to Ajax. "At the end of the day, I don't see how this new wrinkle changes your responsibilities. Teach the Kitanja how to fight and teach him how to enter and exit the Dreaming."

"I just thought you might want to hear about what he did," said Ajax.

Gaius' expression softened. "I'm glad you told me, but we need more information. If he builds some kind of protective barrier, or magically moves from one spot to another—"

"It's called Telepurrtation," interjected Loki.

"Don't interrupt me—"

"I was just saying—"

"Silence!" shouted Gaius, holding up a paw.

Ajax did his best to muffle his chuckle. He knew Loki was teasing Gaius. That cat's momma named him well. Loki was quite the trickster.

"Look," said Gaius after taking a deep breath, "one way or another, that Kitanja is going to express his true Calling, and then we'll be able to put this whole Conjurepurr business to rest. Personally, I'm hoping for another Guardian, Wildseeker, or even a Catsassin. Anything but a Spiritchaser will be acceptable."

"Why not a Spiritchaser?" asked Loki. "You seem fine with another Guardian or Wildseeker."

Gaius regarded Loki cooly. "Never in a million naps would an Uhl Cah'ten Ra allow two Spiritchasers to live beneath the same roof. We're too rare, and far too important." Gaius reached up with his back paw and scratched his neck.

"What would they do about it?" asked Loki.

"They'd reassign him to a different house."

"Oh," said Loki. "Well, that wouldn't be so bad."

Gaius swished his tail aggressively. "Do you have any idea what that would do to our hoomans? They love that Kitanja!"

"Oh, I guess so," said Loki.

"Besides, we already do too much for this Catsland," said Gaius. "I have little interest in going through the trouble of training a new Cah'ten, only to have him ripped away from us."

Ajax looked down. He seemed to be the one doing all the training. Even after the other cats worked with the little one, Ajax expected most of the parenting duties would revert to him. It was how it was with Loki. He expected it would be the same with this new Kitanja.

He didn't mind. In fact, he kind of liked the little guy. Ajax hoped the Kitanja wouldn't become a Spiritchaser. He didn't want to give him up.

5.
CATNIP DREAMING

The nameless kitten tried to jump on the glass table, but it was too tall. He got his paws over the top, but he couldn't grab the smooth glass. Ajax sat on top of the table, patiently waiting, but the kitten didn't think there was any way he could join the big brown cat.

"Climb the chair. The one next to the table," said Ajax. "It has a pillow on it. You can use your claws."

The kitten felt like a fool. The solution was right next to him all along. Excited by the prospect of starting his new adventure, the kitten leapt at the chair. His legs were exhausted from trying to climb the table, but he managed to sink his claws into the red pillow on top of the chair and pull himself up. From there, it was just a short hop over to the glass table.

"Good job, little guy," said the big brown cat. "There's probably an important lesson here. Something about working smarter and not harder, but screw that. We're here to talk about catnip!"

The kitten sniffed the closest clump of green leaves. There were piles of the stuff scattered across the glass table. The sharp minty aroma tickled his nostrils, nearly forcing him to sneeze. Deciding he liked it, the kitten licked up a few shredded leaves.

"Be careful, Kitanja," warned Ajax. "This stuff can pack a wallop. It won't take much to get you in the right frame of mind. If you take too much, you might struggle to leave the Dreaming, and we don't want that."

The nameless kitten licked up another clump of catnip. He loved how it made his tongue tingle. He wanted to dive, headfirst, into the largest pile, but he didn't want to make Ajax angry. The large cat seemed serious about the danger of him taking too much. With a sigh, the kitten backed away from the tasty catnip.

"So, your first lesson about catnip is to take it slow," said Ajax. "You might think you're okay to take more, but catnip can have a delayed reaction. If you have too much in one sitting, you might be in for a world of hurt."

"How will I know when I've had enough?"

Ajax shrugged. "It hits you differently every day, and the hoomans buy several blends, some stronger than others. There's really no way to be sure."

The kitten rested his chin on his paws. "So, are you saying I have to sit here and wait, with all this catnip in reach? I don't think that's a good idea."

"Nah, little guy," said Ajax. "Let me show you something." The big brown cat carefully positioned himself above the catnip before flopping onto his side. He rolled around for a few moments before climbing back to his feet. The fur on his left side was completely covered with green speckles of catnip.

"Why'd you do that?"

"Catnip to go, my friend," said Ajax with a grin. "I can walk anywhere I want in the house, snacking on this catnip all day long. Each cat does it a little differently, but I like to load up my fur, find a nice patch of sun, and nap."

The kitten wiggled his butt and swished his tail before springing. He slid along the glass table, plowing through several clumps of catnip. Some of it flew in the air, coating his cheeks and shoulders, but most of it stuck in the fur along his underside.

"We might want to improve your technique, but I guess that works," said the Ajax.

The kitten climbed to his feet, licking a few pieces of catnip from his nose. "What's next?"

"Well, since you're too small to go outside, we're going to enter the Dreaming from inside the house."

"Is it harder that way?"

Ajax shook his head. "Not really. Gaius and Loki usually enter the Dreaming from inside, but I like to be outside when I do it."

"Why?"

"You're going to learn a lot of lessons today, little guy, but I want you to really take this one to heart," said the big brown cat. "You'll be asleep when you enter the Dreaming. Wherever you bed down, that'll be where you enter. When you want to escape the Dreaming, you need to return to your body, you follow?"

The little kitten shook his head. He didn't quite understand.

"In the Dreaming, you'll run around, sometimes traveling miles. You need to understand, your body isn't really moving. Wherever you curled up for your nap, that's where you are. You need to return to your body to get out."

"I think I get it," said the kitten. "I need to enter and leave the Dreaming from the same place."

"Not quite. If someone picks you up and moves you while you're sleeping, you'll need to find your body before leaving the Dreaming. Hoomans tend to pick up sleeping cats and cuddle them. We've tried to communicate how dangerous it is, but for some reason, hoomans never seem to understand."

The kitten thought about Ajax's words and even pictured how it might happen. The hoomans often picked him up and dragged him to a couch or a bed to cuddle. He enjoyed it, but now he wasn't so sure. Maybe he needed to hiss and bite anytime a hooman picked him up to teach them to stop doing it. Then again, he really didn't know how to hiss yet. Gaius was great at it. Maybe he could learn from him.

"So, that's one reason I like to nap outside," said the big brown cat. "The hoomans rarely move me when I'm out there."

The little kitten nodded. "Got it."

"See that nice patch of sunlight over there?" said Ajax, nodding towards an invitingly bright patch of flooring.

"Race ya to it!" chirped the kitten as he tumbled off the glass table. He planned to leap to the ground gracefully, but it didn't quite happen that way. Maybe the catnip was hitting him harder than he expected.

Ajax gently landed next to him and helped him to his feet. Determined to win the race, the kitten initiated his most powerful butt-wiggle, preparing his back legs to sprint at incredible speeds. In the meantime, Ajax calmly walked toward the sunlit section of the floor.

Satisfied with the intensity of his butt-wiggle, the nameless kitten sprinted after the big brown cat. If he were on carpet, his plan might have worked, but the wooden floor wasn't well suited for sprinting kittens. He quickly slipped, tumbling into a tangled mass of whiskers and limbs.

Ajax turned to face the kitten before sitting on the sun-warmed floor. "I 'spose there's another important lesson here. Probably something about the tortoise and the hare, with the slow and steady pace winning the day, but let's not worry about it. Come on over, there's plenty of sunlight for both of us."

Embarrassed and defeated, the nameless kitten carefully climbed to his feet. It didn't take him long to reach Ajax and the sunlit floor. Maybe Ajax was right. Was all that butt wiggling necessary? In the time it took him to get his legs pumping, he could have walked most of the way to his destination. He'd need to think about that later. Right now, he just wanted to bask in the warm sunlight.

"There you go, little Kitanja, snuggle yourself in against my fur," purred the big brown cat. "Get yourself nice and comfortable, and close your eyes."

The kitten did as instructed. Somehow, Ajax's fur felt warmer and even more inviting than normal. Everything was so relaxing. He felt safe, warm, and loved. The kitten purred as he closed his eyes. He wanted this moment to last forever.

"Good," whispered Ajax. "You're probably seeing a golden glow through your eyelids right now. That's the sunlight, but concentrate on that glow. I bet you can see a faint green color seeping in from the sides of it. Nod if you're seeing that."

The kitten nodded. The rich yellow glow was comforting. It reminded him of the warm sun, and even warmer fur of his friend, but he definitely saw the green aura around the edges of his vision.

"You're doing great, Kitanja," said Ajax. "I want you to welcome in that green light. Draw it down from where it's pooled. Let that green light wash across everything. Let me know once you've done that."

The kitten scrunched his nose and tried to force the green aura to expand across his vision, but it didn't work. He was working too hard at it. He needed to slow down and let things happen. Gradually, the green finally began to expand. Once it did, he gently encouraged it, nudging it until it finally stretched all the way across his vision. Satisfied, he gently pressed his head back, nuzzling under the Ajax's chin.

"You're almost there, little one. There's only one thing left to do," purred Ajax. "Open your eyes, Kitanja. Open your eyes…"

The kitten opened his eyes and gasped. Everything about the world was different. If he squinted, he could see through the wooden floor he was resting on. It wasn't light brown anymore, either. It was a mixture of white and yellow. Glancing up, he found the ceiling similarly less solid, but it was mostly grey.

Climbing to his feet, the kitten was surprised to see the faded, see-through bodies of Ajax and him curled up on the floor. His tiny heart pounded in his chest as he backed away from the strange ghostly cats. Did he die? Was this what it was like to be dead?

"Calm down, little guy," soothed Ajax. "Everything is going to be alright. You're in the Dreaming, that's all. Those are our sleeping bodies. They look ghostly because they're in the real world."

The kitten spun around until he found Ajax, or what he assumed was Ajax. The big brown cat was positively enormous. His shoulders were ten or more kittens high, and his body was much broader. His fangs, the tips of which used to peek out beneath his upper lip, were replaced with large tusks. His gleaming claws extended inches from his paws, and they looked to be razor sharp. Most impressively, his eyes shone with smoldering golden light.

"Don't be afraid of my appearance, Kitanja," said Ajax. "In the Dreaming, we take on forms that support our Callings."

The kitten arched his back. He tried to be brave, but he couldn't stop his tail from bushing. Ajax was really scary. It looked like he could tear a kitten apart with a single swipe of his paw!

"I am a Guardian," explained Ajax. "My role is to defend this place, and all who live here, both hooman and Cah'ten. You have nothing to fear from me, Kitanja. In fact, should anything try to harm you, I will be there to protect you."

"Oh, that sounds okay, I guess," said the kitten timidly. "I just feel tiny right now."

"I understand completely," said Ajax as he approached the kitten. He swept his tail off to the side, and the kitten couldn't believe how thick and long it was. Ajax possessed a mighty tail in the real world, but in the Dreaming, it was nearly six feet long! The tail gently circled around the kitten, picked him up, and deftly placed him on Ajax's massive back.

"Hey!" blurted the kitten. He wasn't sure he liked being picked up without permission.

"It will be safer if you ride me, my friend. This is your first trip to the Dreaming," said Ajax.

"That makes sense, I guess."

Ajax turned in a slow circle before facing the glass doors to the backyard. In the Dreaming, veins of silver, that seemed to throb with a pulse, streaked the normally clear panes of glass. "Wow," breathed the kitten.

"Barriers are important in the Dreaming," explained Ajax. "Unlike the real world, you can pass through solid objects in the Dreaming. You may have noticed you can see through the floor. If we wanted to, we could sink through to the basement. If I jumped, we could pass through the ceiling and enter the second story of the house."

"How does it work? I mean, we seem to be standing on the floor. We're not sinking."

"Excellent observation," said Ajax as he approached to within inches of the strangely veined glass doors. "Crossing through physical objects requires thought and intent. The more natural the material, the easier it is to pass through."

"I don't understand."

"This floor is made from hardwoods, and the panes of glass from melted sand. Both are more natural than whatever strange hooman material forms the ceiling, not that passing through the ceiling poses any real challenge. Metals are the only thing I struggle to pass through."

"How do you actually do it? How do I walk through a wall or a window?"

"On this trip, you won't need to worry about it. Give me a moment. I'll Bind you to me." Ajax issued a deep, rumbling purr. Gradually, waves of warm amber light rose from Ajax's rich brown fur. Slowly, the light flowed around the kitten, encasing him in an almost invisible bubble. "There, that should do it."

"What just happened?"

"I've accepted you as my rider for this voyage into the Dreaming. When I pass through an object, you will come with me. You won't fall off my back, no matter how fast I run, or how high I leap, and nothing will hurt you without first hurting me. For the duration of this journey, you are my ward."

"Wow… Neato!" gasped the kitten.

"Well said, Kitanja," said Ajax as he pushed his nose against the silver-veined glass. It shimmered, for just an instant, before rippling like water. A moment later, Ajax stepped through the glass. The kitten felt a little tickle against his whiskers as he passed through, but nothing more than that.

The back yard took his breath away. The kitten was used to seeing it through the windows, and even then, it mystified him, but this was something wonderful and new! Everything seemed to glow, and the colors were amazing and vibrant. The smells were strange to him, but he expected he'd get used to them.

There was a long, curved retaining wall, and each of its stones glowed from within. Most of the stones were varied shades of red, orange, or yellow, but a few of them glowed blue. The kitten wondered if they were hot or dangerous. He didn't feel any heat coming from them.

The ground surrounding the retaining wall featured large patches of foliage. In the real world, the foliage was a bland mixture of greens, but here, glowing oranges and purples were more common. What's more, the kitten saw what looked like pulsing red snakes beneath the orange and purple leaves. He was scared, at first, but then he realized he was seeing the roots and vines that supported the field of foliage.

A forest of broad-leaved plants dominated the terrace above the retaining wall. He overheard the other cats calling them hostas. In the Dreaming, each leaf was a blend of ever-shifting colors. Strangely, the ground beneath the hostas didn't seem to change colors. The kitten surmised the underside of the leaves didn't change colors like the tops. It made little sense to him, but then again, nothing about the Dreaming did.

"It's breathtaking, isn't it?" whispered Ajax.

"It's amazing," breathed the kitten. "How often do you come here?"

"I try to spend six or more hours a day in the Dreaming, mostly in this backyard. I keep watch over the trees," said Ajax. "Do you see where the upper branches connect, there, above the middle of the yard?"

The two enormous oak trees fascinated the kitten. The outside of the bark didn't glow, but all the nooks and crannies pulsed with light. The colors shifted and blended in places, but stuck to cooler tones, like blues and greens.

Studying the trees, the kitten noticed a pattern to the pulsing lights. It looked like they were flowing up from the base of the tree and radiating out across the branches. He followed the pulsing lights until they led them to the spot Ajax was talking about. High above the ground, the two trees touched. He couldn't be sure, but it looked like the branches and tree trunks formed part of a circle. The ground prevented the shape from being completed.

"That's the Abyssinial Gateway, or at least one of them. Gaius said there were nineteen," said Ajax. "You're only seeing part of it. The roots of both trees touch beneath the ground. Between the roots, trunks, and branches, it forms a circle."

"What's an Aby… Abysinsin Gateway do?"

Ajax chuckled. "The Abyssinial Gateways connect various places in the Dreaming. They are named after one of the oldest, most famous breeds of cats."

"What do you mean, connect?" The kitten was worried he was asking too many questions, but if Ajax was growing tired of them, he wasn't showing it.

"I don't pretend to know how they work, but beings can move between the Gateways, stepping through one and appearing outside another."

"Can we do that?"

"No, little Kitanja," said Ajax. "We don't know how. At least, not yet."

The nameless kitten thought the Gateway sounded absolutely fascinating, but then again, everything in the Dreaming fascinated him. To his left, an endless expanse of colorful trees stretched out into the distance. The colors faded as the trees grew farther away from him, until the forest eventually descended into darkness. The kitten didn't know if it was just a trick of his vision. He wondered if the colors continued, and they were just too far away for him to see. Then again, maybe the forest was truly dark. "What's over there, Ajax?" he asked.

"The Forest of Shadows."

The kitten didn't like the name. "What's it like? Have you explored it?"

"I have enough troubles dealing with the things that come out of there. No sense in looking for trouble when my paws are already full. I only enter that forest when I absolutely have to," said Ajax. "If you really want to know more about it, ask Loki. He scouts it often."

The kitten shivered. Something about Ajax's response scared him. If the kitten wasn't sitting on his tail, he might have bushed. He resolved to ask Loki about it, but not anytime soon.

6.
CATNIP NIGHTMARES

Ajax sniffed the air. Many of the crawling denizens within the Forest of Shadows carried the faint scent of spoiled milk. There was a light, favorable breeze. If any of those creatures were sneaking up on them, Ajax should have smelled it. Regrettably, not everything in the Forest of Shadows carried such a distinct odor.

"Is it always day in the Dreaming, or is there night?" asked the inquisitive little kitten.

Ajax was happy the Kitanja was asking so many questions. It made his job easier. "There are four time periods within the Dreaming. Dawn, day, dusk, and dark, but it works differently than in the real world. It's hard to explain."

Ajax leapt up into the hostas, putting some distance between them and the Forest of Shadows. He felt like they were being watched. "Day and night roughly follow along with the real world, but dawn and dusk, the places in between day and night, they last longer. Sometimes for several hours."

"I'm not sure I understand."

Ajax didn't think there was any good way to explain it. The Kitanja needed to experience it. Then he'd understand. "It will all make sense after you've spent more time in the Dreaming." A whiff of acrid air tickled Ajax's nostrils. He padded over to the tree next to the Abyssinial Gateway.

"What's wrong?" asked the kitten.

"Nothing."

"I'm sitting on you," said the kitten. "I can feel the tension in your back and shoulders."

"I think we're being watched," whispered Ajax.

"Who's watching us?" asked the kitten.

"I don't know, but it's something in the Forest of Shadows," breathed Ajax. "Don't worry. It's probably nothing." Ajax faced the forest, studying the tree line. The leaves were rustling more than they should for a light breeze, but Ajax didn't see any silhouettes between the trees.

"What happens if it isn't nothing?"

"Then we fight."

"But I'm just a kitten!"

"Stay on my back, and you'll be fine," said Ajax. His magic would protect the Kitanja. It wasn't a spell he used often. Neither Gaius nor Loki allowed him to protect them with this spell. He didn't blame them. Loki was much faster. The last thing he wanted to do was tie himself to Ajax, and Gaius needed to move freely to call spirits.

"Okay," said the kitten. "You don't have to tell me twice."

A crackle, followed by a faint humming, interrupted their conversation. The kitten dug his claws into Ajax's back. The little guy was probably scared. "Something is using the Gateway," said Ajax.

"Is it safe for us to be here?"

"Yes." They were standing in the safest place Ajax could think of. Things that used the Gateway generally appeared in the middle of the yard. Standing off to the side, near one of the trees, offered them some protection. Most beings that came through the Gateway were ambivalent, or even friendly, but it wasn't always the case.

"How long does the Gateway take?"

"Not long." Ajax waited until the humming faded. "It just finished. Whatever is coming, it should be here any second." Ajax caught a whiff of spoiled milk on the breeze. Nothing stepped through the Gateway yet, so he reasoned the smell must be coming from the Forest of Shadows.

"What's taking so long?" asked the kitten.

"Be patient, little guy," said Ajax, but he was beginning to wonder the same thing. It never took more than a few seconds for something to materialize, but there was nothing there. He glanced up, wondering if a flying creature perhaps appeared up in the sky, but he saw nothing.

Ajax leapt the instant he felt the ground shake. The Gateway existed both above and below ground. Whatever came through must have come through under the surface. Hostas flew as spikes exploded from the earth. Ajax was lucky he jumped, because the spikes crashed and snapped together right where he was standing, just a moment ago.

The kitten gripped Ajax's back and began frantically purring. The little Kitanja was terrified, and Ajax didn't blame him. Sinking his claws in the soft bark of the tree, Ajax sprung, launching himself across the yard. Spinning in midair, he landed on the far side of the yard, facing whatever was emerging from the earth.

The creature that burst through the hostas made Ajax's blood run cold. Its body was divided into two massive sections, each supported by four multisegmented legs. Sheets of glowing purple chitin covered its thick body. Its head was an enormous beak, covered with glowing red eyes. Long, writhing tentacles surrounded its head. A thick, serrated blade of midnight black chitin tipped each tentacle. The tentacles extended nearly thirty feet from its body.

It was an Elder Nightmare, something from the deepest, darkest depths of the Dreaming. It didn't belong here. How did it access an Abyssinial Gateway in the first place? "Hold on, little Kitanja. It's going to be a bumpy ride."

"Whiskers, what is that thing?" screamed the kitten.

Ajax felt a wet spot form on his back. The kitten was right to be terrified. Ajax was scared, too. Off to the side, a flicker of motion caught his attention. Sparing a quick glance, he watched a writhing mass of terrorlings race into the yard. They were what he smelled. He didn't take time to count, but he thought there were at least a half dozen of the disgusting things.

One on one, they were no match for him. A sea of stumpy legs propelled their three-foot diameter bodies. Pairs of long, chitinous arms sprouted from their backs. Each arm ended in a mass of eyes and needlelike teeth. They were terrifying to behold, but they lacked any real armor.

"What do we do?" whined the terrified kitten.

"I'll get us back to our bodies. We're getting out of here," growled Ajax. With the terrorlings charging from the side, and the Elder Nightmare between them and the house, Ajax wasn't sure how he was going to accomplish it, but he was a crafty cat. He'd figure something out.

Tendrils of translucent gold sprouted from Ajax's fur on either side of his face, forming a glorious, glowing mane. At the same time, a thin field of golden light formed around his body. His Spirit Armor would protect him from simple dreams, like the terrorlings, but it wouldn't hold up against the Elder Nightmare.

Springing to the right, Ajax sprinted at the pack of charging terrorlings. Tracking his motion, the Elder Nightmare snapped its head forward, like a whip, sending a writhing storm of tentacles in his direction.

Ajax leapt, kicking off a nearby tree to change directions. The terrorlings seemed confused by his movements, because several of them stumbled into each other, tumbling to the ground. Those that kept their footing quickly turned and raced toward the spot where he was most likely to land.

Regrettably, the Elder Nightmare wasn't confused by Ajax's evasive leap. Its tentacles fanned out, creating too wide a web for Ajax to avoid. The first serrated blade of chitin failed to cut through his Spirit Armor, but it forcefully knocked him to the side. Ajax tried to adjust, but he was leaping through the air. Without a branch or wall to kick off of, there was nothing he could do.

The kitten screamed.

Ajax landed hard, rolling several feet before righting himself. Fortunately, the Kitanja was protected by his magic, or he would have been crushed. The time it took Ajax to right himself was all the time the Elder Nightmare needed to redirect its army of tentacles. The world darkened. There were so many of them.

Seeing no obvious way out, Ajax raced toward the house. He knew it was going to be bad. His only hope was to somehow charge past the crashing web of chitin and flesh before it tore him to shreds. The skittering terrorlings were little more than an afterthought at this point. They were nothing compared to the Elder Nightmare.

Ajax growled as the first tentacle ripped through his body. He coughed as the second one burst through his lungs. He yelped as the third shattered his leg, and he howled as the fourth tore through his heart, bringing his life to an end.

"No!" screamed the kitten. "Please don't go, Ajax, I need you!"

Spitting and coughing, Ajax stumbled back to his feet. Marshaling as much magic as he could muster, Ajax leapt high into the air. Excruciating pain raced through his body as he ripped himself free from the tentacles and their serrated blades.

He was down one life already today, leaving him with six. Ajax thought he'd be lucky to make it back to his body without losing one or two more, but he didn't see another solution. Even with nine lives, he couldn't hope to win against the Elder Nightmare. It was too big, too fast, and too strong.

Sprinting, Ajax raced for the house. For a moment, he thought he might make it, but his hopes were dashed when the Elder Nightmare crashed down in front of him. It understood his intentions, and it wasn't going to allow him to escape. Why was that thing here in the first place? Creatures like that belonged deep in the Dreaming, in the dark places Cah'ten dare not tread. Why was it after him?

Then again, maybe it was after the Kitanja.

The monstrous creature roared, and its chaotic mass of tentacles came crashing down. Ajax considered giving up, but he wasn't that kind of cat. Meowing at the top of his lungs, he charged the creature. If he was going to lose more lives, he planned to make the monster suffer. Smoldering flames erupted from his golden mane as he coaxed his dwindling magic into action.

The world around him seemed to fade until only the sounds of his pounding heart and the Kitanja's pulsing purr remained. The swarm of tentacles eclipsed the light as they surrounded him. He prepared to feel them rip through his body. He knew it would hurt.

But it didn't happen.

A barrier of scintillating sapphire light sprung into existence around him. The tentacles crashed against it, producing a cascading rain of tiny blue sparks, but they didn't pierce it. Ajax didn't understand what happened. It sure as fur wasn't his Spirit Armor. Whatever the blue barrier was, it wasn't anything he did.

"I'm so tired," breathed the kitten on his back.

And then Ajax knew.

The Kitanja made the barrier!

Taking advantage of the moment, Ajax sprinted past the Elder Nightmare. Fortunately, the magical barrier must have confused it, because it didn't gather its tentacles in time to stop him. Ajax would have preferred to enter the house by passing through the glass doors, but there wasn't time. Instead, he forced his way through the siding, the wooden studs, and the strange material hoomans used to make walls. It stung, leaving his limbs tingling, but that was far better than the alternative.

Without losing a step, Ajax raced over to their ghostly sleeping bodies. They needed to get out of the Dreaming before it was too late. The walls of the house wouldn't stop the Elder Nightmare for long. "Kitanja!" he shouted. "I know you're scared, but close your eyes for me. I need you to close your eyes."

"Okay, Ajax," called the kitten.

The Elder Nightmare's beak exploded out of the wall. It was less than twenty feet away. Its tentacles lanced out in front of it. Fortunately, Ajax moved after entering the house.

"You should see green light. I want you to push it away. Make the green light flee to the edges of your vision."

The horrifying monster swept its head left and then right. Its countless red eyes flashed when it saw Ajax.

"Is it working?"

"Yes, I think so."

"Good," said Ajax. "Keep going. You're doing great." Purring, Ajax unwound his Spirit Armor. He formed it into a single shield in front of him. He felt the weight of the kitten disappear from his back as the Elder Nightmares' tentacles crashed into his meager defenses. His shield deflected much of the impact, but several of the tentacles tore through it. Ajax felt two rip into his body as he closed his eyes, and willed the green light to the edges of his vision.

7.
GHOSTLY WHISPERS

Gaius watched the swirling spirits flit about the room. There were more than usual for this time of the day. Far more, actually. He didn't like it. So far, none of them invaded the sleeping hooman, but he didn't think that would last. With this many spirits in the air, a few were bound to get aggressive.

Spirits often possessed hoomans. Normally, it wasn't a big deal. Most of the time, they delivered minor illnesses, brief fits of sadness, strange cravings, or other manageable maladies. Sometimes, though, they inflicted dangerous conditions upon their hosts.

Any cat could remove a spirit, but Spiritchasers excelled at it. Gaius removed two or three foul spirits from his chosen hooman, Jeff, each night. It only took a few minutes of sitting on his hooman's chest to accomplish it. Regrettably, Jeff preferred to sleep on his side.

Gaius gazed at the ceiling and gently allowed his vision to drift into the Endless Tide, the spirit world. It wasn't the Dreaming, but instead, a place reserved for the dead. There, he witnessed a line of hundreds, if not thousands, of spirits drifting by. Spiritchasers referred to it as the Procession. Normally, the Procession of spirits moved quickly, but today, they were shuffling along at a snail's pace. The glacial flow explained why so many spirits were crossing over into the real world. They were probably bored.

Off to the side, a flicker of motion caught his eye. A spirit was standing on the far side of the room. While most spirits were shapeless, like clouds of mist, this one looked much like a hooman woman. Only powerful spirits could take on a clear shape and form. It wasn't uncommon to encounter a strong spirit like that, but it wasn't a daily occurrence either.

Deciding it was best to investigate, Gaius leapt from the bed and padded over to the spirit. At first, he thought it might be a Muse, attracted by the harp in the corner of the room. Several Muses regularly visited the house to listen to Jeff's daily piano practice, but as Gaius approached, he realized this spirit was far more powerful than a Muse. It was a Celestine. What was a Celestine doing here? Neither of the hoomans in this house were religious.

"Follow me. I would like to exchange words with you, but not here," said the spirit before drifting from the room and out into the hall. Gaius followed along. He wanted to hear what the spirit had to say, and having a conversation in the bedroom would probably wake Maureen or Loki.

"This should be far enough, Gaius. We'll be able to speak without disturbing the others."

"Why do you know my name?" asked the cat. He doubted it was hard for the Celestine to discover his name. Gaius was a Spiritchaser, after all. He frequently made deals with spirits. Why the spirit bothered to learn his name, that was the more interesting question.

"Because you've suddenly become important," answered the spirit. She smiled, and her wispy, wavering face gradually became more substantial, if not solid. She was quite striking, with silver hair, sharply pointed ears, and large, expressionate eyes.

"My clowder guards one of the nineteen Abyssinial Gateways," meowed Gaius. "We've always been important."

"Perhaps, but never more so than now."

Gaius lazily cleaned a paw, feigning indifference. He knew if he waited long enough, the Celestine would explain it to him, but if he appeared eager or desperate for the information, the spirit would attempt to exact a price.

"We don't need to engage in performative dance, Gaius," whispered the spirit. "Me, tantalizing you with information, and you feigning indifference. In the end, we'll strike a bargain. You won't have a choice. The events that are in motion… they're far too important."

Celestines drew power from religious belief. In ancient times, they were each dedicated to one particular religion or another, but that led to war. At some point, they realized it was better for them to share equally in the fruits of religious belief, regardless of what faith it came from. Even after setting their internal differences aside, they weren't without enemies. Nothing was, but few spirits were strong enough to oppose the Celestines directly. "I'm listening," meowed Gaius. "Patiently, even."

"Such a clever cat," cooed the spirit. "For starters, it may come as a surprise, but an Elder Nightmare stepped through your Gateway, just a few minutes ago."

Gaius looked away, trying to hide his shock. An Elder Nightmare… here? Hopefully, Ajax and the Kitanja weren't out there when it arrived. He needed to warn them to avoid the Dreaming! Something like that could strip nine lives from a cat in mere moments. "Excuse me, but I must warn my clowder, great spirit," he said, trying to control the panic in his voice.

"It's too late for that."

Gaius' heart sank. He knew Ajax since he was a Kitanja. He raised that cat.

"The Guardian and the kitten both survived," said the spirit. "They're downstairs, sleeping, but the Elder Nightmare is close. It hungers for them."

Gaius couldn't believe what he was hearing. "Why? Creatures like that care little for the lives of mortals."

The Celestine pursed her lips and shook her head. When she did, her hair rattled and shifted. It only lasted a moment, but during that time, her hair was no longer supple and flowing. If Gaius wasn't mistaken, her hair momentarily turned into silver chains. "I must leave your question unanswered, clever cat. Just believe me when I say it hungers for them. In fact, if it is not dealt with in the Dreaming, I suspect it will eventually find a way to cross over into this world, and none of us wants that."

"Into this world?" asked Gaius. "Wait, you mean the real world?"

The spirit nodded. "It must be prevented, at all costs. The monsters that live in the Dreaming need to stay there. Humanity isn't prepared to see such horrors."

So, that's why the Celestine was here. It was worried about the Elder Nightmare breaking through into the real world. "Well, feel free to go remove it from my backyard. You certainly have my permission."

The spirit laughed. At first, the sound was crystalline and beautiful, but dissonant notes quickly appeared, spoiling the beautiful laughter. "You must think me a fool. If several of my sisters joined me in battle, perhaps, but alone, this is not a fight I would choose."

"You don't have the luxury of choosing your battles," said Gaius.

"Neither do you, clever cat," said the Celestine. "The Elder Nightmare isn't here for me. It is here for members of your clowder. If anyone needs to destroy it, it's you."

Queasiness crept into Gaius' throat. It was like a horrible hairball he couldn't quite cough up. "You're suggesting we work together to destroy it, aren't you?"

The Celestine nodded. "Unlike you cats, I only have one life to give. I will support you, but this fight isn't mine to lead."

"How will it work… specifically?" asked Gaius. It was unwise to allow a spirit, especially a Celestine, to make vague offers. "How will you support us in this battle?"

"You don't trust me," said the spirit. She plastered an exaggerated, sad expression across her face. "You've hurt my feelings."

Gaius went back to lazily cleaning a paw. Patience was of the utmost importance when dealing with spirits, and besides, his paws were actually quite dirty. Either the Celestine would start telling him what he wanted to know, or she'd spend the afternoon watching him clean himself.

"Very well, clever cat, I'll answer your questions," hissed this spirit.

Gaius stopped cleaning his paws and looked at the spirit. He lightly flicked the tip of his tail back and forth. "I'm waiting."

"I will gather several spirits for you to summon during the battle. These spirits are special. They're far more powerful than what you'd normally summon."

"Powerful spirits are often costly to summon," said Gaius. "They know their worth, so they bargain hard."

The Celestine shook her head. Once again, her hair momentarily shifted, and this time, Gaius was certain her hair became gleaming chains. "I've already purchased their participation, clever cat. Each of these spirits owes many debts to me. The upcoming battle is their opportunity to satisfy those debts."

Gaius didn't like the joyous tone that crept into her voice each time she said the word debt. His mentor warned him about Celestines. Now he understood why. "And to be clear, no one in this house, hooman or cat, is incurring any debt to you from this arrangement. We are joining forces to defeat a common enemy, no more, no less."

The Celestine bowed her head. "Very well, for now."

"What's that supposed to mean?"

The spirit smiled broadly, exposing rows of fangs. "I suspect we'll do business again, in the future, clever cat."

Gaius wasn't so sure. "When do we have to do this? I need to speak with the other cats. We're certainly not jumping into this without a plan."

"I need a day to gather my spirits," said the Celestine. "Shall we meet again tomorrow afternoon?"

Gaius hoped that would be enough time, but what did he know? He never faced anything like an Elder Nightmare. He needed to speak with Ajax and find out what kind of monster they were truly dealing with. "Tomorrow it is."

"Agreed," said the Celestine.

"Oh, one last thing."

"What is it, cat?"

"We're only doing this because we have to. If the Elder Nightmare gets bored and moves on, this entire arrangement is null and void. No harm or foul to either party." Gaius didn't really think the creature was going to wander off, but it was nice to have hopes and dreams.

"Of course, but this monster won't leave on its own," said the spirit. "If we don't defeat it, it will find a way to kill its target."

"Who's it after?"

"Nice try, clever cat," said the spirit, shaking her head. "We can bargain for that information, of course, but I suspect it won't be hard to figure it out on your own. Besides, you're asking the wrong question."

Gaius pondered the spirit's words and smiled. She shared a lot with him in this conversation, perhaps more than she intended. "Since you want to bargain with me again in the future, what is your name? What shall I call you?" Gaius didn't expect the spirit to give him her Truename, but it never hurt to ask. Every once in a while, it worked.

"Even if I told you, my name is unpronounceable to mortals. For now, call me Sybil. I've always liked that name."

"Very well, Sybil," said Gaius. "While I will not say I've enjoyed meeting you, I must admit, I found this negotiation rather pleasant."

"Until tomorrow, clever cat."

"Until tomorrow." Gaius watched the spirit drift back into the bedroom. He considered following her, but he needed to check on Ajax and the Kitanja first. Once he knew they were safe, they'd wake Loki and plan their next moves.

8.
MOMMA TAUGHT ME RIGHT

Loki yawned as he studied the other cats. He really wished Gaius would have let him sleep longer. Gaius woke him while he was holding paws with his hooman, Maureen. It was his favorite time of the day. Well, second favorite time of the day. He enjoyed running through the woods and spying on the neighbors even more.

Both Ajax and the Kitanja looked positively shook. Whatever they saw out there in the Dreaming, it scared the heck out of them. Loki was half-tempted to step into the Dreaming and look for himself. He was super-fast. He didn't think anything out there was quick enough to catch him, but Gaius strictly forbid him from taking the risk.

"I know things were rough out there. I've tried to give you time to recover, but there is much to discuss." said Gaius softly. He was a nearly perfect cat. His pointed markings gave him the appearance of a long-haired Siamese, but as he aged, the fur beneath his nose lightened, making him look like he had a mustache. His tail was luxurious, and his fur never tangled or clumped. "What happened out there, Ajax?"

The big brown cat's golden eyes were wider than Loki remembered seeing them before, and his normally proud tail was tucked behind him. He never saw Ajax scared like this. He didn't even think it was possible for a cat that big to be scared.

"It was underground when it stepped through the Gateway. We didn't even know it was there. Not until it attacked us."

"So, it attacked you from beneath the earth?" asked Gaius.

Ajax nodded. "I felt a slight tremble and managed to jump to safety at the last second. Both the Kitanja and I would have lost lives if I hadn't."

Loki's mouth hung open. Ajax was a Guardian. In the Dreaming, he was one tough kitty. "Are you sure, big guy?" asked Loki. He didn't want to contradict Ajax, but he was having a hard time believing him. "Maybe it would have hurt real bad, but how can you be so sure it would have cost both of you lives?"

"Because the one time that thing got a hold of me, it ripped me apart like I was a roll of toilet paper," growled Ajax.

Gaius held up a paw. He was probably trying to calm things down. Loki was tempted to tease the Cah'ten Ra until he got mad and shouted, 'Silence!' Loki always found that really funny, but he decided now wasn't the right time. "First, I'm truly sorry to hear about your lost life," said Gaius. He paused a moment before continuing. "The spirits told me it was an Elder Nightmare. Is that true?"

The big brown cat nodded.

"I'm not doubting you, but help me understand. How do you know?"

"It's part of being a Guardian," said Ajax. "When we face something, we know if it's just a bad dream, or something truly powerful, like an Old One, an Elder, or an Ancient."

"Thank you," said Gaius. "I understand now."

As a Wildseeker, Loki knew something about creatures in the Dreaming. Simple, weaker creatures were simply referred to as dreams. Powerful beings were often described as Old Ones. Elders were the next strongest, with Ancients being the most powerful. The nastiest thing Loki ever crossed paths with in the Dreaming was an Old One. Fortunately, it wasn't fast enough to catch him.

"I knew this thing was an Elder the moment I saw it," said Ajax. "Oh, and a bunch of terrorlings came after us from the Forest of Shadows at roughly the same time. I don't know if that's important, but I thought I should bring it up."

Loki's ears perked up. Terrorlings were fairly common in the Forest of Shadows. They often hunted in groups, so he wasn't surprised about there being a pack of them, but in his experience, terrorlings were cowards. "So, they came after you even with the scary nightmare monster nearby?"

Ajax nodded.

"That's not normal," said Loki with a shake of his head. "Terrorlings are kind of skittish. The only way they would have approached a really powerful monster is if they were on its side." Something about the involvement of the terrorlings set Loki on edge. Packs of them roamed the Forest of Shadows, hunting, but for them to show up right when the scary monster did was too much of a coincidence. They would have needed to have been close by.

"Thank you for pointing that out, Loki. That's an important detail," said Gaius.

"Hey Ajax, did you smell them?" asked Loki.

The big brown cat nodded. "I caught a whiff of sour milk right before they charged out of the Forest of Shadows."

"But you didn't smell them earlier?"

Ajax shook his head. "It felt like we were being watched the entire time we were out there, but I didn't smell the terrorlings before they attacked."

There was something significant there, but Loki couldn't put his paw on it. Glancing down at the kitten, he wondered if there was something wrong. This whole time, the Kitanja was curled up against the side of Ajax's body. Loki couldn't blame the kitten for being tired after his ordeal, but shouldn't he have woken up by now? "Hey, is that thing alright?" he asked, pointing at Ajax and the kitten sleeping against him.

"Who, me?" asked Ajax. "Of course, I'm not alright! I just lost a life. I would have lost two or three, if not for the Kitanja."

"Not you, I'm talking about the Kitanja! Is he alright?" Loki couldn't have been the only one to notice. "He's been sleeping this whole time. Has anyone tried to wake him up?"

"Of course, I tried, but the little guy can't seem to keep his eyes open," said Ajax. "After what he did out there, I'm not surprised he's tired."

"What exactly did he do?" asked Gaius.

"He made a big blue forcefield," said Ajax. "It was strong enough to deflect the Elder Nightmare's tentacles, which means his forcefield was a lot stronger than my Spirit Armor."

Loki didn't like the Kitanja, but if he did that, maybe Loki needed to rethink things. "There's your proof, Gaius. That kitten is a Conjurepurr."

"We don't know that."

"Yes, we do," said Loki. "You said it yourself. We were waiting for a clear expression of his power. Ajax just described a Purrtection spell."

"Oh, come on. Like anyone knows what a Purrtection spell really looks like," scoffed Gaius.

"I do."

"What… how?"

"Back when I was just a kitten, my momma used to tell me stories. She told them every night as I was drifting off to sleep." Loki savored those memories. He was fortunate enough to spend nearly half a year with his mom before coming to this home. "Her favorite stories were the ones about Purrsephone, the first Conjurepurr."

"Great," sighed Gaius. "We're relying on bedtime stories."

"Do you have a better idea, oh great Cah'ten Ra?" asked Loki, his tone clearly mocking.

"No, not particularly," admitted Gaius.

Ajax climbed to his feet, careful to ease the Kitanja's body to the ground gently. "Actually, he feels sort of limp, you guys. I'm getting kind of worried," said Ajax. "Did any of the stories your mother told you talk about this issue?"

Loki thought hard about it. His mother told him so many stories, they ran together in his head. He missed her so much. "Well, Purrsephone was a bit of a trickster. In many of the stories, she stole little items from her hoomans. She often did it before taking on a dangerous mission, or after returning from one. It was her special way to rest and recover."

"What kind of items?" asked Ajax. "Like socks, underwear, and combs?"

"Or writing implements, bottle openers, and remote controls?" asked Gaius.

"Wait, are you guys thieves?" asked Loki. He often stole hair ties, but nothing more than that.

"Thieves… Um, no," said Ajax casually. Gaius started cleaning a paw, ignoring the question. "But what about Purrsephone?" asked Ajax.

"She stole minor items. Pretty much like the stuff you and Gaius listed."

"And you think they recharged her?" asked Ajax.

Loki shrugged. "How do I know? I mean, it's worth a try."

Gaius walked over to the sleeping kitten and gently nudged him. "He's out cold. I don't think he's in any condition to steal, at least not anytime soon."

"Maybe it's not so much the stealing that recharged Purrsephone," suggested Loki. "What if just possessing a stolen item helped? If someone can give him a stolen item, maybe it will energize him. Once the Kitanja wakes up, I'm sure he can steal things on his own."

"Worth a try," said Ajax as he casually padded over the dining room's storage cabinet and slipped a paw beneath it. He fished around for a moment before producing a sock and a pair of underwear.

"So, you are a thief!" gasped Loki.

"What, me?" said Ajax, glancing at the ceiling. "No, not at all. These just happened to be here… under this cabinet… nowhere near the bedroom…" Ajax looked away for a moment. "Okay, yes. I steal socks and underwear."

"Ajax!" gasped Gaius. "I'm so disappointed in you."

"What? Like you don't steal?"

"Silence!"

Loki snickered. It was fun watching the other cats argue, but he didn't think it was helping the Kitanja wake up. "So, Ajax," he blurted, quickly gaining the big brown cat's attention. "Maybe place the sock and underwear between the kitten's paws? Honestly, I'm not sure how it works."

Ajax grabbed both items in his mouth and carried them over to the sleeping kitten. He carefully worked one piece of clothing beneath the kitten's head, and the other between his front paws. When he was done, he leaned down and nudged the kitten before cleaning his forehead. Loki was often surprised by how gentle Ajax could be when he wanted to.

Ever so slowly, the Kitanja yawned and opened his eyes. It took him a few breaths to react to his surroundings. Loki could sympathize. He often struggled to wake up. "Ajax!" breathed the kitten. His eyes went wide, and a tiny puddle of urine spilled out behind him. "You made it? Did we both make it?" he panted. "Are we safe?"

"Yeah, little buddy, we made it. We're safe."

"For now," said Gaius.

"Would you just chill, man?" growled Ajax. "Let the little guy wake up before getting all serious and stuff."

Loki agreed with Ajax, but he said nothing. Gaius was a decent enough leader, but he often took himself too seriously. Loki's mom taught him that a cat earned respect through his actions, not his words. Gaius acted with more authority than he'd earned. Loki understood Gaius was trying to fill some pretty big paws, but that cat needed to learn some patience.

"I'm sorry, Ajax, but we don't have a lot of time," said Gaius as he sat down next to the bleary-eyed kitten. "I need to ask you a few questions, little Kitanja. Do you think you can answer them?"

Loki didn't like the Cah'ten Ra's tone. "I think Ajax is right. You need to lighten up. Give the kitten a few minutes."

"It's okay," yawned the kitten. "I'm awake."

"What happened out there?" Gaius swished his tail impatiently. He was nervous, maybe even scared. "Ajax said you created some kind of forcefield to protect him. Is that true?"

The kitten nodded. "It was going to kill Ajax! I was so scared. I just started purring and thinking how I wanted Ajax to be alright, and how I wanted us to get away, and it just happened. Did I do something wrong?" The kitten looked like he wanted to cry.

"No, Kitanja," said Gaius softly. "You did nothing wrong."

Ajax nuzzled the kitten. "You did well, little guy. You saved us."

Gaius cleared his throat. "That thing you faced in the Dreaming." He paused and looked away. "We need to kill it."

"Have you been rolling around in the nip again?" snapped Ajax. "There's no way we're going anywhere near that thing!"

"I'm sorry, friend, but we have to."

"We don't have to do anything!"

"I'll explain later, but regrettably, this is a fight we can't avoid." Gaius leaned down and gently planted a single lick on the kitten's nose. "The forcefield you built, little Kitanja… do you think you can do it again?"

"I don't know," whispered the kitten. "I'm just so… tired." He yawned and placed his head on his paws.

"Loki thinks he has a way to help wake you up. If we can do that, Kitanja, do you think you can make another forcefield? It's important," said Gaius.

Loki's mother named him when he was just a wee little thing, much smaller than the Kitanja. He understood Gaius' reluctance to name the kitten before knowing his Calling, but that wasn't an issue anymore. Gaius was asking the kitten to cast Conjurepurr spells. There seemed to be little debate about the Kitanja's Calling. "I think it's time we give the little guy a name."

Gaius shook his head. "There's no time for that. We'll do it after we deal with the Elder Nightmare."

"No," said Loki sternly. He fought the urge to bush. Confronting Gaius was difficult for him, but his momma taught him to speak up when he knew he was right. "If we need the kitten for this fight, the least we can do is give him a name."

"He's right, Gaius," said Ajax. "The little guy deserves a name."

Gaius sighed. "I guess you're right."

The kitten slowly lifted his head off his paws, but it was a struggle. "I'm finally getting a name?" he asked between breathy purrs.

"After what you did out there, you earned it, little kitten," said Ajax.

"Now let me see," said Gaius. "The hoomans call you Chairman, so we probably need to find a name that sounds similar, otherwise it gets confusing."

Loki was glad his mom named him. The hoomans called him Justin. He didn't want to think about what name the Cah'ten Ra might have given him. He thought about it from time to time. Justice might have been nice, but that was about the only option he liked.

"Wait," said Gaius, holding a paw in the air. "I think I have it. Yes… that will do nicely."

"Come on, man, don't keep us waiting," said Ajax.

"Since our little Conjurepurr is so magical, I think we should call him Shaman."

Loki whispered the name a few times to try it out. It was simple enough to say, and it sounded enough like Chairman, where it would be easy to tie his hooman name to his Cah'ten name. "Wow, that's actually pretty good."

"What do you think, little Kitanja?" asked Gaius softly. "Do you want to be called Shaman?"

The kitten positively beamed. He tried to climb to his feet, but his legs were wobbly, and he tumbled onto his side, but he kept purring the entire time. "Shaman. My name is Shaman!"

"Now listen up. We have much to do," said Gaius.

Loki listened as the Cah'ten Ra explained the situation, and all that needed to be done. The first task was helping Shaman recover from his recent ordeal. Loki volunteered to help with that. He enjoyed playing little pranks, and teaching Shaman how to steal from the hoomans sounded like a great way to spend the afternoon.

Everything that needed to happen afterwards sounded dangerous and scary, but there would be time to be terrified about all that stuff later. For now, he needed to teach the kitten how to steal!

9.
THE CLEVER CAT'S PLAN

Gaius wished there were more time. He didn't like relying on the Celestine, Sybil. He wanted time to question a few spirits about her. Even if Sybil proved true to her word, Gaius needed time to work with Shaman and explore his abilities. He also needed time to get word to the Uhl Cah'ten Ra, the director of all feline activities in the region.

They needed help.

But they didn't have time for any of that. Sybil thought the risk of the Elder Nightmare breaking into the real world was too severe to wait, and Gaius went along with it. Why didn't he bargain harder? At a minimum, he should have pushed this battle off for another day or two.

Gaius sighed. It was too late to second guess himself now. After wracking his brain for hours, he cobbled together a plan he thought might work. But then again, he knew very little about the monster they were about to face. That was a pretty serious flaw in his plan.

Hopefully, it wouldn't become a fatal flaw.

At least the weather was in their favor. A few raindrops were falling here and there. The hooman was smoking the brisket Shaman recently convinced him to buy. The sparse rain striking the smoker was causing the infernal stinking box to smoke even more. That smoke manifested as fog within the Dreaming. It might be enough to conceal them.

A heavy rain would have been a disaster. Water attracted spirits, and powerful rains attracted dangerous spirits. Gaius hated summoning during downpours. The risk of the wrong spirits answering his call was too great. But a scattered drizzle was perfect. It was just enough moisture to make summoning easy, while still keeping it safe.

"Loki just climbed back into the yard," said Ajax. He was peering out the glass doors, watching the backyard. "Are you sure about this? It's not too late to call this off."

Gaius wasn't remotely sure about his plan, but he wasn't about to share his concerns. "Has he given you the sign?" Loki was scouting the woods surrounding the yard, essentially the real world version of the Forest of Shadows. While the Dreaming and the real world didn't exactly mirror one another, the health of one world was often reflected within the other.

"He's curling up under the tree right now."

"Alright, wave to him," said Gaius. The kitten was too small to go outside, forcing most of the cats to enter the Dreaming from inside the house, but given the plan, it was safest for Loki to enter from out in the yard.

"Is it time?" asked Shaman. He was sitting on the catnip-covered glass table. His tail was tucked between his legs. Gaius didn't blame him for being scared.

"It's time, little one."

Shaman bent down and licked up a few clumps of catnip before jumping from the table and trotting over to the patch of sun-warmed floor. Ajax sauntered over and joined him. The big brown cat lay down first. Once he was settled, Shaman curled up against him.

"Do it just like last time, Shaman," said Ajax. "Close your eyes, until all you see is the glow of the sunlight through your eyelids. Find the green light at the edge of your vision. Welcome it. Coax it to cover everything you see."

Gaius remembered using that method to enter the Dreaming, back when he was just a kitten. Now, he could pretty much do it at will, but back then, small concentration tricks helped tremendously. He smiled, remembering how he taught Ajax the same method, back when the big brown cat was just a tiny little kitten. It seemed like lifetimes ago.

"Once we cross over, I'll toss you on my back and Bind you to me, like before, but we're moving pretty fast this time. Loki is going in first. With any luck, it chases him. Whatever it does, we can't afford to waste time."

"I understand," said Shaman.

Confident Ajax and his student were about to enter the Dreaming, Gaius curled up into a neat ball and closed his eyes. It only took him a pair of deep breaths to enter the Dreaming. He appeared a dozen feet from where Ajax and Shaman were crossing over. They weren't in the Dreaming yet, but Loki was.

Gaius never tired of seeing Loki in the Dreaming. His body was long and low to the ground, and his fur was sleek, perhaps even oily. In the real world, Loki displayed an adorable blaze of white, running the length of his nose. In the Dreaming, his snout and face were elongated, like you might see with a badger. The blaze was thick and long, but not always white. It changed colors, depending what Loki needed it to do. Sometimes, it even glowed.

Loki's claws were also more akin to a badger's than a jungle cat's in the Dreaming. They were thick and sharp, capable of rending flesh, shattering wood, or digging through dense earth. The only thing that wasn't impressive about Loki was his tail. In the real world, Loki's tail was rather short. In the Dreaming, his tail didn't lengthen like the rest of his body, making it seem almost comically small.

Gaius heard the sigh of Ajax and Shaman crossing over as he watched Loki carefully sneak through the vibrant back yard. He was prowling along the edge of the glowing retaining wall, just outside the colorful canopy of hosta leaves. The stripe on his nose was glowing blue, bathing the ground in front of him with its light.

"That nose of his sure comes in handy, doesn't it?" said Ajax.

Gaius spared a glace to his left. Shaman was riding on Ajax's back. A thin field of amber energy surrounded the kitten. It meant Ajax was protecting him. "Yes, it certainly does. Hopefully, he finds the creature before it finds him."

"Or us, for that matter," added Ajax.

The stripe on Loki's nose, among other things, detected hidden, even invisible threats. Since Loki was casting blue light against the ground, Gaius surmised that blue was used to detect underground threats. He wasn't used to seeing it. Loki most often colored his blaze green, red, or silver.

"I think he found something," whispered Ajax.

Loki stopped prowling and backed up a step. He was staring intently at a section of earth in front of him. Gaius wondered if Loki was just being extra careful, but in the next moment, the ground exploded in a sea of writhing tentacles, each tipped with a serrated blade.

Loki jumped back, spinning 180 degrees before landing. He didn't wait to see if the monster was pursuing before sprinting away from it. It's a good thing he didn't delay, because the thing that emerged from the earth moved far faster than it should, given its size.

"I'm scared," cried Shaman.

The Elder Nightmare was simply enormous. Extending from its head, long ridges of serrated bone came together, forming a huge beak. Dozens of glowing red eyes ran the length of the beak, but the thick tentacles flowing around the edges of the beak likely obscured the creature's peripheral vision. At least Gaius hoped so, otherwise the creature could probably see them.

Loki ran, and the creature's tentacles followed. Fortunately, Loki was just fast enough to escape the range of the tentacles, forcing the creature to lurch after him. It moved at an angle, charging the center of the yard. From there, it could reach most of the yard with its tentacles, but Loki wasn't afraid to enter the Forest of Shadows if he needed to. So far, the plan was working perfectly.

"That's our cue," said Gaius as he pushed his way through the silver-veined window he was observing from. Once outside the house, he crept behind a swirling cloud of white smoke. He wished the smoke was thicker, but he'd just have to make do.

Axel and Shaman followed suit. They entered the Dreaming close to the large glass doors. The white smoke shrouded them the moment they exited the house. Hopefully, Ajax's golden Spirit Armor didn't give away their position. So far, they seemed safe.

Loki was doing an excellent job of distracting the Elder Nightmare. He was running back and forth along the far side of the yard. The horrifying monster was fanning its tentacles wide as it whipped them at him, but Loki stayed just out of range. He probably needed to dip in and out of the Forest of Shadows to do so, but so far, that didn't seem to be a problem.

"Whatever you're going to do, Gaius, you best do it soon," said Ajax. "That thing will be on us the second it notices us."

"Are you ready to build a forcefield, Shaman? Are you ready to cast Purrtection?"

"I think so."

Gaius would have preferred a more confident answer from the kitten, but he kept his concerns to himself. "Wait until it turns on us before casting your spell, Shaman."

"Got it."

Shifting his vision into the Endless Tide, Gaius quickly located the Celestine spirit. True to her word, she was following along, and she wasn't alone. A group of four spirits stood behind her. Surprisingly, each of them was armed. One held a bow, and another a katana. The third carried a spear, and the fourth a longsword and shield.

Weapons were incredibly rare within the spirit world. Most spirits fashioned weapons out of portions of themselves. Spirits could take any form, after all. If one wanted to wield a sword, it could simply make a sword appear at the end of its arm. But these spirits were holding real weapons.

Gaius didn't understand why real weapons were any more powerful than spiritual weapons, but that's what his mentors taught him. He studied many stories. In all of them, only ancient, powerful spirits carried such things, and they always wielded them to tremendous effect.

After nodding to Sybil, Gaius chose the first spirit to summon. He decided that the one with the sword and shield was the best choice. He needed to summon the spirits individually. Each spell would take a fair amount of time to complete. Hopefully, the combination of the spirit's shield, and Shaman's Purrtection spell would buy Gaius time to bring all four spirits into the Dreaming.

Meowing softy, Gaius started his spell. He skipped to the right, and then back to the left. He leapt into the air, waving his paws above his head. After landing, he flopped to his back and rolled around. As expected, the spirit became intrigued by his cute, if not crazy, antics. Slowly, a bond formed between Gaius and the spirit. When Gaius finally climbed back to his feet and pawed at the air, a tiny rip appeared, connecting the Dreaming to the Endless Tide. The spirit quickly leapt through the tear, joining Gaius in the Dreaming.

"Sybil sends her regards," said the spirit, his voice like wind rustling leaves.

"Greetings, spirit. Defend us until I can bring your brethren across."

The spirit pointed out into the yard. "It seems the creature has noticed us, cat. You had best make haste."

The Elder Nightmare was advancing toward them. Its army of tentacles was above it, sweeping down at them in a deadly arc. Gaius couldn't spot Loki, and he didn't have time to search for him. Hopefully, the Wildseeker managed to avoid harm. Now, it was up to Shaman to protect them. "Anytime, Shaman!" shouted Gaius.

The kitten on Ajax's back raised a paw and closed his eyes. A moment later, a barrier of scintillating sapphire light sprung into existence around the area. The tentacles crashed against it, producing a thunderclap, followed by a torrential rain of tiny blue sparks. The ground shook from the weight of the impact.

Gaius staggered, but easily maintained his balance. He was a cat, after all. The strength of the Elder Nightmare's attacks concerned him. He was amazed that Shaman's barrier survived the first blows, but he couldn't be certain it would survive many more.

Ignoring the queasiness taking hold of his stomach, Gaius selected another spirit and started the intricate dance necessary to summon him.

10.
THE QUICK CAT'S DANCE

Loki was relieved when the Elder Nightmare lost interest in him. He thought Ajax was exaggerating about the length of the monster's tentacles, but if anything, Ajax undersold them. Loki barely escaped its initial ambush, and matters improved little from there.

Fortunately, within the Dreaming, Loki was a quick kitty. He lacked the sheer power of Ajax, but he more than made up for it with speed and agility. Loki could turn on a dime, leap high into trees, and even burrow into the earth, when need be. He was the perfect choice to distract the Elder Nightmare. Despite that, he still almost lost a life.

Loki was the only cat in the clowder with nine lives, and he hoped to keep them all.

To avoid the Elder Nightmare's incredibly long tentacles, Loki retreated into the Forest of Shadows. Regions were important within the Dreaming. Even though he only traveled a couple of feet into the Forest of Shadows, it represented something significant. It was like crossing into another dimension. One moment, he was in the backyard, or the Oaken Grove, as they liked to call it. In the next, he was in the Forest of Shadows.

It was much cooler in the Forest of Shadows. The air was heavy and wet, and it reeked of sour milk, which meant terrorlings were nearby. Loki shouldn't have been surprised. Ajax warned him about the terrorlings, but Loki didn't expect their smell to be so pronounced.

There was another smell buried beneath the rancid milk. Something acrid, almost alien.

Loki didn't have time to dwell on it. Gaius' instructions were simple. Distract the Elder Nightmare as long as he could. Once the monster lost interest in him, he was to sneak up behind it and harass it. Gaius made it absolutely clear that the Elder Nightmare was their priority. If terrorlings attacked, they needed to be dealt with, but only after the group killed the Elder Nightmare.

Loki crept out from beneath the foliage lining the Oaken Grove. He knew the plants offered him no protection against the horrifying monster's heavy tentacles. Even so, he felt more comfortable beneath them. He hated being out in the open. It made him feel naked and vulnerable. Stealth was a critical survival tool.

The Elder Nightmare was facing away from him, giving Loki a clear path to its back. It was slamming its tentacles against a bright blue dome of light, most likely Shaman's Purrtection spell. Brilliant sparks exploded from the barrier every time the monster struck it.

Flattening himself out as much as possible, Loki made his way across the yard. He didn't expect the monster to turn on him, but it never hurt to be careful. Loki slowed down as he approached within ten feet of the creature. He wasn't sure how to attack the thing.

The Elder Nightmare was covered in glowing purple chitin. Loki assumed the glow meant the chitin was magically reinforced, but he didn't know that. Maybe the monster simply liked the color purple, or perhaps it was broadcasting to the world that it was in a rather 'purple' mood, but he doubted it. He was pretty sure the purple light was some kind of armor, similar to the golden light that often protected Ajax.

A trio of slender antennae extended from the monster's back, and there was a thick, nasty-looking stinger protruding from its butt. Four chitinous legs supported the rear section of the creature, two on each side. He wondered if he could take out one of the legs. His digging claws were pretty powerful. The glowing chitin couldn't be that strong, could it?

The Elder Nightmare slammed its massive tentacles against the bright blue forcefield once again. This time, a section of it shattered, sending several shards of blue light spinning off to the side. Much of the Purrtection spell was still intact, but there was definitely a hole in it. Loki couldn't see past the creature to get a good assessment of the damage.

Off to his right, he saw motion along the edge of the Forest of Shadows. He suspected it was the terrorlings he smelled earlier, but he didn't pay them much thought. Carefully avoiding the stinger, Loki approached the outside of the Elder Nightmare's rear leg, on the left side. He figured if the terrorlings were approaching from his right, he wanted to put the creature between him and them.

The Elder Nightmare smashed its tentacles against Shaman's forcefield again, and it sounded like glass shattering. Sparing a glance, Loki saw Ajax flee to the left. The forcefield was completely gone. Gaius was rolling around on the patio, probably in the process of summoning something. Interestingly, there were three spirits standing near him.

Wisps of silver light rose from the spiritual trio. It looked a lot like smoke. Each spirit was carrying a glowing weapon. One, carrying a shield, stood protectively above Gaius. The other two, one with a sword and one with a spear, gracefully rose into the air before launching themselves at the Elder Nightmare. Neat, he thought. Flying spirits!

Focusing on the task at hand, Loki forcefully drove his claws into the Elder Nightmare's leg. Its antennae whipped back and forth, and it swept its stinger toward him, but Loki was too quick. He danced around the leg until he was sure the stinger couldn't hit him before resuming his attacks.

At first, he couldn't pierce the glowing chitin. The purple light functioned as a shield, and a strong one at that. It felt like he was trying to claw into metal. Eventually, hairline fractures appeared. Loki struck them, over and over again, until he finally forced his way through. The black chitin underneath was strong, but it was no match for his digging claws.

Loki yelped when the Elder Nightmare took a step. With his claws lodged into the beast, it dragged him along with it. Fortunately, its legs were segmented, and Loki found a safe place to perch, a place where he wasn't likely to get knocked off. The last thing he wanted to do was fall and get stepped on. That would be a silly way to lose a life.

Seeing no better plan, Loki kept clawing the Elder Nightmare as it walked. He was making steady progress, but he figured it would take him a while to break or disable the leg. It looked like the creature was chasing Ajax, which meant it was all but ignoring Gaius and the cool flying spirits. That was curious.

The monster shook, howling in pain. Loki wondered if he struck a nerve while digging around inside its leg, but a quick look around showed him what really happened. The flying spirits were attacking it. Their weapons seemed to all but ignore the protective field of purple energy. There was another spirit now, off in the distance, with a bow. Loki watched as it launched a shining silver arrow at the Elder Nightmare.

Whatever they were doing, they must have been hurting it, because it wasn't long before the Elder Nightmare stopped chasing Ajax and turned its attention on the spirits. Loki was glad they were there. He didn't want the monster focusing on him as he continued to dig a deeper hole in the thing's leg. He expected his claws to come out the other side soon.

Tentacles whipped all around him as the Elder Nightmare defended itself. Loki was forced to hide behind the leg he was perching on, otherwise he might have been hit. With all the tentacles flying around, it was hard to keep track of the action. The Elder Nightmare eventually found its mark. It landed a solid blow, driving the spiritual spearman into the ground a short distance away.

The spirit climbed to its feet, but the Elder Nightmare was too fast. A sea of writhing tentacles surrounded the spirit, each dragging a serrated edge across its body. Loki wasn't sure 'body' was the right word. Did spirits even have bodies? In any event, whatever the spirit was, it quickly faded into nothingness. Loki was certain it wouldn't be back.

Returning his attention to the leg, Loki continued to dig. Eventually, he forced both claws clear through to the other side. He was surprised the leg could still support the creature's weight, but it wouldn't be able to for much longer, not if Loki had anything to say about it. Wedging his back against one side of the hole, he began frantically clawing at the other side, working to expand the cavity. It didn't take him long to dig out another healthy chunk of chitin.

The Elder Nightmare went to take another step and its rearmost left leg shattered, sending Loki tumbling to the ground. Being a cat, he landed on his feet, but regrettably, the monster was still standing. Between its two major segments, eight legs supported it. Taking out one leg wasn't enough to unbalance it.

"An excellent idea, badger-cat," said the spirit with the long curved blade as it drifted next to the monster. A writhing mass of tentacles followed the spirit, but he didn't seem concerned. Lining up his cut, the spirit spun, swinging his sword in a deadly arc. The blade struck the closest leg, right at the joint. It passed through the magically reinforced chitin with ease. Loki thought it was horribly unfair. He worked really hard to sever a leg, yet this spirit did it with a single cut!

The Elder Nightmare howled in pain. Loki retreated as the swirling sea of tentacles struck like vipers, trying to catch the spirit with the curved sword. The spirit spun, and his blade cut through several of the tentacles, but there were more. Still, with two of its legs missing, the Elder Nightmare struggled to keep its balance. It was forced to press some of its tentacles against the ground to stay upright.

Gaius shouted, "Help Ajax!" as he raced by. Loki thought the primary goal was the Elder Nightmare, but if Gaius was giving an order, he wasn't about to question it, at least not until later. Besides, the farther away he got from the massive beast with all its writhing tentacles, the better.

Loki sprinted after Gaius. He was much faster, and it didn't take him long to catch up with the Cah'ten Ra. "What's happening?" he asked.

"They're all after Ajax and the Kitanja," said Gaius. "The Elder Nightmare is crippled. The spirits will finish it, but it'll be all for naught if the terrorlings kill Ajax and Shaman."

Loki was so focused on the Elder Nightmare that he lost track of the terrorlings. He expected perhaps six or eight of them, but it was much worse than that. Ajax already killed several, but Loki spotted at least a dozen still giving chase.

He quickly glanced over toward the spot where the terrorlings exited the Forest of Shadows, and his heart sank.

There were more of them. They were still coming!

11.
THE STRONG CAT'S GAMBIT

Ajax roared and swept his enormous paw at the closest terrorling. As he did, his Spirit Armor adjusted, building extensions of smoldering energy around his claws. The heat was so intense, he left a trail of wispy smoke in the air.

His paw struck the terrorling beneath the ball of fangs that served as one of its heads. The creature pulled back, just enough to avoid Ajax lopping its head clean off, but the damage was enough to crack its long chitinous neck. The round monster spun off to the side, crashing into another advancing terrorling.

There were so many of them.

Too many of them.

"You got any juice left, little guy, or did making that forcefield knock you out?" asked Ajax, scanning the yard for a safe place to retreat to.

"I'm so… tired," answered Shaman, his voice barely a whisper.

"Alright, I get it," said Ajax. "Let me try to get us out of this mess."

Energy crackled and hissed as Ajax's Spirit Armor absorbed several blows. He was completely surrounded by the terrorlings. With their toothy heads mounted at the end of long, insectoid arms, the terrorlings attacked by thrusting their heads at their opponents. Ajax's Spirit Armor was holding, but he didn't want to rely on it too heavily.

With a roar, he reared up on his hind legs and pounced, mauling a pair of terrorlings. He outweighed them by a fair margin, but then again, the terrorlings greatly outnumbered him. Turning in a tight circle, Ajax fanned out his mane, sending long tendrils of golden light spinning around him. Terrorlings sizzled and hissed as the tendrils struck them, causing several of them to retreat, which was all he needed.

Capitalizing on the moment, Ajax charged past the retreating terrorlings, escaping their containment. He knew they'd keep chasing him. With only so many places to run, it was only a matter of time before they cornered him again. He thought about leaping into a tree, but terrorlings were strong climbers. Besides, he didn't want to make himself a target for the greater threat.

The Elder Nightmare was close to the center of the yard, and it was very much alive. Several of its legs were broken, and it was struggling to move. Three of the spirits Gaius summoned were still fighting it, but Ajax saw no sign of the fourth. The one with the katana was chopping at the monster's legs, while the archer was sending a constant stream of silvery arrows at the thing. The spirit with the shield was in front of the Elder Nightmare, surrounded by tentacles. Ajax didn't expect him to survive much longer.

"How ya doing, big guy?" asked Loki as he raced past. That cat was crazy fast in the Dreaming. He was almost too fast.

"Been better," growled Ajax as he turned to face the charging terrorlings.

"It's about to get worse," said Loki. "More terrorlings are coming from the Forest of Shadows. They'll be here soon."

Ajax took a deep breath, wiggled his whiskers, and wrinkled his nose. Thrusting his head forward, he exhaled a stream of sweltering fire. Desperate to avoid being incinerated, the chaotic mass of charging terrorlings skittered to a stop. The three closest to Ajax burst into flame, while several others crashed into one another, tumbling to the ground. Ajax shook his head to chase away his growing exhaustion. Breathing fire was incredibly taxing.

"That was really neat," said Shaman.

"Well, the good news is that the Elder Nightmare is nearly dead," said Gaius. Ajax didn't notice the Cah'ten Ra's arrival, but that didn't surprise him. In the Dreaming, Gaius was barely larger than a house cat. His only distinctive features were his white Fu Manchu mustache, his glowing silver eyes, and his trio of tails.

Ajax lashed out at the closest pair of terrorlings. The rest were fanning out, forming a ring around the cats. Ajax guessed they were waiting for reinforcements. Once their numbers were sufficient, they'd attack as a group. "Can you summon something to help us, Gaius?"

"Sorry, friend. It took everything I had to summon those four warriors. They're ancient, powerful, and, regrettably, rather expensive."

Ajax shot Gaius a glance. "Then why are you still out here? Why didn't you leave the Dreaming?"

"Because this was my plan," said Gaius. "If it leads to a bitter end, then so be it. I will walk that path alongside you."

It spoke well of the Cah'ten Ra. Ajax never pegged Gaius for a coward, and this confirmed it. His willingness to die with the rest of them showed courage. Well, or stupidity. Perhaps both.

"The reinforcements have arrived," said Loki.

Seizing on that flicker of hope, Ajax looked for anyone or anything to help them out of this mess, but nothing was there. Just an army of terrorlings, and the Elder Nightmare off in the distance. "What are you talking about?"

"Sorry, I guess I should have been more specific," said Loki. "The terrorlings… Their reinforcements have arrived."

Ajax sighed. He started counting the disgusting creatures, but quickly stopped. There were more than enough to kill them. It didn't really matter if it was one, two, or twelve more than necessary. "Anyone have any ideas?"

"I'm kind of surprised they haven't leapt on us yet," said Loki. "They're probably afraid of me."

"They're ignoring you, Loki," said Gaius, shaking his head. "In fact, they're ignoring me, too. They only seem interested in Ajax and Shaman."

"Yeah, well, that's not too comforting," grumbled Ajax. He turned a slow circle, evaluating the situation. They were completely surrounded. The terrorlings were a few rows deep now, and it looked like another dozen were on their way from the Forest of Shadows.

"Actually, I don't think they're interested in you either," breathed Gaius.

The sudden realization stopped Ajax in his tracks. "They're here for Shaman!" Everything started happening after Shaman arrived in their home. None of it was a coincidence. Ajax cast a glance toward the house. The Elder Nightmare was lying on its side now. Ajax didn't think it would present much of a problem. All he needed to do was to get back to their sleeping bodies and they could escape the Dreaming.

"I know what you're thinking," said Gaius. "I don't think you'll make it."

"Maybe he doesn't have to," said Loki.

"What are you getting at?" asked Gaius.

"Right now, Ajax's Spirit Armor is protecting Shaman," said Loki. "I say, he makes a break for it. I'll run alongside him. Once they mob him, I'll grab Shaman and run the rest of the way." Loki sounded proud of himself. "Will that work? You can let Shaman out of your Spirit Armor without turning it off, right?"

Ajax nodded, but he was lying. He needed to drop his Spirit Armor to release Shaman, though he didn't expect it would be a problem. His Spirit Armor wouldn't last forever. It would fade on its own.

"I don't have a better plan, and there are more terrorlings on the way. We gain nothing by waiting," said Gaius.

With as many terrorlings as there were, Ajax didn't think making a break for it was wise. One of them was bound to trip him up. His best bet was to focus on defending himself. He could take the brunt of their attacks, at least for a little while.

"Keep them off me, if you can," growled Ajax. Breathing deeply, he withdrew his mane of golden tendrils and absorbed the fiery energy surrounding his paws. He focused everything into his Spirit Armor, strengthening it.

"We'll do our best," said Gaius.

Lunging forward, Ajax pressed into the first rank of terrorlings. He roared and swung his claws, but he didn't waste his energy on offense. There were far too many of them to kill. His focus was putting one foot in front of the other.

Ajax's Spirit Armor sputtered and crackled as it absorbed blow after blow from the swarming terrorlings. Fortunately, there were only so many that could hit him at once. They might have stopped him from moving entirely if they all just tackled him, but that idea must not have occurred to them.

Avoiding the Elder Nightmare was the highest priority. Even in its death throes, its tentacles were lethal, so Ajax set a path toward the far end of the house. If he could just make it inside, Loki would have time to grab Shaman. The cats lived in that house. Passing through the walls wasn't difficult for them, but the terrorlings would struggle to pass through. It would take them a few seconds.

A stinging pain erupted in Ajax's shoulder. One of the terrorlings landed a blow past his Spirit Armor. He expected that to happen, but not so soon. The Spirit Armor would continue to weaken as it absorbed more damage. Without it, he wouldn't last long. Not against so many opponents.

Roaring, Ajax plowed forward. He swept his head back and forth like a battering ram. He drove his claws into the ground, driving himself farther. The house was far away, but he had to keep trying. The closer he got, the easier it would be for Loki.

Needles of pain raced through Ajax's body. His protective magic was failing. It was only deflecting portions of each attack. The terrorlings were everywhere. He didn't think there was any way Loki could grab Shaman and get out of there, not without help.

"Get on my back, Loki," shouted Ajax. He was being hit so often now, he couldn't track the location of each distinct strike. Still, he trudged forward, step after painful step.

"I'm here, big guy," said Loki. Ajax never even felt the Wildseeker jump on his back. Taking a deep breath, wiggling his whiskers and wrinkling his nose, Ajax exhaled a searing stream of blistering flame. His Spirit Armor immediately faded as he coaxed every last drop of his magic through his lungs. Ajax swept his head back and forth, using his fire to clear the immediate area of terrorlings.

"Here I go!" shouted Loki. A moment later, he leapt from Ajax's back, with Shaman held firmly in his mouth. The terrorlings hissed and leapt at Loki, but with so many of them burning and smoking, they struggled to see, let alone leap. Ajax guessed he lit at least a dozen of the foul things on fire.

Most of the terrorlings pursued Loki, but a few terrorlings remained. They continued to slam their toothy heads against Ajax, and it hurt bad, but he didn't have the strength to deal with them. He was utterly exhausted. He could barely keep his eyes open. Every step was an exercise in agony.

Out of the corner of his eye, Ajax saw Gaius. The tiny white cat jumped on a terrorling's back and raised his left paw. He struck the creature repeatedly. His paw gained speed and power with each strike until it became a blur. Eventually, the terrorling collapsed, and he leapt to the next.

"Just keep walking, my friend," called Gaius from the back of a terrorling. "I'll take care of these."

Keep walking, thought Ajax.

Step after painful step.

His vision blurred, but the house wasn't far away. Only a few terrorlings were gnawing on him now, and Gaius was dealing with them quickly enough.

All in all, he couldn't complain. He did his job, and as far as he could tell, so did all the other cats. It wasn't a perfect plan, but it worked. They got it done, and that was good enough for him.

12.
REST AND REVELATIONS

Gaius pressed his head against his hooman's hand and purred. He jumped up on the table the moment he saw Jeff come back inside from tending the brisket. Loki raced back into the house when Jeff opened the door. He nodded at Gaius before running upstairs, likely to hold paws with his favorite hooman.

Both Ajax and Shaman were sleeping near the catnip table. Gaius made absolutely sure they were safe before considering his own needs. Both cats were traumatized by the battle, and he couldn't blame them. It was a miracle Ajax didn't lose another life.

Hell, it was a miracle any of them survived.

"Here you go, Genghis," said Jeff as he deftly worked his fingers alongside Gaius's face, occasionally sweeping them back behind his ears. Moments like this made Gaius appreciate the special connection he shared with his hooman. Right now, he desperately needed comfort and attention, and Jeff seemed to understand.

Hoomans were always so busy. If they weren't working, they were racing about, taking care of the house, the yard, or doing other trivial things. It was rare to find one willing to spend the time to pet a cat properly. Both the hoomans in this house understood cats, and because of that, they needed to be protected.

Gaius already lost one hooman. He swore to never let it happen again.

He knew he shouldn't blame himself for Kelly's passing. The dark spirits inside of her were surprisingly strong, and they were there long before Gaius met her. Every night, he tried to draw them out while she slumbered, like he often did for Jeff, but they were buried too deep to dislodge.

In the end, the spirits destroyed her. Once they took away her ability to experience joy, it was all downhill from there. She grew sullen and abusive. Fortunately, she never turned on Gaius or the other cats. Even if they couldn't save her, it meant a lot to give her a few moments of peace whenever possible.

Purring, Gaius pressed his face against Jeff's cheek. He wanted to keep enjoying this moment, but he knew he couldn't. He was tired, and even though a nap sounded absolutely heavenly, he couldn't risk falling asleep. Gaius pulled away, gently biting his hooman's hand.

"Enough pets for now?" asked Jeff. He held his hand out, inviting Gaius to rub against it.

Gaius sighed and leapt from the table. Every part of him wanted to press his body against his hooman's hand, curl up in a ball, and nap, but there was too much to do. His clowder just defeated an Elder Nightmare, a being of myths and legends. A creature that, until recently, Gaius doubted existed.

"Alright, Genghis," said Jeff. "I need to keep an eye on the brisket, anyway. It's cooking a little faster than I planned." He opened the sliding door and went out to the backyard, closing the door behind him.

Gaius waited until Jeff was out of sight before letting his vision drift into the Endless Tide. The all too familiar Procession of spirits greeted him. They were drifting by more quickly than before. He wondered if the changing speeds had anything to do with the Elder Nightmare, but there was no way to really know.

As expected, Sybil, the Celestine, was waiting for him. Two of the spirits Gaius summoned to fight the Elder Nightmare were there as well, standing far enough away from the Celestine to be out of earshot. Interesting, mused Gaius. All three spirits were clearly waiting for him. He expected to have a conversation with the Celestine, but not the warrior spirits.

"Greetings, clever cat. Come close, so that I might speak with you," said Sybil. She glanced over at the pair of warrior spirits before adding, "Privately."

Gaius trotted over to Sybil and began lazily cleaning a paw. He definitely needed to speak with her, but she was the first to request the discussion. Feigning indifference might give him a slight edge in the conversation.

"You and your clowder did very well out there today," said the Celestine. "I trust you've figured out which cat it was after?"

Gaius stopped cleaning and nodded. "Shaman, our new Kitanja."

"Yes," said Sybil with a slight nod. "The Conjurepurr."

It didn't surprise Gaius that she knew Shaman was a Conjurepurr. She watched them fight the Elder Nightmare, after all. She saw him create a magical forcefield. "Is that why it went after him? Because he's a Conjurepurr?"

"Are we bargaining for this information?"

Gaius started shaking his head, but stopped. "Do you know the answer?" It was a fair question. She couldn't bargain with him, in good faith, if she didn't know the answer. Having an educated guess was one thing. Knowing was something entirely different.

The Celestine held his gaze for a moment before shaking her head. "Clever cat," she mumbled. "I'm sure it's related. I mean, it wasn't mere coincidence." The Celestine sighed. "Regrettably, I have earned no knowledge to sell you, at least not regarding this."

"Then I suggest we are both free to speculate, with no bargain struck."

"Agreed, cat."

Gaius didn't think he won any real victory. He suspected the Celestine had as much to gain from the discussion as he did, but there was nothing wrong with a mutually beneficial conversation. Since Sybil seemed to be waiting for him to start, he said, "Conjurepurrs are incredibly rare. To be honest, I thought they were just a myth. Then again, until yesterday, I thought Elder Nightmares were myths as well."

"I have heard of at least one other," said Sybil, before adding, "Conjurepurr, that is. If I'm not mistaken, there are eighteen remaining Elder Nightmares. The one we killed was named Uohr'Koren, often referred to as the Devourer Beneath the Dark Earth. He was considered one of the weakest."

Gaius suspected there was much of value in what the Celestine told him about the Elder Nightmares, but he would ponder it later. "Do you know where this other Conjurepurr is?"

"No, but I imagine I could find out," said Sybil. She smiled, revealing her rows of fangs. "Would you care to bargain for that information?"

Gaius decided to play along. "What's your price?"

The Celestine ran her hand through her hair. Beyond her fingers, her hair shifted into chains, but only beyond her fingers. Everywhere else, her hair appeared normal. It was unsettling. "One of your lives."

"Out of the question!" snapped Gaius before even thinking it through. He expected Sybil to overcharge him, but the thought of paying a life for information he might discover on his own was unfathomable. "If you could arrange a meeting, I might consider it." He emphasized the word 'might'.

"So, you expect me to find it, talk to it, and earn its trust before you'll pay up?"

Even though they were just talking, with no chance of a bargain being inadvertently struck, Gaius wanted to be cautious with his words. "If we were to strike such a bargain, I would only render payment after the meeting."

Sybil cocked her head to the side. "If you won't pay until the meeting actually happens, you're asking me, on top of everything else, to arrange transport for one or both parties. I think you're grossly overvaluing your lives, clever cat."

"Don't pretend you won't profit from every step of the journey," said Gaius with a haughty hint of derision in his voice. "Meeting and befriending this other Conjurepurr, for instance, is of great value." Gaius carefully studied her reaction. A smile crept across her lips. He was right! "Besides, you're invested here. You and I already struck one bargain, and together, we did something great."

The Celestine nodded. "While we've forged no formal arrangement, I plan to look into this matter. I hope our discussion today has been in good faith, and that you'd be willing to go through with such an arrangement, should I be able to make it happen. I understand I can't bind you to it, of course."

Gaius considered backing out of the prospective agreement. The thought of letting this thing rip a life from him made his blood run cold. But then again, she more than lived up to her end of the bargain with the Elder Nightmare. "Assuming conditions don't change, I would entertain it. I'm certainly going to make my own inquiries. Understand, I'll only pay you if I can't get the job done on my own."

"Understood," said Sybil, bowing her head. "I shall take my leave of you, for now. Expect to hear from me again in a couple of days."

Gaius resumed cleaning his paw until Sybil faded away. Once he was certain she was gone, he beckoned for the pair of warrior spirits. For a moment, it looked like they were going to force him to come to them, but eventually, they drifted over. Both spirits bowed deeply. Suspecting it might be something cultural and important, Gaius returned the gesture by bowing his head. Doing anything more would be decidedly un-feline.

"Greetings, Spiritchaser, I am Tokugawa. My companion is Kiyo." He smiled warmly, his Asian eyes sparkling. "We would like to thank you for freeing us from the Chaining One."

"The Chaining one?" mused Gaius. "Is that how you refer to the Celestine?"

They both nodded. "We've been bound to her for more than a century," said Kiyo, the woman with the bow. "Be careful when bargaining with her. Once she slips a single chain around you, others will soon follow."

So far, his interactions with Sybil have been productive, but Gaius appreciated the warning. "I trust the other two didn't make it."

Tokugawa nodded. "Uohr'Koren claimed their lives."

"I'm sorry to hear that."

"All four of us understood the risks when we agreed to answer your summons," said Kiyo. "We were happy to risk death, if it meant a chance to earn our freedom."

Gaius was getting the impression these two hated Sybil. "I'm happy to have been of assistance. I must thank you as well. Without your help, the Elder Nightmare would have surely defeated us."

"That is true," said Tokugawa matter-of-factly. "Which is why we wish to make you an offer."

"An offer?"

Tokugawa glanced at Kiyo and nodded. She stepped forward and held out her hand. A tiny glowing blue sphere rested in her hand. "Do you know what this is, Spiritchaser?"

"I think so," said Gaius. "It's a Calling Stone, isn't it?"

"Very good, cat," said Kiyo, her musical voice soothing. "We wish to present this to you as a gift. Use it to call upon us, should you need assistance."

Gaius held out his paw, and Kiyo placed her hand above it. Even though they were both in different worlds, Gaius felt the tingling chill of the Calling Stone. When Kiyo pulled her hand away, the Calling Stone rested in Gaius's paw. "Thank you."

"You've earned it, Spiritchaser," said Tokugawa. "We must take our leave of you. Understand, it may take some time for us to respond to your call, so plan ahead. Also, understand that we must exact a price from you, should you summon us. We have no choice, but we promise we'll make it more than worth your while."

None of it surprised Gaius. He didn't expect spirits as powerful as these two to hang around, waiting for his call, and he never expected to summon them for free. They were noble creatures, almost as noble as cats. They deserved to be rewarded for their efforts. "I understand, and once again, you have my thanks. By the way, my name is Gaius."

Kiyo smiled. "It is a good name, Gaius." She waved and quickly faded from view. Tokugawa bowed his head before also fading from view.

With the spirits gone, Gaius considered his options. He wanted to work with Shaman, but he thought it best to let the Kitanja sleep for a little while. Even if he wanted to wake Shaman, he wasn't certain he could. It cost Ajax a sock and some undergarments to wake the Kitanja. Gaius probably needed to part with one of the bottle openers he stole from the hoomans if he hoped to wake him. As long as he didn't have to part with one of his precious remote controls, he didn't mind too much.

But he would deal with that later. Right now, he needed to send a message to the Uhl Cah'ten Ra. He needed to let the Feline Council know what happened here. Hopefully, they'd know what to do. With any luck, they might have a lead on where to find the Conjurepurr Sybil told him about.

Gaius was exhausted. He desperately needed a nap, but summoning a messenger spirit wasn't difficult. He could nap after sending a quick message to the Uhl Cah'ten Ra. He'd work with Shaman after resting.

13.
GHOSTS IN THE LITTER

Shaman curled his paws around the strange metal object, hugging it tight. He didn't want to wake up. It felt so good to sleep against Ajax's soft fur, basking in the warmth of the sun, but something was nudging him awake. He snuggled deeper into Ajax's fur, hoping to fall back asleep, but it was useless.

After a long yawn, Shaman opened his eyes. He wasn't familiar with the strange metal object he was hugging. It had a pointy end and a small open slot. The minty smell of catnip tickled his nose. He was resting his head against one of Ajax's arms, and the big brown cat was covered in catnip.

"Sorry to wake you," said Gaius softly. "I wanted to let you sleep a little while longer, but we have a few things to work on."

Shaman looked around until he spotted Gaius. The immaculate cat was standing off to the side. "What is this?" asked the kitten as he pushed the strange metal object away.

"The hoomans call it a bottle opener. They use it to open certain types of smelly, colored liquid they seem to savor." Gaius crept closer to Shaman and whispered. "I enjoy stealing them."

It suddenly made sense. Loki explained it to Shaman while he taught him how to steal. Conjurepurrs needed to steal things to recover after exerting themselves. Shaman put every ounce of energy he had into that Purrtection spell. Gaius must have used the stolen bottle opener to wake him up. "The bottle opener woke me up, didn't it?"

Gaius nodded. "Come along, little Kitanja. There are a few things I would like to show you." Gaius didn't wait for an answer. He gracefully turned around and walked away.

Shaman considered closing his eyes and going back to sleep, but he didn't want to anger the Cah'ten Ra. Yawning, he climbed to his feet and padded after the older cat. They navigated a long hallway, stopping next to a door near the end.

"Do you see them?" asked Gaius, gazing at the ceiling.

Shaman looked up, but he saw nothing. What was Gaius seeing? Were there tiny flies up there? "I don't see anything. What am I looking for?"

"You're looking for spirits, Shaman. All cats can see them, though some have an easier time than others," said Gaius. "Close your eyes, halfway, and relax. The worst thing you can do is actively try to see them. Just relax and let it happen."

Shaman did as he was told, but he struggled with the notion of not trying. He was supposed to be looking for spirits. Didn't that mean he was trying to find them? He pushed the confusing thoughts from his head and sighed. Gradually, wispy shapes materialized. Most were floating near the ceiling. Some were passing through the door, apparently moving in and out of the closet.

"You see them, don't you?"

Shaman nodded. "I see many by the ceiling, and some are coming in and out of that closet."

"Excellent," praised Gaius.

"Does this mean I'm a Spiritchaser, or is that different?"

"A Spiritchaser is something much different," said Gaius. He was so close his breath tickled Shaman's whiskers. "All cats can see free-roaming spirits, and in time, learn to spot which ones are dangerous. The spirits you are looking at are outside of the Endless Tide."

"What does that mean?" asked Shaman. He enjoyed watching the spirits, but a few of them made him uncomfortable. One of them was pushing its head through the closed closet door, watching him. Every time Shaman focused on it, it retreated into the closet.

"The Endless Tide is the spirit world. It is the place spirits go after they finally move on from this material place."

"What happens to them there?"

"Most spirits who enter the Endless Tide join the Procession, where they wait in line to be reborn. Other spirits make different choices," said Gaius. "Spiritchasers can see into the Endless Tide. We learn the ways of spirits. We learn how to call them, and how to bargain with them. It's quite complicated."

Shaman found it incredibly interesting. He liked the thought of calling spirits to do his bidding, like Gaius did out in the Dreaming. "Was it hard to summon the spirits who helped us fight the scary monster?"

"Incredibly hard," said Gaius solemnly. "I needed to strike a deal to do it. I suspect I'll be paying for it for some time to come, but let's not dwell on that. Tell me about the spirits you're seeing. Do some of them scare you?"

Shaman nodded. "There's one that keeps slipping in and out of the closet. I don't like him."

"You learn quickly. Now, step aside, please."

Shaman shuffled to his left. He didn't know why he was asked to move, but he wasn't about to argue. A moment later, Gaius approached the door and leapt high in the air. He wrapped his paws around the door handle and hung from it. As the handle slowly turned from his weight, he kicked his back paws against the molding next to the door. When he landed, he quickly snaked a paw beneath the door and pulled. It swung open.

"Wow!" breathed Shaman.

"Is that the spirit that scares you?" asked Gaius, pointing. Now that the door was open, the creepy spirit was cowering in the corner. For whatever reason, it seemed terrified of Gaius.

"Yes, that's the one."

Gaius jumped, kicking his feet against the wall inside the closet. When he did, he meowed loudly. The spirit raced from the closet, quickly disappearing from sight. Gaius gracefully landed and faced Shaman. "Infected spirits, we call them Banes, are terrified of cats. Leap and meow at them. If you're convincing enough, they'll run."

"What's a Bane?" asked Shaman.

"While most spirits are harmless, some wish to harm the world. We refer to those as Banes."

"Are they dangerous?"

Gaius nodded. "Banes can infect living things. When they do, they spread their sickness to their host. Most times, the infections are mild. A cough or a cold. Perhaps a sore paw, or weepy eyes, but their infections aren't limited to physical ailments. A Bane can make someone sad, or nervous, or even cause a lapse in memory."

Shaman was confused. He was often scared. Sometimes, he was even sad. Was that all because of Banes? "Are these bad spirits the source of all sadness?"

"A good question, little Kitanja," said Gaius. "Cats, hoomans, animals… we can all get sick or become sad on our own, but when a Bane causes it, it's much worse. When you or I become sad, the feeling eventually passes. When a Bane makes someone sad, they'll remain sad until someone removes the spirit."

The Cah'ten Ra's explanation made sense. "How do you remove a Bane?" asked Shaman. It seemed the next logical question.

"I'll show you sometime. Cats aren't the only creatures that can remove Banes, but, of course, we're the best at it. There are spirits in the Endless Tide who remove Banes, but let's save that discussion for another day."

Just then, the back door slid open, and Jeff entered the house. He was carrying a large tray of steaming meat. It didn't take Shaman more than a second to recognize the smell. Brisket! The brisket was done cooking!

"Let me set this here to cool, and it's off to the bathroom with me," said Jeff as he set the tray of meat on the counter. The hoomans in this house liked to talk to themselves.

"Perfect timing," said Gaius.

"I know, right?" purred Shaman. "Let's get some brisket!"

Gaius gently swatted his nose. It didn't hurt. It was just surprising. "I meant the bathroom."

"Huh?"

"Follow me," said Gaius as he padded after Jeff. "Banes are most commonly found in bathrooms."

Shaman followed Gaius to the bathroom. By the time he made it there, the hooman was already sitting on the cool white bowl.

"Really, Genghis?" said the hooman, shaking his head. "Are you teaching the Chairman to watch me on the throne? Sometimes, I just don't get you cats."

"Keep your eyes focused on the flushing device," said Gaius as he sat down, his tail twitching. "Water attracts spirits, and for reasons I don't understand, hoomans like to do their business when sitting on this device. It's filled with water, but that's not the worst of it. It connects to an entire system of water pipes."

"Okay," whispered Shaman. He knew the hooman couldn't hear them, but he thought he should be quiet, all the same.

"When mass leaves a hooman, sometimes a Bane enters, filling the void," said Gaius. He crept closer and meowed. "Just like I thought. One was trying to infect him."

Shaman thought he saw something, but he wasn't certain. "Did I just see one?" he asked. "I'm not sure."

Gaius nodded. "They're harder to see against the white flushing device, but there was definitely one there. I chased it off."

"What would have happened if you didn't?"

"It would have infected my hooman. Several spirits infect him every day. It's unavoidable, but the more I prevent from getting inside of him, the less I have to remove while he sleeps." Gaius turned and left the bathroom. He looked back at Shaman, encouraging him to follow.

The thought of spirits racing into his delicate areas made Shaman incredibly uncomfortable. "Do spirits do the same thing to cats? I mean… when we're doing our business?"

"Yes, but it's very rare," said the Cah'ten Ra. He turned and faced Shaman. "Unlike hoomans, cats have the common sense to do their business in dry places. There's a reason there is no water in our litter boxes."

"But it still happens sometimes?" asked Shaman nervously.

"Yes."

"So, what do we do about it?"

Gaius leaned forward and licked Shaman's nose. "If you feel it happening, you run from the litter as fast as your little legs can carry you, and you keep running. Meowing helps too. The spirit will chase you, but spirits tire easily. As long as you keep running, you'll get away."

Shaman remembered seeing Ajax run from the litter once. He didn't understand why the enormous brown cat ran around the house, meowing at the top of his lungs, but it made sense now. "But what happens if you don't feel it in time? What happens if you don't get away?"

"It's difficult to remove a spirit from a cat, but it's possible," said Gaius. "But do your best to avoid getting infected, all the same. Deal?"

"Deal."

"Jeff will be in there for a few minutes." Gaius noticed the succulent scent of meat in the air and licked his chops. "How about we take the opportunity to help ourselves to some of that brisket?"

The promise of rich, juicy meat chased away Shaman's fear of scary spirits invading his private parts. He nodded eagerly. "I cast, Summon Brisket!"

14.
THE HUNTER'S GLADE

Shaman gazed at the vibrant night sky and gasped. This was the first time he saw the Dreaming at night, and its beauty took his breath away. An assortment of colorful stars peppered the dark sky. A bright purple moon was the focal point, but between the stars and the swirling patches of multicolored dust, it was quite the show.

"Any sign of the terrorlings?" asked Gaius.

Loki raised his long snout and sniffed the air. "They definitely stayed in the Oaken Grove for a while, but I don't smell any of them nearby."

Ajax relaxed. Shaman was, once again, protected by the Guardian's magic. He was tiring of riding Ajax. He wanted to walk around, feeling the grass and soil of the Dreaming beneath his paws, but Gaius said it was still too dangerous. Shaman wasn't about to challenge the Cah'ten Ra.

"Excellent. That's one less thing to deal with," said Gaius. "Loki, I have a task for you."

"Why does it always have to me?" pouted Loki.

"Why does it have to be you?" huffed Ajax. "What about me? I'm the one constantly getting attacked by everything."

"Silence!" snapped Gaius, holding up a paw. Both of the other cats immediately quieted. "I need someone to reach out to the neighboring domain. We seek an audience with the Hunter."

Loki's ears twitched. "Oh, why didn't you say so?"

"I was trying to, but no one would let me," grumbled Gaius.

"Give me a few minutes. I'll see if he's in the mood." said Loki as he padded to the far side of the yard. Creepy trees surrounded much of the Oaken Grove. Ajax said those trees were part of the Forest of Shadows, but one corner of the yard seemed to lead to a verdant clearing.

Despite all the creepy trees, the Oaken Grove was beautiful at night. Sure, everything glowed during the day, but in the darkness, the countless glowing things painted the entire region in a collage of lights. Everywhere Shaman looked, he saw distinct patterns of colors. He could spend hours out here, just studying how the colors all blended together.

Once Loki reached the edge of the yard, he disappeared from sight. Shaman wasn't sure what happened to him. He could see inside the clearing. Why couldn't he see Loki? "Where did he go?" asked Shaman.

"Some regions in the Dreaming are private," explained Gaius. "That glade over there belongs to the Hunter. We can't see inside it."

"But I can see it from here. It's pretty. Everything is green, and there is a pond and a waterfall."

"Yup, that's what it looks like," said Ajax. "The tricky thing, little guy, is we can't see what's going on inside there right at this moment."

"I don't get it," sighed Shaman.

"Think of it like a picture," said Gaius. "What you're seeing is a picture of what it looks like inside the Hunter's domain at night. The picture doesn't change often. It doesn't show us if the Hunter is bathing in his pond, or if a flock of flapfeathers stopped by for a refreshing drink. It also doesn't show us Loki, but rest assured, he's in there right now."

"Is he going to be okay?" asked Shaman, suddenly nervous. "Is he safe?"

"Loki is friends with all the neighbors. He'll be fine," said Ajax.

Shaman didn't like losing sight of Loki, but if Ajax said everything was alright, he would not question it. Sure enough, a few moments later, Loki materialized at the edge of the yard. He appeared out of nowhere. Reflecting on the way Gaius explained it, Shaman thought of it as if Loki stepped out of a painting.

"Well?" asked Gaius.

"The Hunter is home. He said it was alright if we wanted to come over and visit." Loki sat down near the border to the Hunter's domain and cleaned a paw.

Gaius trotted over to Loki, and Ajax followed. Shaman studied the verdant clearing as they approached it, and sure enough, it looked more and more like a painting to him. A few of the leaves and branches moved as if blown by the wind, but their motions seemed inconsistent to Shaman. Why would certain leaves move, and others remain still? The pond and waterfall looked even more fake.

"Hold on, little guy, this may tickle," said Ajax as he pressed his snout against what Shaman was increasingly thinking of as a picture. Sure enough, after a moment, Ajax's head disappeared from view. Shaman closed his eyes and turned his face away as he was pulled against the barrier. It didn't hurt, but he couldn't quite describe it as a tickle, either. It felt like he was being squeezed, but only for a moment.

Shaman opened his eyes and was greeted by another world. This place contained a glowing retaining wall, much like the Oaken Grove did, but this retaining wall was much taller, and featured a series of steps. Glowing plants covered each step. The first hosted light green plants. The second displayed orange plants, and the top step featured a mixture of yellow and white plants.

Rows of trees towered around the edges of the round clearing. Several of them were twisted and dark. Shaman immediately understood those to be part of the Forest of Shadows, but the rest of them glowed with soft amber light from within. The trees were so close together, they formed a wall.

An enormous pool of shimmering turquoise dominated the center of the glade. A cascading waterfall fed the pool, though Shaman didn't see any river supplying the waterfall. He suspected the waterfall was somehow circulating the water inside the pool. He guessed it worked a lot like the endless water bowl the hoomans kept in the kitchen. One of the hoomans took it apart the other morning. There was a little black box inside that sucked up water and spit it out the top.

"Greetings, noble Cah'ten Ra," called a rumbling voice. "Tonight, you and your clowder are welcome guests within my domain. No harm will come to you."

"Thank you, great Hunter. We appreciate your hospitality," said Gaius with a nod.

Shaman gasped as the Hunter stepped out from behind the waterfall. His body was unmistakably that of a large dog, but a hairy human torso sprouted from where the dog's head and shoulders should have been. The Hunter's head wasn't human. It was broad and covered in white feathers. Two huge, golden eyes rested in recessed sockets, and a sharp beak poked out from the center of his face. He topped everything off with a droopy tan hat.

"Funky, isn't he," said Ajax. "He's kind of a cross between a dog, a man, and an owl."

A decoratively carved wooden bow rested diagonally across his back, and he held a curious spear in his right hand. Instead of having a long wooden shaft, the shaft of the Hunter's spear ended about midway along the length. Several spikes of glistening metal twisted together, forming the rest of the length. They concentrated into a sharp point at the top.

"I trust you're here to speak with me about yesterday's events?" said the Hunter.

"Yes," said Gaius, stepping forward. "I'm curious about your take on it. What did you observe? What was happening within the Forest of Shadow yesterday, before and during our fight? Were things different after we defeated the Elder Nightmare?"

The Hunter whistled. "I knew something powerful took up residence in your Grove, but I didn't know it was an Elder Nightmare." The Hunter stepped into the shallows of his pond. The water came up to just beneath the top of the dog portion of his body. "Have the Blooms started yet?"

"What's he talking about?" mumbled Ajax beneath his breath.

Gaius shot Ajax a quizzical look. "No, but to be honest, I'm not sure what to look for. This is the first time we've fought something so powerful. If I'm not mistaken, it has been more than a century since any Cah'ten have fought a foe like this."

"I don't study Cah'ten history, so if you say it has been that long, I'll take your word for it," said the Hunter with a shrug. "When a great creature perishes, some of its power seeps into the land. If the thing you killed was one of the Elder Nightmares, that domain of yours is going to change."

"How so?" asked Loki.

"It's hard to say," said the Hunter as he adjusted his droopy tan hat. "This pond of mine, for instance, used to be pretty darn small. It only grew into what it is today after I hunted a pair of Old Ones."

"Cool," breathed Loki. "I never knew that, neighbor."

The Hunter tipped his cap.

"Thank you for the information, great Hunter," said Gaius. "We will certainly let you know how the Oaken Grove changes, but what of my other questions?"

"To tell you the truth, I avoided the Forest of Shadows for the past few days. There's been an awful lot of terrorling activity, but there's something else going on in that place. I suspect something is organizing and directing them."

"I noticed an acrid smell the other day," said Loki. "It's not a smell I've encountered before."

The Hunter nodded. "I don't have a fraction of your sense of smell, but the fact that you picked up something out of the ordinary confirms my fears. Terrorlings rarely travel in large groups. Something gathered them."

"What about the Elder Nightmare? Couldn't it have gathered the terrorlings? They were aiding it in battle, after all. That seems the likeliest explanation," said Gaius.

"If we're thinking the acrid smell is part of it, I have bad news for you," said Ajax sheepishly.

"What are you talking about?" asked Gaius.

"I smelled something strange before the Elder Nightmare stepped through the Abyssinial Gateway."

"What did it smell like?" asked Loki. "Did it burn your nose? Was it sweet, or perhaps sour? Are you sure it wasn't just a stray terrorling or too?"

"I may not have an enormous snout like you, but I know what a damn terrorling smells like," growled Ajax.

"So, what did it smell like?" asked Gaius.

"Kind of like the stuff hoomans use to take the fake colors off their nails," said Ajax. "It tickled and burned my nose. I only caught a brief whiff, but that's what I remember most."

"Well, whiskers," cursed Loki. "That's the same thing I smelled."

Shaman smiled at the Hunter, and the strange creature returned the friendly gesture. Shaman was afraid of the odd mixture of a dog, an owl, and a man, but the smile went a long way toward comforting him.

"Well, I think that settles it," said the Hunter. "If the smell appeared before the Elder Nightmare entered your Grove, it couldn't have been the Elder Nightmare. You cats had to be smelling something else."

"Agreed," sighed Gaius. "So, how do we find out what it was? Is there any way you can help us, Hunter?"

The Hunter backed deeper into his pond until the waters climbed to halfway up his human torso. "Sure, I can help, but why should I?"

His answer surprised Shaman. He wondered if he could make the strange creature do what he wanted. He made the hooman go out and buy a brisket, after all. Ajax even admitted feeling compelled by Shaman's commands.

"I would think it is in your best interests to help," said Gaius. "We are neighbors. The problems that haunt us also haunt you, and vice versa."

The Hunter cocked his head to the side. "Funny you should mention that, Cah'ten Ra. I have a problem you cats might help me with. Are you interested in trading favors?"

"What do you need us to do?"

"There have been many Banes in the region, as of late," said the Hunter. "They've infected the local chipmunks, forcing them to attack the real world version of my retaining wall. We all know what will happen if that goes unchecked."

"Of course," said Gaius.

Shaman didn't know what would happen. This was all new to him. Maybe Ajax or one of the other cats would explain it to him later, but he wanted to be a part of the conversation. "What will happen? I'm just a kitten. I don't understand."

The Hunter quickly glanced at Gaius. Shaman didn't know if he was angry, or asking permission, or what. "Banes are spirits that possess others."

"I know what Banes are," said Shaman with a nod. "Gaius explained them to me. What I don't understand is the part about the wall."

"Things in the real world are mirrored in the Dreaming, little guy," said Ajax. "If chipmunks start knocking rocks out of the retaining wall in the real world, it will damage the retaining wall in the Dreaming."

"Basically, yes," said Gaius. "It's a little more complicated than that, especially given the exact nature of the Hunter's wall, but I think Ajax's explanation is sufficient."

The Hunter nodded. "My offer is this. In exchange for reducing the local chipmunk population, I will investigate this new threat in the Forest of Shadows. Do you agree to my terms, Cah'ten Ra?"

"I agree in principle," said Gaius. "The duration of our hunt, and the exact quantity of chipmunks we purge, needs to be established."

The Hunter shrugged. "Let's keep it open-ended. For all I know, I won't be able to discover anything for you."

"Very well," said Gaius. "We've always dealt fairly with one another. I suspect this arrangement will be no different."

"You know what this means, little guy?" purred Ajax. He sounded positively overjoyed. "We get to teach you how to hunt chippers!"

As much as Shaman was content eating brisket and napping on comfortable floors, he couldn't deny the excitement he felt every time he spied a furry rodent running across the yard. He wondered what it would feel like beneath his claws, or taste like between his teeth.

Hunting sounded like a good time! He couldn't wait to get started, but he wasn't sure how it would work. The hoomans never let him outside. They said he was too small. He needed to grow before they'd let him outside.

Hopefully, the other cats knew a solution to the problem. He suspected they did. They were quite clever, after all.

15.
HUNTING LESSONS

Shaman tugged and scratched at the uncomfortable collar, but it wouldn't budge. It wouldn't be so bad if it was just the collar, but there was a leash attached. As far as he was concerned, leashes were for dogs and other lesser creatures. Leashes were definitely not for cats.

"You know, if the hoomans see you trying to escape like that, they'll put you back inside the house," said Ajax. "It's probably best if you forget about the collar. Besides, it's only temporary."

Shaman glared at Ajax and pointed at how his leash was tied around a tree branch. "This is so unfair," he whined. "I should be free to roam around, just like the rest of you."

"You should be grateful they let you outside," said Ajax. "Between you and me, I'm surprised Gaius' plan worked."

Initially, the hoomans kept Shaman inside. They claimed he was too small to be outside without supervision, but Gaius had a plan. Every couple of minutes, one of the cats begged to come back inside. Once inside, they waited a minute or two before demanding to go back outside. Shaman thought the plan failed when the hoomans got fed up and kept all the cats inside, but the sound of all the cats meowing at the top of their lungs was too much for them.

Eventually, the hoomans relented and left the door open, just enough for cats to come and go as they pleased. Shaman raced for the open door, but one of the hoomans grabbed him by his tail before he could make it outside. Evidently, their decision to leave the door open relied on Shaman wearing a collar and a leash.

It was so undignified!

"How am I supposed to catch a chipmunk if I'm tied to a tree?" asked Shaman. "Gaius is chasing them around the yard, and Loki is over in the neighbor's yard."

"Gaius is just scaring them," said Ajax. "He's hoping the smart ones will realize we're out here hunting and hide in their holes. We're only after the infected ones, and they're pretty dumb. Must be something the Banes do to them."

Shaman sighed and lay down beneath the hostas. The ground was covered in woodchips. He preferred lying in the grass, but the woodchips weren't too bad. Although it was a hot day, a gentle breeze blew, delivering cooler air and interesting smells.

Ajax pointed to a nearby hole in the ground. "While it's fun to chase chipmunks around the yard, the best way to hunt them is to sit down next to one of their tunnels and wait."

"Really? That's how we hunt?" Shaman wanted to creep through the underbrush, sneaking close enough to his prey, before triumphantly charging. That's what hunting meant to him.

"It's all about hunting smarter, not harder," said Ajax with a nod. "I mean, look at me. I'm a pretty big kitty. Sure, I can climb trees and run around with the best of them, but I'm more interested in letting the chipmunks come to me." He licked his chops. "Besides, they taste the same either way."

"Do you eat the chipmunks you kill?"

Ajax shrugged. "Sometimes, but not all that often. I mean, brisket tastes a lot better than chipmunk. Every now and then, though, I get a hankering for some chipper meat."

Shaman was nervous about the next question. He was worried asking it would somehow make him less of a cat. "How do you… um…" Shaman looked away. "How do you kill a chipmunk?"

"Don't worry, little guy, I'll teach you," said Ajax. "I've got Loki looking for mice and smaller chippers as we speak."

"What happens if a chipmunk comes out of this hole while we're waiting?"

"Then we'll kill it, but I don't expect one to show up so soon," said Ajax. "It'll probably be a few hours before chipmunks start popping their heads out of this hole, but if it happens sooner, it's pretty simple." Ajax leaned in and nuzzled the Shaman. "If you see a chipper, bite it, and don't let go. If you want to play with them, the best place to grab them is the scruff of the neck. If you're going for the kill, bite the rest of the neck."

Shaman didn't like the sound of that. He could handle grabbing something by the scruff. He knew what that felt like, and it didn't hurt or anything. Biting something in the neck seemed awfully violent to him. There had to be a gentler way to kill chipmunks.

"Here comes Loki now," said Ajax with a nod. "It looks like he's got a mouse for you."

Shaman stood so he could see above the hostas. Loki was perched on top of the flimsy, floppy fence surrounding the yard with a mouse hanging from his mouth. He leapt from the fence and padded over to them.

"Nice mouse. Was it hard to catch?" asked Ajax.

Loki dropped the mouse, quickly placing a paw over its tail before it could run. "It was hard to find, but easy to catch. There's a ton of chippers back there, but not a lot of mice."

Shaman remembered what the Hunter said about the chipmunks being possessed by Banes. "Do the infected chipmunks chase the mice away?"

"I don't know. Never thought about it," said Loki with a shrug. When he shrugged, he lifted his paw just enough to let the mouse escape. It ran away from Loki as fast as its little legs could carry it. Unfortunately, it ran directly at Ajax.

"Hey, Shaman," called Ajax as he swatted the mouse. "Comin' at ya!"

It skittered and rolled toward Shaman, desperate to escape, but with three cats sitting right there, there was no place for it to go. Shaman swatted the mouse more out of instinct than anything else. It felt nice to sink a claw into its soft fur. The mouse went absolutely still. For a moment, Shaman wondered if he killed it, but he noticed it was still breathing.

"Good job, Kitanja," said Loki. "While you're having fun playing with that mouse, I'll go grab us a chipmunk."

Shaman gripped the mouse with both paws and tossed it into the air. It twisted and spun, flailing its little legs as it started its descent. Shaman waited until it was roughly eye level with him before slamming a paw down on it, driving it into the ground.

Playing with rodents was fun!

"Hey, little guy, you might want to be careful with mice," said Ajax. "They're a lot smaller than chippers. You don't need to bite them in the neck to kill them. A few swats like the one you just delivered will do the trick."

Shaman peered at the big brown cat. "I thought I was supposed to kill this. Why should I be careful with it?" The mouse slowly rose to its feet. Its legs were wobbly. Shaman smacked it, knocking it on its side.

"If you kill it, we won't be able to play with it later."

Shaman sniffed the terrified mouse. It was back to playing dead. Waiting for it to stop playing dead seemed pretty boring, but tossing it in the air would be fun. "It's not really doing much."

"Sure, right now, it's not doing anything, but what do you expect?" said Ajax. "It's trapped between a pair of cats. If we want to play with that one, we need to let it go. Then we can catch it again."

"Doesn't that defeat the purpose?" asked Shaman, shaking his head. "Why catch it in the first place if we're just going to let it go? Won't it dive into a burrow, never to be seen again?"

Ajax smiled. "Not if we bring it into the house."

"The house?"

Ajax nodded. "Whenever we catch something we want to play with, we bring it into the house. Then, after we get bored, we let it run away and hide."

"And the hoomans allow this?"

"Not much they can do about it," said Ajax. "Sure, they get mad, from time to time, but it's well worth it. I can't even begin to describe how much fun it is when you get two or three chippers running around in the basement."

Shaman pulled at his collar. "My leash isn't long enough for me to bring this mouse into the house."

Ajax shrugged. "Well, it's just a mouse. You might as well kill it."

Shaman grabbed it with both paws and tossed it high in the air. He swatted it with his right paw as it fell, driving it into the ground once again. Shaman waited for it to get back to its feet, but it didn't. He swatted it a few more times to be sure it was dead.

"Good job, Kitanja," called Gaius as he approached. "Where's Loki?"

"He's off fetching us a chipmunk. He should be back soon," said Ajax.

Shaman wondered how quickly Loki could catch a chipmunk. He only left a minute ago. Was he really that fast?

"I see him coming back over the fence now," said Gaius. "It looks like he caught a small one."

"Is it that easy to catch chipmunks?" asked Shaman.

"Not really," said Gaius. "Normal chipmunks spend most of their time hiding in their burrows, but these are infected with Banes. They seem more concerned with destroying retaining walls than avoiding us."

Loki padded over with a chipmunk dangling from his mouth. He dropped it in the midst of the gathered cats. It turned and leapt at him. Shaman was surprised how fast the thing moved, but Loki wasn't. He swatted the rodent with his right paw, sending it tumbling to the ground. "Take that!" said Loki.

"Now that we're all here, there's been a change in plans," said Gaius.

Shaman pounced on the chipmunk the moment it tried to climb back to its feet. It wasn't overly large, but then again, neither was he.

Still, he was heavy enough to collapse its legs. It coughed out a tiny squeak of protest.

"Regrettably, chipmunk hunting will have to wait."

"Why?" asked Ajax. "What happened?"

"The other day, I sent a messenger spirit to the Uhl Cah'ten Ra, informing him of our plight. I didn't expect to hear anything back, but apparently, he is quite interested in our story." Gaius paused to clean a paw. "The Uhl Cah'ten Ra is convening an emergency Cah'ten Moot tonight."

"Tonight?" asked Loki. "Where? Wait, he's not holding it in the normal spot, is he?"

Gaius nodded.

"Whiskers!" cursed Loki.

"That's a long journey. Even if we left right now, we wouldn't make it," said Ajax.

"I know," said Gaius softy. "The only way we can possibly make it in time is by traveling the Wilds. The Uhl Cah'ten Ra would know that as well."

"I don't like this," grumbled Ajax.

"Neither do I, but I don't see much of an alternative," said Gaius.

"Can't you just send another messenger-thingy and tell him we can't make it?" asked Shaman. He was sitting next to the chipmunk, with one paw resting on its haunches, waiting for it to move.

"I don't think that's wise," said Gaius.

"Yeah, well, neither is traveling through the Wilds," growled Ajax.

"I gotta say, I agree with Ajax on this one," said Loki. "I hate walking through that place, and I'm a lot faster than the rest of you."

Gaius sighed. "I know it's dangerous, but I don't think there's an alternative."

"Of course, there's an alternative," said Ajax. "Refuse the meeting!"

Gaius shook his head. "I think the Uhl Cah'ten Ra expects that. That tells me there will be repercussions, should we refuse." Gaius met Ajax's gaze. "Serious repercussions."

"How bad can it be?" asked Loki.

Gaius sighed. "The Uhl Cah'ten Ra has made it no secret that he thinks he should be the one watching over the Abyssinial Gateway. If he convenes a special meeting for us, and we cannot attend, he'll use that to his advantage."

Ajax took a deep breath and closed his eyes. "Even traveling the Wilds, we'll need to leave before sundown if we hope to make it in time."

Gaius nodded. "Tonight's journey will be a dangerous one. We all need to be at our best, so I suggest everyone rests." Gaius paused, glancing at Shaman and the chipmunk. "You can kill that one, Shaman, but after that, we need to get you inside so you can rest. Have you stolen enough items to recharge your abilities?"

Shaman beamed with pride. "I stole a bunch of hair ties from the hoomans. They both stash them on the tables next to their bed. I think I'm as ready as I'll ever be."

"Excellent," said Gaius. "That's what I wanted to hear."

The chipmunk beneath Shaman's paw sprung to its feet, but Shaman extended his claws fast enough to stop it from escaping. Lunging, Shaman snapped his jaws shut around the chipper's neck. It squeaked and struggled, but his bite was precise.

The way the other cats reacted to the prospect of a journey through the Wilds made Shaman nervous. If Ajax was scared, he knew he should be as well. Still, he was growing stronger by the day. He was learning how to use and replenish his powers, and he just learned how to hunt chipmunks.

Shaman thought he was well on his way to becoming a full member of this clowder, and he couldn't be happier.

16.
HOLDING PAWS

Loki cradled Maureen's hand as he watched her from the pillow at the top of the bed. He didn't understand why she slept during the day, given that the other hooman slept at night, but he appreciated it. It was nice to have one of the hoomans constantly awake for pets, cuddles, and treats.

He also enjoyed having one in bed, sleeping, most of the time. Loki liked resting with both of the hoomans, but he only really held paws with Maureen. Somehow, he identified with her. Jeff was organized, regimented, and often sad. Without Gaius regularly pulling Banes out of him, he'd be much worse. Maureen, on the other hand, was a free spirit. She understood Loki's need to jump the fence and roam the neighborhood. She often told him so.

Gaius and Ajax favored Jeff over Maureen, and Loki understood why. Both those cats were raised by Jeff's lost mate, Kelly. Loki knew Gaius blamed himself for Kelly's passing, and he suspected Ajax harbored similar feelings. Kelly was still alive when Loki first came to the house, but they never grew close. She was too riddled with Banes by the time he entered her life to help her. Loki was good at scaring evil spirits, but he didn't know how to pull them out of people. The best he could do was chase them away before they entered a hooman.

The Banes that lived deep inside Maureen were powerful, but Loki didn't think they were strong enough to destroy her. Gaius extracted many of Maureen's Banes, but he decided the deepest ones shouldn't be removed. According to Gaius, some Banes eventually became a part of a person. Removing them did more harm than good.

Maureen adjusted in her sleep, pulling her hand toward her face, but Loki pulled it back. He enjoyed feeling her steady pulse while she slept. It comforted him. Her pulse served as a constant reminder of his purpose in this house. She was his hooman, and he needed to protect her. It was as simple as that.

He remembered when she first arrived. It was a sad time in the house. The loss of Kelly devastated everyone. They were aimlessly wandering, with no real destination, but the arrival of a new hooman changed things. Despite some of the cats' misgivings, Maureen was good for Jeff. Loki saw it right away. That's why he adopted her.

But that was years ago. Eventually, life settled into a new rhythm. The passage of time gradually softened the pain of loss, and as it did, the other cats grew to accept Maureen as a member of the household.

Loki often wondered if the hoomans knew how hard he and the other cats fought for them. He liked to think they understood how dangerous the Dreaming could be. He imagined they cuddled the cats as a way of saying thank you. Deep down, he knew hoomans didn't know about the Dreaming, and that they cuddled for their own reasons, but it was nice to pretend.

The upcoming mission terrified Loki. He generally avoided the Wilds, especially at night. In the real world, the Wilds were an overgrown patch of wetlands, starting several hundred yards from the house. Loki rarely explored the area. He knew turkeys and deer liked to bed down in there, but they weren't the only creatures to be found in the dense woods. At night, a three-legged coyote and his pack often hunted there.

In the Dreaming, the Wilds stretched for miles. Giant stags and enormous, omnivorous birds roamed the territory. Loki suspected they were the Dreaming's versions of deer and turkeys. Using that logic, Fenris, and his pack, must be the coyotes.

"You should come downstairs," said Gaius softly as he hopped up onto the bed. "We're almost ready to go."

Loki held Maureen's paw tight. "I don't think we should go. I've got a bad feeling about this."

"We've been over this before," said Gaius with a sigh. "We don't have a choice."

"But what about Fenris?" Loki shuddered as he remembered the time a coyote nearly got him. He was outside the yard, hiding in the bushes. He didn't know why, but something set him on edge. Jeff was walking through the woods, trying to chase him back into the yard. He must have startled a bunny, because one hopped out from the underbrush. A breath later, a coyote leapt out of nowhere, instantly killing the bunny.

Loki cowered in the bushes as Jeff and the coyote faced off. Jeff was powerfully built for a hooman, but Loki sensed his fear. If Loki could sense it, he knew the coyote could smell it. The two of them stood barely a dozen paces apart, each waiting for the other to move. Eventually, the coyote turned and trotted away. It wasn't after any bunny. Loki knew it in his soul. That horrible beast was after him.

"It's been weeks since we've heard the coyotes yapping and howling at night. I'm just as scared of Fenris and his pack as you are, but they roam a nearly endless territory. If they were in the area, we would have heard them by now," said Gaius.

Loki wasn't so sure. The coyote that almost got him was hunting in broad daylight. They never heard it howling either, not in the nights before or after the incident. "They don't always howl, Gaius. You know that, right?"

The Cah'ten Ra nodded, ever so slightly. "Look… I wish there were another way, but there isn't."

"I know," whispered Loki. "But with everything that's happened lately, we both know this will be dangerous."

Gaius looked away for a moment. "Take a little while longer, but not too long. For what it's worth, you're not the only cat who's scared. I can see it in Ajax's eyes."

"What about you?"

Gaius met Loki's gaze. "I'm terrified. The only reason I'm not curled up with my hooman is because he's not home. He's at work."

Loki nodded. The fact that Gaius and Ajax were scared shouldn't have brought him solace. It should have enhanced his fear, but it comforted him instead. "Thanks, Gaius."

The Cah'ten Ra said nothing. He simply turned and gracefully leapt from the bed, leaving Loki alone with his hooman. Somehow, holding Maureen's paw wasn't enough for him. He needed more contact… More comfort.

Loki gently worked his way beneath the covers and snuggled up against Maureen's chest. She instinctively wrapped an arm around him. Normally, he avoided being held. He was a wild and free kitty, after all, but right now, he needed to be hugged.

Maureen stirred as Loki purred his heart out. Slowly, she began drawing her hand across his cheek and down his sides. Her breathing pattern changed as she woke. She continued petting him for a few moments before lifting the covers and planting a kiss on his forehead.

Loki closed his eyes, snuggled against Maureen's body, and continued purring. This was what he needed most. Later today, when he set foot in the Wilds, he'd be doing it for a reason. He didn't understand everything that was happening, but Gaius warned him that problems in the Dreaming could bleed into the real world. The monsters of the Dreaming could cross over. They could hurt or kill his hooman.

"Is everything alright?" said Maureen with a yawn. "You can stay as long as you like. You know I like to snuggle."

Loki carefully crawled free from Maureen's arm and out from under the covers. He knew she wouldn't try to stop him. Once he was free, he gently pressed his face against her cheek and rubbed. They were cheek to cheek.

He stayed there for several deep, throaty purrs. It was his way of telling her that everything was going to be alright. He was going to go out there and face the scary monsters, so she didn't have to.

Maureen reached up and gently massaged him behind the ears. Loki pressed his head back, but only for a moment. Gaius and the others were downstairs. He didn't want to keep them waiting. As much as he wanted to cuddle, there was work to do.

Loki leapt from the bed and quickly trotted out of the bedroom.

17.
INTO THE WILDS

Ajax sniffed the air before cautiously creeping down the trail. Unlike many areas in the Dreaming, a clear border did not define the Wilds. Loki guided them along a winding path leading out of the Hunter's Glade. At first, the grassy path felt cool and soft, and the smells of the foliage lining the path were pleasantly peppery, almost like catnip.

But that didn't last.

Ajax couldn't put his paw on the exact moment they left the path and entered the Wilds. He just knew it happened. The grass gradually became slick and wet, and the peppery smells of the foliage gave way to the foul tang of rotting vegetation.

The change in the ambient lighting was even more disturbing. The plants here glowed, just like everywhere in the Dreaming, but the quality of the lighting was different. Back home, in the Oaken Grove, glowing plants bathed the area with their light. Here, in the Wilds, light didn't seem to travel. Ajax even tested it. He held a paw next to a glowing green branch. The light didn't splash any color against his fur. It was eerie.

"I don't like this place," whispered Shaman. As usual, he was riding on Ajax's back, protected by the Guardian's Spirit Armor.

"None of us do, Kitanja," said Gaius.

"Do you want me to scout ahead again?" asked Loki. "As much as it scares me, if anyone is going to stumble into something dangerous, I guess it should be me. I'm the quickest, after all."

"No," said Gaius, shaking his head. "For now, let's stick together."

"You won't get any argument from me."

Ajax pressed on. While he would have preferred Loki to scout, he couldn't argue with the Cah'ten Ra's logic. The last thing they wanted was to get separated. None of the cats knew the Wilds well, not even Loki. Sticking together was probably for the best.

Up ahead, the path dipped sharply. Ajax stopped at the top of the hill and peered down at the land below. Murky water covered everything. He didn't think it was deep, but he expected it to be unpleasant, nonetheless. "Are we sure this is the right way?" asked Ajax. "I don't want to get all muddy if I can avoid it."

"The tracker spirit tells me this is the correct path," said Gaius. "I'm sorry, friend. I wish I had better news."

Gaius summoned a spirit to lead them through the Wilds. Loki seemed a touch offended by the decision, but Ajax thought it was the right call. Even if Loki could safely lead them through the region, it was nice to have backup. If the past few days were any sign, Ajax didn't expect this trip to go smoothly. Something would happen to them. He knew it in his bones.

Digging his claws into the moist, soft earth, Ajax carefully descended the hill. The chilly water below was covered with an oily film. It stank like car farts. Ajax knew the strange metal boxes the hoomans rode in didn't actually fart, but as far as he was concerned, it smelled just as bad.

Ajax crept forward, reassured by the splashing of the other cats following him. Between the foul smells, the cold oily water, and the squishy mud beneath his paws, Ajax was majorly creeped out. He needed to know he wasn't the only cat experiencing this unpleasantness.

The area grew progressively darker as they walked. It took Ajax a moment to understand what was happening. The trees and foliage around them were growing thicker the deeper they pressed into the Wilds, but that wasn't the only problem. Before, the leaves and branches glowed with a blend of greens, yellows, and blues. Now, the colors were more often brown, indigo, or even black. It was like the trees literally devoured the light.

"This is getting difficult, Gaius," grumbled Ajax. "I can't see a damn thing."

"I know, friend. If it's any consolation, the spirit tells me we're going the right direction."

Ajax considered arguing, but what good would it do? Sighing, he plodded forward. He hated barely being able to see more than a few inches in front of his face. Suddenly, his Spirit Armor crackled and flashed.

"What just happened?" yelped Loki. He sounded scared.

"I don't know," said Ajax. He took another step, and his Spirit Armor flashed again. "No one move. I think there are thorns or something on the ground." Ajax hoped it was thorns. What if it were snakes, beetles, or even spiders? He shuddered just thinking about it.

"Do we go back?" asked Loki. "There's probably another path through here."

"I'm not sure," said Gaius after a long pause.

Ajax took another step, causing his golden Spirit Armor to flash again. Whatever was attacking him, it was on the ground. Nothing seemed to happen if he stood still. Maybe there were blades or thorns of some sort on the ground. "It's something I'm stepping on. With my Spirit Armor, I should be fine."

"That doesn't help the rest of us," sighed Gaius.

"It'll be tiring, but I bet I can carry you all on my back."

The sounds of Shaman's breathy purr rang out across the cold darkness. Ajax didn't know what the Kitanja was doing, but a shimmering blue light flashed into existence. It was dim at first, but gradually grew bright enough to fill the area with scintillating light.

"Neat," said Gaius. "Shaman can create light."

"I'm guessing it's a Purrception spell," said Loki.

"Knock it off!" hissed Gaius. "His abilities can't be defined by stupid purr-puns. That's just silly."

Loki snickered. "Nope. Definitely a Purrception spell."

Ajax studied the recently lit area, and sure enough, a forest of thick, black, glistening thorns poked up from the surface of the water. Milky blue paste coated their tips. Ajax wasn't about to test them, but he suspected they were poisoned.

"That's a neat spell, Shaman," said Loki. "Very handy."

"It looks like there's a narrow path leading through the thorns," said Gaius.

Ajax started navigating the path, carefully testing each step. His Spirit Armor flared up on two occasions, but the path was otherwise clear. With him out front, testing things, the other cats avoided stepping on any thorns.

"Did I do good?" whispered Shaman.

"You did great, little guy."

"Can I turn off the light now? I'm getting tired."

Ajax took a moment to get the lay of the land. The field of thorns was safely behind them. They were still walking through greasy water, but brighter colors were returning to the surrounding leaves and trees. The area they just walked through was clearly some kind of trap. Ajax didn't want to think about who or what set it up. "Sure, Shaman. I think we can continue without your light."

Gaius cleared his throat, but said nothing.

Ajax realized he pounced on Shaman's question too quickly. He should have let the Cah'ten Ra make the decision, but he couldn't change that now. Gaius seemed to handle the slight well enough. Ajax would apologize later.

With the thorns behind them, he picked up the pace. He led the cats through muddy pools for several minutes before the ground gently climbed out of the nasty water. Once back on dry land, they took a few moments to scrape the oily filth from their paws before pressing onward.

Over time, tall trees gave way to dense bushes. Most of the bushes glowed with a mixture of yellow, blue, and green light, but a few were in the early stages of shifting to oranges and reds. Autumn was just around the corner. Ajax loved fall colors within the Dreaming. Autumn was his favorite time of the year.

They traveled peacefully for the better part of an hour. From time to time, Ajax caught flickers of motion off in the woods. None of the other cats mentioned it, but they definitely noticed. Shaman snuggled against Ajax's back. Gaius grew silent, and Loki stopped running ahead of the group, as he was apt to do occasionally. They were spooked.

Along the way, they passed a group of enormous brown and yellow birds with strangely toothy beaks. Ajax gave the birds a wide berth. Loki called them Dreaming turkeys, but Ajax wasn't so sure. They looked nothing like turkeys to him, but he wasn't about to argue about it.

Ajax continued leading them through the forest until a guttural huffing caught his attention. He looked around until he saw a gigantic stag. It snorted, pawed at the ground, and charged. In place of antlers, a forest of thick, sharpened spikes sprouted from its head. Long tendrils of silver light trailed behind it as it ran. Given how thick its body was, it must have weighed a couple of tons.

"Get behind me!" meowed Ajax as he spun to face the charging creature. Taking a deep breath, he gathered his Spirit Armor, forming it into a thick shield in front of him. He hoped it would be strong enough to absorb the impact. Fortunately, it took barely whisker's worth of energy to deflect the thorns in the water. His Spirit Armor was at full strength.

The staggering collision knocked him back several feet and made his vision blur, but his Spirit Armor held. His legs felt wobbly as he tried to right himself, and his breathing was labored. Damn, that thing hit hard!

"Wow," breathed Shaman from his back.

The enormous stag fared little better from the impact. It backed away after the collision, shaking its head, and its legs looked unsteady.

Loki was off to one side of it, trying his best to hiss. He really needed to work on his hissing. It wasn't very scary. Gaius was standing in front of it, with one paw held high. He was getting ready to unleash his Hundred Paws of Justice attack. It was one of his better combat moves.

The stag must have realized it wasn't going to win this encounter, because it turned and trotted back the way it came. The cats gathered around Ajax, watching the stag retreat. Gaius spoke shortly after it disappeared from view. "Are you alright, Ajax?"

His vision was still a touch shaky, and his legs felt like jelly, but other than that, he couldn't complain. "I could be worse."

"Hopefully, that thing doesn't come back," said Loki. "But if it does, I'm ready for it."

"Why did it attack us? We didn't do anything to hurt it," said Shaman.

"The Wilds is a dangerous place, little Kitanja," said Gaius. "It gradually twists the minds of all creatures who call it home. Even peaceful animals become aggressive."

"I don't like this place," said Shaman.

"I don't like it too much either," said Ajax.

"Take a moment to recover, if you must, but we should keep moving," said Gaius.

"I'm okay," said Ajax as he resumed his journey. He adopted a slow pace until his vision stopped shaking, but that didn't take more than a couple of minutes. Once he recovered, he moved faster to make up for lost time. The sooner they made it through the Wilds, the better.

He continued to spot silhouettes, shadowing them off in the distance. Whatever they were, he wondered what they were doing. He hoped they were just local creatures, trying to keep tabs on a group of adventurous cats moving through their lands, but he doubted that was the case.

The first howl confirmed his fears. Coyotes were terrifying enough in the real world. Ajax couldn't imagine how scary they might be in the Dreaming, but he was about to find out. The initial howl was answered by a second, and then a third. A series of short barks followed. They sounded like they were coming from all across the forest.

"Whiskers!" cursed Loki.

"What do we do?" cried Shaman.

"We've traveled far," said Gaius. "We must be getting close to the Moot site. Run, Ajax! We'll follow."

The big brown cat didn't need more encouragement. Fearing what might happen should the coyotes catch them, Ajax ran down the trail. Howls and barks rang out across the Wilds, and the forest exploded into motion. Before, the coyotes seemed content to follow the cats from a distance. Now that Ajax and his group were running, the coyotes were closing in.

Ajax didn't think they'd make it. The Wilds stretched out endlessly in front of them. He knew the Cah'ten Moot site was hidden. Just because he couldn't see it didn't mean it wasn't close. Still, with howling coyotes closing in from seemingly every direction, Ajax didn't think there was any way they'd make it.

18.
THE LAST STAND

Gaius' heart sank as he watched the circling coyotes surround them. In the Dreaming, their elongated claws and fangs were serrated. Their eyes burned like molten fire, and faint flames danced across their fur. Puffs of yellow smoke burst from their mouths with each bark. They were, in many ways, the hell hounds Gaius always imagined them to be.

But one of them was different. He was much larger than the rest, and his eyes pulsed with frozen blue light instead of anything fiery. His left rear leg was missing. A structure of ice and snow took its place. The icy limb wasn't built like the other legs, but Gaius assumed it functioned like one.

"I hope you have a plan," whimpered Loki. "You do have a plan, don't you?"

Gaius knew there was a possibility of encountering coyotes in the Wilds, but he wasn't expecting this many of the blasted things. "Yes, Loki," he said, but it was a lie. There was no way they could fight them all off. Ajax was more than a match for any of the coyotes, except maybe the larger one, but the entire pack would make quick work of the cats.

"Not to rush you, but now would be a good time for that plan of yours," said Loki. His eyes were wild, and his tiny tail was bushed.

"Run and get help, Loki," said Gaius. "We'll hold them off as long as we can, but our survival is in your paws. I'll send the tracker spirit with you. It will guide you, should you lose your way."

"Man," sighed Loki, sounding dejected. He took a deep breath and nodded. A moment later, he dashed to the left. A pair of coyotes leapt at him, while others moved into position to block him.

Loki ran a few steps and stopped. Gaius didn't understand what he was doing. The two leaping coyotes were about to pounce on him. In the next instant, Loki disappeared, only to reappear a dozen feet from his previous position. Gaius knew Loki possessed many powers for movement, but he never saw the Wildseeker do anything like that. The pair of leaping coyotes slammed into each other, howling as, together, they tumbled in a tangle of limbs.

Three more coyotes raced to intercept Loki, but the Wildseeker was too quick. He didn't wink in and out of existence this time. Instead, he raced forward so fast, he became a blur. The sudden burst of speed caught the trio of coyotes off guard. One tumbled as it tried to change directions, and another skidded to a halt. Only one of them continued its pursuit of the Wildseeker.

"Let him go," growled the enormous coyote with the leg made of ice. "The one we want is right here."

"And you must be Fenris, I presume?" said Gaius. Gazing into the Endless Tide, Gaius was satisfied to see his tracker spirit racing after Loki. The rest of the spirits in sight were Lost Ones. That was odd. Gaius thought of them as angry ghosts, spirits that let their rage consume them until there was little left. Why were there so many gathered in one place?

"Ah, my reputation precedes me," barked the terrifying coyote. "If you know me, then you must know you are lost."

Ajax let out a low growl as he backed away from Fenris. Golden strands of searing energy extended from his mane, and the Spirit Armor surrounding his claws lengthened and smoked. Shaman pressed himself flat against Ajax's back. The Kitanja was probably terrified, and Gaius couldn't blame him. The coyotes kept a safe distance as they circled the Guardian. Gaius counted nine of them, plus Fenris.

"Take them," growled Fenris.

The coyotes barked and howled as they charged, and Ajax roared in response. He looked like he was preparing to pounce, but a dome of shimmering azure light sprung into existence. It was just big enough to surround Ajax, Shaman, and Gaius.

Showers of bright blue sparks rained down from the barrier as the coyotes slammed into it, but it held strong. Fenris padded forward and swiped the barrier with one paw, creating his own cascade of sparks. "What kind of vile cat magic is this?"

"It's really none of your concern, Fenris," said Gaius, with as much confidence as he could muster. "The barrier will protect us until our Wildseeker arrives with reinforcements. You've lost. Save us all some time and move on. In fact, if you need something to hunt, there is a stag, likely with a tremendous headache, back the way we came."

Fenris chuckled. "Not so fast, cat. I can smell your fear." He raked his claws against the shimmering blue energy field again. A shower of cascading sparks flashed into existence before quickly burning out. "All power has limits. I suspect this barrier is no different."

Gaius sighed, but kept an aloof expression plastered across his face. "Of course, there are limits, but I expect it'll take hours for you and your pack to exhaust them."

Fenris shook his head. "You're a good liar, cat, I'll give you that, but I'm no fool. Surrender the kitten, and you're free to go. He's all I care about."

"You must be referring to Shaman, our Conjurepurr." Gaius wasn't about to ignore an opportunity to extend the conversation. He needed to buy time.

"A Conjurepurr, you say?" said Fenris, clearly surprised. "Interesting."

"Based on your reaction, it seems you didn't know."

"What does it matter?" growled Fenris. "I wasn't given many details."

"If you ask me, your employer withheld valuable information from you," said Gaius. He spoke slowly. He wanted to drag this conversation out as long as possible. "Let me offer you a piece of friendly advice, Fenris. An employer who withholds critical information can't be trusted."

"I don't need your advice, cat," said Fenris. "I'll make the offer once again. Surrender the Conjurepurr and you're free to go. You needn't throw your lives away on a hopeless battle."

Even if Gaius believed Fenris would keep his word, he wouldn't take the deal. "I'm afraid I must decline."

"Have it your way, then." Fenris barked a command, and his pack of coyotes began savagely attacking Shaman's Purrtection spell. Blue sparks rained down all around Gaius and the others.

"I know you're exhausted, little guy, but I need you to dig deep," said Ajax. "Keep your spell running as long as possible."

"Okay," coughed Shaman.

Gaius regretted not contacting Tokugawa and Kiyo earlier. They warned him it would take them some time to respond to his summons, so calling them was out of the question. Besides, he left the Calling Stone at home, under a cabinet. Shifting his focus back into the Endless Tide, he considered his options. He didn't like the prospect of summoning Lost Ones, but he was running out of options.

Skipping back and forth, left, and right, Gaius started building his spell. In this instance, he didn't need to concern himself with individual spirits. He merely needed to create a rift between the worlds. Once the doorway was opened, the Lost Ones were certain to come.

The coyotes attacked with increasing ferocity, causing tiny cracks to spiderweb across the vibrant blue energy field. "Keep going. We're almost through it!" shouted Fenris.

Gaius pushed his fear aside and focused on his spell. Many of the Lost Ones were gathering at a specific point. It meant his magic was working. The barrier separating one world from the other was weakening. Gaius spun in a tight circle, as if he were trying to chase his tail. Gradually, a jagged dark grey tear appeared in the night air.

Gaius was careful to place it outside Shaman's Purrtection spell, and it was a good thing he did.

A cacophony of windy howls rang out across the Wilds as a series of wispy, shadowy beings raced through the rift between worlds. The jagged tear closed an instant later. Gaius didn't know how many made it through, but he guessed at least six. They immediately charged him, slamming their shadowy bodies against the Shaman's blue forcefield, but the spell repelled them. Prevented from pursuing their preferred prey, they descended upon the next best option.

The coyotes.

The coyotes yipped and yelped as the Lost Ones swept their shadowy arms through them. Patches of frost and ice spread across any flesh the Lost Ones touched, but the coyotes were far from defenseless. Once they recovered from the initial shock and surprise, they turned on the Lost Ones, slashing with burning claws and belching gouts of flame.

"Damn you!" growled Fenris. He seemed completely unbothered by the Lost One that was attacking him. Unlike the other coyotes, who were aligned with fire, Fenris was a creature of ice. The freezing touches of the Lost Ones had little effect on him. "I didn't expect a Spiritchaser, but no matter," he barked. Ignoring the surrounding battle, Fenris savagely attacked the Purrtection spell. The spiderweb of cracks across the forcefield grew.

The coyotes were holding their own against the shadowy Lost Ones, with both sides experiencing losses. By Gaius' count, both sides lost two, but he didn't think it would continue that way. There were more coyotes than Lost Ones, and the element of surprise was gone. The shadowy spirits would soon start falling more quickly.

Fenris barked as he slashed a gaping hole through one side of Shaman's Purrtection spell. With his pack otherwise engaged, he didn't wait for reinforcements. With a triumphant howl, Fenris leapt through the breach. His icy blue eyes flashed, and blasts of frosty mist escaped his mouth with each breath.

Ajax roared and met the coyote's charge. Fenris was larger, but it didn't seem to matter, at least not in the initial exchange. Both beasts slammed into one another, neither giving an inch. Fenris bit and slashed, causing Ajax's Spirit Armor to crackle and flash, but Ajax attacked with equal ferocity.

Gaius pressed himself into the back corner of Shaman's Purrtection spell. With Ajax and the enormous coyote locked in mortal combat, he wanted to be as far from the action as possible. Even in the Dreaming, Gaius was a small cat. The last thing he could afford was to lose a life by being stepped on by one of the larger combatants.

Ajax and Fenris fought to a standstill for what seemed like ages. The Guardian's fire seemed the perfect match to Fenris' ice. Regrettably, things weren't going nearly as well outside Shaman's protective forcefield. All but one of the Lost Ones were gone. It looked like the spirits killed or seriously wounded four members of Fenris' pack, but it wasn't nearly enough. With the Lost Ones defeated, the coyotes resumed their attacks against the Purrtection spell, opting to bring down the rest of the forcefield over entering through the breach.

Gaius frantically searched the Endless Tide for more spirits to summon, but there were few to be found. He saw another pair of Lost Ones, but nothing else. He assumed they didn't make it through the rift before it collapsed. Summoning them wouldn't be worth the energy, and with the Purrtection spell failing, they'd likely ignore the coyotes and attack him.

"You're strong, but you're fading, big cat," teased Fenris as he lunged. Ajax lowered his head and barreled into Fenris' chest, knocking the coyote back, but not before getting clawed on the haunches. Ajax's Spirit Armor flared as it absorbed the blow, but it looked like it was fading.

Unable to hold off the coyotes any longer, Shaman's Purrtection spell shattered in a shower of tiny azure stars. Gaius was impressed that the Kitanja maintained it as long as he did, but it was cold comfort.

"You are beaten!" barked Fenris. "You're outmatched, outnumbered, and you're out of tricks."

"I'm not done yet!" roared Ajax as he breathed forth a roiling cone of sweltering fire. Fenris yelped and retreated, but none of the other coyotes seemed fazed by it.

"Before you die, cats, I want you to understand that death won't be the end, not for you," said Fenris, gloating. "Victims of my pack become Lost Ones, condemned to follow us, suffering for all eternity!"

Gaius swallowed hard. At least that explained why the Endless Tide was filled with Lost Ones.

19.
THE CAH'TEN CALVARY

Loki raced between the tangled thickets and the Guardians followed. He was happy Gaius sent the tracker spirit along with him. He would have eventually found a way into the Cah'ten Moot site, but the spirit got him there quicker. Seeing the state of the battle playing out in front of him, he was grateful for the help. It didn't look like there was time to spare.

Hellish, fire-breathing coyotes surrounded Ajax. He was bleeding from countless wounds, spread all across his body. His Spirit Armor only covered a small portion of his back. Loki assumed Ajax was using the last of his power to protect Shaman. Ajax was a good cat, always looking out for everyone else.

At first, Loki couldn't find Gaius, and he feared the worst, but he noticed a small flicker of white hidden behind a rock, a few feet from Ajax and the pack of coyotes. Gaius was hiding, which probably made sense. He wasn't built for paw to paw combat in the Dreaming.

Ajax howled in pain as a coyote clamped its jaws down on his neck. There was so much blood. Loki was sure the big brown cat lost a life from all the damage he was taking. Hopefully, he only lost one.

"You know what to do, Guardians!" bellowed one of the cats, following Loki. Now that they were in sight of the battle, there was no reason for Loki to keep moving at a reasonable pace. The Guardians would be there to help Ajax soon, but Loki wasn't sure it would be soon enough.

Drawing on his power of enhanced speed, Loki sprinted like a cheetah. Most of his abilities revolved around quickness and agility. He rapidly pulled away from the Guardians, who followed him. Few cats could keep up with a sprinting Wildseeker. He leapt at the last moment, just before reaching Ajax and the pack of coyotes.

Loki's front claws sunk into the coyote's flesh as if it were a roll of paper towels. An instant later, his back claws followed suit. The momentum of his charge was enough to knock the foul beast off of Ajax. The rest of the coyotes glanced over at Loki, but they kept attacking Ajax. For whatever reason, they wanted Ajax dead.

"To paws!" shouted one of the charging Guardians. Not wanting to be in the way, Loki leapt toward Gaius. The Cah'ten Ra appeared unwounded, but Loki thought it was best to defend the smaller cat. Besides, if anyone was likely to find the safest place to observe a battle, it was Gaius. If Loki wanted to be out of the way, standing next to Gaius was the right idea.

The Guardians wasted no time wading into the fight. Each was protected by their own Spirit Armor spells. One was emerald, green, and another rusty orange. Pink Spirit Armor protected the third Guardian. This was the first time Loki saw different cats using Spirit Armor. He never realized they came in different colors.

The coyotes spun to face the new threats. They probably didn't have a choice. Ignoring a single Wildseeker was one thing. Ignoring a trio of angry Guardians was another matter entirely. They yipped and barked, spitting gouts of flame, and snapping their jaws at the feline reinforcements, but it was clear they weren't interested in battle anymore. They were retreating.

Scanning the area, Loki located Fenris. He was standing perhaps thirty feet away, atop a slight hill. A section of his fur was burned away, revealing angry red burns. Hopefully, Ajax did that. The big brown cat could breathe fire, after all.

"Retreat!" barked Fenris.

The pack of coyotes carefully backed away from the trio of Guardian cats. Once they realized the Guardians weren't pursuing, they turned and ran, eventually gathering behind their leader, Fenris.

Gaius darted out from his hiding place, running out in front of Ajax and the other Guardians. "I told you how this would end, Fenris," he said. "You've lost. Now leave. Leave while you still can!"

"This isn't over, cat," growled Fenris. "There won't always be magical barriers, angry ghosts, and an army of cats to protect you."

"Perhaps, perhaps not, Fenris," said Gaius. He sounded surprisingly confident, given how poorly things went. "I wouldn't bet against us."

Fenris snorted. "Until next time, cat," he said before turning and trotting out into the night, his pack in tow.

"Whiskers of the Great Void Kitty," breathed the Guardian with the pink Spirit Armor. Loki kind of liked her. Her tail was long and fluffy. "Ajax is hurt, bad. We need to get him to the Cah'ten Moot. There is a Medicat there who can treat his wounds."

"You lost a life, didn't you Brother?" said the biggest of the cats. Given his long fur, huge paws, and massive size, Loki guessed he was a Maine Coon in the real world. It was rare to see a cat larger than Ajax.

"What gave it away?" coughed Ajax. He tried to climb to his feet, but his shuddering legs gave out.

"Only one life?"

"Yeah, only one," grunted Ajax. "Well…so far. The night is young."

"I'm sorry, Ajax," said Shaman. "This was all my fault."

Ajax shook his head. "There's nothing to be sorry about, little guy. You did nothing wrong. We never would have survived without your magic."

"Ajax is right, Shaman. You mustn't blame yourself," said Gaius. "If anyone is to blame, it's me. I should have refused the Cah'ten Moot. We suspected it was a trap all along. Now we know that for a fact."

The Maine Coon exchanged glances with the girl-kitty with the long fluffy tail. "What do you mean, Gaius?" he asked. "How do you know it was a trap?"

"Fenris pretty much told us so. He was sent for Shaman. He offered to let the rest of us go if we gave up the Kitanja."

"That doesn't necessarily mean…" The Maine Coon Guardian stopped mid-sentence and shook his head. "What am I saying? Of course, it means it was a trap."

"How else would Fenris have known where to look?" breathed the girl-kitty.

"And, for that matter, what he was looking for?" added Gaius. "He knew about Shaman. Interestingly, he didn't know about him being a Conjurepurr.

The girl-kitty with the long fluffy tail gasped. "Did you hear that, Marcus? The stories… they're true. He's a Conjurepurr."

The Maine Coon faced her, his mouth hanging open. "But the Uhl Cah'ten Ra said it was just a childish story. He called it a rumor, best ignored. I don't like this, Feyluff. I don't like this one bit."

Loki listened carefully, noting the names. "Feyluff… That's a pretty name," he said softly. Loki looked away, his ears flushing with embarrassment. He didn't intend to say it out loud.

"It's a horrible name," said Feyluff. "My stupid hoomans named me Fluffy, and my Cah'ten Ra insists on naming cats in accordance with their hooman names."

"It's quite a sensible practice," mumbled Gaius.

Feyluff glared at Gaius, her ears flattened out to the sides.

"Can we talk about this later?" said Ajax with a soft cough. "I'm kind of bleeding out over here."

"Oh, good point," said Loki. Ajax looked pretty bad. Loki wished there was something he could do for him.

"Actually, we can't talk about this later," said Marcus. "During the Cah'ten Moot, I don't think you should mention what Fenris told you."

Gaius leaned down and nuzzled Ajax's cheek. "Can you walk, old friend? We'll carry you if we must."

Ajax sighed, and the small patch of glowing golden Spirit Armor protecting Shaman faded. "I need one of you to protect our Kitanja for the rest of the journey." Slowly, tiny points of golden light blossomed across Ajax's body. It took Loki a moment to understand what was happening. He was building magical bandages to cover some of his deeper wounds.

"Of course, Brother," said Marcus. "He may ride me."

"But I want to stay with you, Ajax," said Shaman. He crawled off the big brown cat's back and started licking his face.

"It's alright, little buddy. I'll make it. I just want to make sure you're safe. I can't protect you right now, but you'll be safe with Marcus. He's the strongest Guardian I know."

"I'm not so sure about that," said Marcus as he sat down next to Shaman. "Not after what I just saw you endure."

Shaman clumsily clambered up onto the Maine Coon's back. The green Spirit Armor faded. A moment later, it reappeared with Shaman inside it.

"There we go. Nice and safe," said Marcus. He moved next to Ajax and gently worked his paws beneath the big brown cat's belly. "Try to get up, Brother. I'll help you."

Ajax growled as he tried to rise on shaky legs. True to his word, Marcus gently lifted until the big brown cat was finally standing. "Now that I'm back on my feet, it should be easier."

"Feyluff, Shadow, help Ajax on our journey," said Marcus. "One of you on each side of him. We'll move slowly. He can't afford to take a fall."

The Guardians flanked Ajax as he took his first few precarious steps. Loki considered running out in front of the group, but decided against it. The Guardians probably knew the way, and with how slowly they were traveling, it would be nearly impossible for them to get lost. Besides, he really admired Feyluff's tail. Walking behind the group afforded him the best view.

The group walked in silence for some time. The path wasn't overly challenging, but with Ajax's condition, even tiny hills and valleys proved difficult to navigate. Fortunately, Feyluff and Shadow did a good job keeping the big guy from falling. Since Ajax only bandaged roughly half of his wounds, he was still bleeding. Loki suspected Ajax was getting weaker as they walked, but he didn't want to say anything. He didn't want Ajax to lose another life, but he respected his friend enough not to second guess his judgment.

Eventually, Gaius broke the silence. "You suggested we don't mention what Fenris told us during the Cah'ten Moot. Are you willing to tell me why?"

Marcus glanced nervously at Gaius. "I'd rather not speculate about the Uhl Cah'ten Ra. Remember, I'm a member of the Feline Council. Any allegations that pass my whiskers must be carefully vetted."

"Understood," said Gaius after a long pause. "That being said, I'm not a member of the Feline Council. I'm just a rather foolish Cah'ten Ra. Would you be willing to listen as I blather on about my wild conspiracy theories? I'm told I can be quite entertaining."

The tension left Marcus' tail, and Loki was pretty sure a slight smile crept across the Maine Coon's lips. "It will be a few more minutes before we reach our destination, and our hearts weep for what Ajax has lost. Some amusing banter would go a long way to lighten the mood."

"Where to start?" mused Gaius. "We received notice of the Cah'ten Moot earlier this morning. Our Oaken Grove is far from the Moot site. The safest path takes more than a day to navigate. Of the other two routes, only the Wilds gave us a chance to make it to the Moot in time."

Marcus nodded ever so slightly.

"Since I was the one who requested the Moot, our absence wasn't an option. Giving us less than a day's notice forced us to travel the Wilds. Did members of the Feline Council point this out to the Uhl Cah'ten Ra? Surely, someone suggested a different day for the Moot."

Once again, Marcus nodded, this time more noticeably.

"Perhaps it was all an amazing coincidence, but does anyone else find it odd that Fenris was patrolling the Wilds, specifically watching for a group of cats on their way to the Cah'ten Moot?" Gaius paused, as if considering his next words. "I guess I'd be willing to call it all a coincidence, but then there's that part about being sent to take our Kitanja, who just happens to be a Conjurepurr. I don't know about you, but for me, that seems awfully specific."

Marcus looked at Gaius, studying him. He said nothing. His expression was unreadable.

Gaius took a deep breath. "Maybe I'm crazy, but is it possible someone on the Feline Council, or the Uhl Cah'ten Ra himself, sent Fenris after our Conjurepurr?"

Marcus nodded.

Loki was following the conversion, but a few details were missing. "Does the Uhl Cah'ten Ra even know about Shaman?" asked Loki.

"Rumor has it the entire Feline Council knows," said Feyluff beneath her breath.

Loki assumed as much, but it was nice to hear confirmation. "How did they find out?"

"My messenger spirit told them," said Gaius with a sigh. "I needed to justify the need for an emergency Cah'ten Moot. My message talked about the Elder Nightmare, and the fact that Shaman is a Conjurepurr."

"Whiskers!" Loki didn't want to curse around a girl-kitty, but he felt the situation more than merited it.

20.
THE MEDICAT

Ajax breathed deeply as the colorful cat brushed her paws across his countless wounds. She purred the entire time. He was never treated by a Medicat before. They were well respected in the feline world. Unlike hooman vets, who poked and prodded with their needles and knives, Medicats treated wounds gently, using feline magic.

"Am I gonna make it, doc?" said Ajax. He was touch and go during the journey, but he felt much better now.

"Of course, you are," said the cat with the mottled gold, brown, black, and white fur. She wasn't a Truepaw, not that Ajax cared. Gaius and Loki questioned his Truepaw status so often, he long since stopped worrying about it. "I wouldn't waste my time and energy on you otherwise."

"Hey, I wouldn't call spending time with me a waste."

"I didn't mean it that way."

"I was just messing with you."

The Medicat nodded and continued her work. The feel of her paws brushing across his fur tickled. Ajax kind of liked it. "Some of these wounds are deep. I see dozens of bites, but also several burns. What happened out there?"

Ajax rolled to his back so he could get a better look at the Medicat. Her fur was short and neatly groomed, and she had lovely green eyes. "They didn't tell you?"

She shook her head.

"What's your name?"

"Patches," she said. "It's my hooman name as well. I kind of wanted a different cat name, but once we found out I was going to be a Medicat, I was pretty much stuck with Patches."

"Yeah, there was no way you were getting out of that one," said Ajax with a chuckle. "As for what happened out there, we ran into Fenris and his pack of fire-breathing coyotes. We held them off the best we could, but towards the end, it was just me against the pack."

Patches gasped. "You took on the entire pack?"

Ajax nodded, but as much as he liked the attention, he didn't want to exaggerate. "Yeah, I did, but keep in mind, I lost. I'm guessing you already figured that out."

Patches smiled. "If you and your clowder lived to share the tale, you didn't lose, noble Guardian." She pressed both paws against one of his nastiest bite wounds, and this time, it didn't tickle. It hurt! "As far as I'm concerned, you won."

"I agree with her," called Marcus. Ajax was lying on a bed of soft moss in the center of a small clearing. He guessed it was barely a dozen feet in diameter. Green, glowing hedges partially surrounded the clearing, providing limited privacy.

Patches startled. "You mustn't surprise me like that when I'm working," she said, flashing an angry glance at the enormous Maine Coon.

"Apologies," said Marcus, bowing. "How is he? How long until he's ready to walk? We're hoping to convene the Moot soon."

"Out of the question," said Patches. "I'd like to keep Ajax here for at least a few hours. He's lost an incredible amount of blood. It will take time for him to recover."

Marcus's ears swiveled to the side and his tail drooped. "We hoped to honor him with the Gor'ahska during the Moot. If he needs to remain under your care, will you permit us to perform the ritual here?"

Ajax wondered if he was hearing things. Massive blood loss often made the mind play funny tricks. Did Marcus really mention the

Gor'ahska? It was perhaps the most prestigious honor among Guardians, but it was more than just an honorific. Cats who took part in a Gor'ahska gave a little of themselves to strengthen the beneficiary.

"I don't even know what that means," said Patches, her ears back. "I'll permit it, but only if you promise to leave us in peace afterwards."

Marcus chuckled. "I agree to your terms, oh feisty one."

"Fine. Now, run along," said Patches, waving her paw dismissively. "Gather what you need. The sooner your strange ritual is finished, the sooner my patient can rest."

Ajax stretched and yawned. He wasn't used to being pampered like this. It was kind of nice, and he definitely needed it. "I have to stand for the Gor'ahska. Is that going to be a problem?"

Patches peered at him for a moment, scanning his various wounds. "We'll make it work. Roll on to your side, please. There are a few wounds on your thighs I need to treat."

Ajax did as instructed. He soon felt Patches' paws tickling their way across his hind legs. He was normally quite protective of his haunches. Ajax let his hoomans scritch and pat him back there, but he chased other cats away from the area. Patches didn't bother him, though. Maybe it was because he knew she was a Medicat.

"This might sting a little," she said as she pressed both paws against a deep wound.

She wasn't wrong. It definitely hurt. Ajax remembered one of the larger coyotes locking its jaws around his right rear leg. That must be the wound she was working on. He was probably in shock while Feyluff and Shadow escorted him to the Cah'ten Moot, otherwise the pain of walking would have been excruciating.

"There we go," she purred. "Much better. You should be able to stand now, at least for a little while."

"Thanks, Patches," said Ajax.

"No thanks necessary. I'm a Medicat. This is what I do."

"Still, I want to thank you," said Ajax. He wasn't sure what he was feeling, and didn't want to make things awkward. "I'm not used to gentle treatment from other cats. Given my size, everyone tends to roughhouse and wrestle with me." Ajax paused for a moment. "I mean, I get it. I can take it."

"Hush," said Patches. "I understand. The other cats look at you and see a brute. Sometimes, they don't appreciate your gentle nature."

Ajax nodded. That's exactly what he meant to say.

Marcus cleared his throat from the edge of the clearing. "I hope I'm not interrupting anything."

"That was quick," said Patches. She sounded a touch perturbed.

"You asked me to hurry, so I did." Marcus padded into the clearing. Feyluff and Shadow followed him. "Are you ready, Brother?"

Ajax slowly climbed to his feet. His back legs were still a touch wobbly, but he felt stable enough to stand. "I'm ready, but you don't have to do this. The Gor'ahska will weaken all of you. I'm not worthy of it."

"It's not your decision to make," snapped Marcus. "Feyluff, Shadow, and I discussed it, and this is the right thing to do."

Ajax nodded. He didn't know what to say, so he kept quiet. He glanced at Patches, and she quietly backed away from the Guardian cats.

One by one, each of the Guardians summoned their Spirit Armor, with Ajax coaxing his into existence last. His energy was nearly depleted. He couldn't maintain his Spirit Armor for long.

Marcus purred. The sound was deep, resonate, and much louder than an ordinary purr. Shadow's purr came second. Its pitch was slightly higher than Marcus'. Together, their purring produced a pleasant harmony. Feyluff was the last to add her purrs to the chorus. She purred from her throat and mouth, producing tones that effortlessly drifted across the top of the otherwise rumbling ocean of purring.

One by one, each of the Guardians stepped forward until their glowing Spirit Armor made contact with the energy field surrounding Ajax. A sea of colorful sparks danced across Ajax's Spirit Armor, infusing it with motes of emerald green, rusty orange, and bright pink.

Ajax's heart pounded, and his breathing thickened into a heavy, panting purr. He felt his Spirit Armor evolve as it tasted the other cats' power. It remained golden, but adopted subtle hints and hues from the other styles of Spirit Armor. Ajax's magic was growing stronger as it learned from the others. He couldn't wait to see what he'd be capable of.

Gradually, the chorus of purrs dwindled, with certain tones fading entirely as each cat finished giving their gift. Marcus was the last one to stop. He purred deeply for several moments after the other two stopped. He bowed his head when he was finally done. "How do you feel, Brother?" he asked.

"Amazing," breathed Ajax. "Simply amazing. Thank you so much. I don't know how to repay the three of you."

"Repay us?" said Shadow, his voice throaty and low. "We're the ones repaying you."

"I don't understand."

"Noble cat," said Feyluff. "We are all Guardians, pledged to defend the lives of all Cah'ten, no matter the breed or Calling. Of the four of us here today, you are the only one actively fighting."

"But that's not by choice," said Ajax. "You all are just as willing to do the job as I am."

"That's not the point, Brother," said Marcus softly. "Yes, all of us are willing, but for whatever reason, be it fate, the will of the Great Void Kitty, or just dumb luck, you are the one fighting the battles."

"By allowing us to honor you with the Gor'ahska, you've allowed us to help you with the great struggles that lie ahead of you. Don't thank us for this, Ajax. We should be the ones thanking you," said Shadow.

Ajax sat down, letting his Spirit Armor spell fade. He understood what the other cats were saying, but it was still hard to wrap his head around it. "I think I understand, but I'm going to need some time to think about it."

"Of course," said Marcus with a nod. "We'll take our leave from you for now. We wouldn't want to risk the vengeance of Patches, the Feisty."

"Yes, please leave us," said Patches. "Ajax needs rest. Come find him after the Moot is over."

"Will you not be attending the Moot, Patches?"

The Medicat shook her head. "I have a patient in need of my care. You can fill us both in on what was discussed afterwards."

"Very well," said Marcus. "Come on, let's go," he said to the other Guardians as he left. The others followed him.

"Roll over on your side," said Patches. Her tone was soft, yet insistent. She was purring.

Ajax rolled to his side, resting his head against the soft, mossy ground.

"There we go," whispered Patches as she gently worked her body next to his. She felt soft and warm. Ajax found her rumbling purr quite soothing. "Rest, gentle Ajax. Allow me to snuggle, cuddle, and comfort you. You've earned a small measure of peace, don't you think?"

Ajax nuzzled his cheek against the colorful shorthaired cat and purred. He was always the one looking after the other cats. He was always the responsible one. The parent.

The Guardian.

It felt wonderful to be the one looked after and taken care of, even if only for a few precious hours.

21.
CAH'TEN MOOT

Gaius patiently cleaned his paws as the Feline Council mumbled its way through the opening statements. Cah'ten Moots were full of proclamations, speeches, and silly procedural votes. Gaius was certain the cats who came up with the concept stole it from the hoomans. Cats were ordinarily far too practical for such nonsense.

Each member of the Feline Council perched proudly on a narrow wooden seat, suspended by two chains that stretched high into the sky. Gaius guessed there must be some kind of crossbar up there supporting the chains, but he couldn't see one. The ground beneath the suspended seats was golden brown. In places, it glowed orange and red, like embers, but it produced no heat.

The cat in the rightmost seat, Theodore, was prattling on about the history and accomplishments of the council. Once he was done, the Moot would finally begin. Theodore, like many orange cats, was a Scholar. When cats joked about orange cats sharing one brain cell, they were referring to the odd way Scholars shared thoughts with one another. Their minds were connected, even across great distances.

The Uhl Cah'ten Ra, Azimov, sat in the middle seat. He was large, by Abyssinian standards, which made him small compared to most Ragdolls. Gaius wasn't particularly large, but he easily outweighed Azimov. Then again, size didn't determine status within the feline world. If anything, it worked against rising in the ranks. Large cats, more often than not, were Wildseekers or Guardians, the two Callings least likely to climb the leadership ladder.

The surrounding chorus of random side conversations gradually quieted as it became clear Theodore was coming to the end of his historical recounting of the Feline Council's accomplishments. Few cats were in attendance tonight. If Gaius were to guess, he'd put the number at fifty. A well-attended Moot hosted three times that number of cats. Then again, this one was announced with little notice.

Was that was why the Uhl Cah'ten Ra rushed this meeting? Maybe he didn't want many cats in attendance. This wouldn't be the first time the Feline Council engineered a low attendance meeting. It was far easier to pass controversial rules, for instance, with a smaller voting body of cats.

"Greetings," meowed Azimov. He waited several moments for the crowd to quiet down. "I welcome you, esteemed cats, to this emergency Cah'ten Moot."

The cat to the left of Azimov, a wrinkled, hairless one, with large ears and even larger eyes, leaned over and whispered in his ear. Her name was Echo, and she was the Feline Council's official Spiritchaser. Gaius didn't know if the hoomans gave her that unfortunate name. Perhaps some cruel Cah'ten Ra was making a joke about how hairless cats looked like weird bats. Either way, he didn't trust her as far as he could throw her.

"Ah, yes," said Azimov with a nod. "In accordance with our traditions, let the record show that this emergency Moot was requested by Gaius, a Truepaw, and Cah'ten Ra within our Catsland. Since he is, as of now, in good standing, we granted his request."

Gaius flicked his tail in agitation. Azimov went out of his way to sneak a threat into his statement. It shouldn't have come as a surprise. Azimov often worked subtle insults and threats into his statements. He was surprisingly good at it for an Abyssinian. Reading Azimov's statements without knowing him, one might assume he was a Persian.

"I heard Gaius' request secondhand," continued Azimov. "Since the message was sent to you, Echo, would you be kind enough to restate it for the record?"

"Of coursssse, Uhl Cah'ten Ra," said the hairless cat.

Gaius hated the way she dragged out some of her S-sounds, like she was some kind of snake. As if being a cat who looked like a bat wasn't bad enough! Echo was trying to be a cat who looked like a bat who spoke like a snake.

"I received a messssssenger spirit from Gaiusssss," continued Echo. "He claimed an Elder Nightmare came through the Abyssssinial Gate in the Oaken Grove and attacked them. He claimed it was after their new Kitanja. He claimed the Kitanja was a Conjurepurr."

All around Gaius, cats gasped or laughed. He didn't expect them to believe his stories. Elder Nightmares and Conjurepurrs were the stuff of fanciful stories momma cats told their kittens. The possibility that they were real was probably too much for many of these cats to accept.

"Absolutely preposterous!" blurted Theodore. "Gaius claims there was an Elder Nightmare in the Oaken Grove? Perhaps he's been hitting the nip too often."

"Kinda thought this might be rough," mumbled Loki.

Gaius spared Loki a reassuring glance before stepping forward. Loki was in charge of keeping Shaman calm throughout the Moot. He would have preferred Ajax to do it, but the Guardian was still being treated by Patches.

"Please, we must let him speak," said Azimov, raising a paw to quiet Theodore. "What do you have to say in your defense, Gaius? Even you must realize that your stories are rather hard to believe."

"Of course, they are hard to believe, but that doesn't make them any less true," said Gaius. "The Elder Nightmare that attacked us was known as Uohr'Koren. I believe its more common name was The Devourer Beneath the Dark Earth."

Theodore, the orange cat in the rightmost seat, closed his eyes for a moment before facing Azimov. "That name exists in the historical records. Gaius has indeed named an Elder Nightmare."

Azimov snorted. "That proves nothing. He could have discovered the name through research."

Gaius momentarily cleaned a paw. "I assure you, and all the esteemed cats present, I'm far too lazy to perform research."

"Then how did you come by thissss name?" hissed Echo.

"Don't you already know?" asked Gaius. He suspected she did. She had a reputation for spying on other Spiritchasers. "A Celestine helped me kill it. She told me its name." A murmur went through the crowd.

"A Celestine, you say?" said Azimov. "Cats should not have dealings with such creatures."

Gaius shook his head. "While it isn't recommended, it isn't forbidden. Isn't that correct, Echo?"

The hairless cat bowed her head. "He speaksssss the truth."

"Fine, fine," said Azimov, waving a paw. "Let's say we believe it. Let's say an Elder Nightmare attacked you. What, precisely, do you expect us to do about it? If you're powerful enough to kill an Elder Nightmare, the Feline Council should be asking you for help, not the other way around."

"I'm not here asking for help. I'm here to warn the Feline Council, and all cats present, about the new dangers within our Catsland. In just the past few days, an Elder Nightmare attacked us. We learned our new Kitanja is a Conjurepurr, and just a few hours ago, we fought off Fenris and his pack. Surely, this can't be coincidence," said Gaius.

Another round of gasps, punctuated by scattered laughter, rumbled across the assembly. The cat to the immediate right of Azimov, a stout Savannah Cat named Archer, held up a paw. "That's enough!" he shouted. He waited until the assembly quieted before speaking. "You said you battled Fenris. When and where did this happen?"

"In the Wilds, on the way to the Cah'ten Moot. I'm surprised no one told you," said Gaius.

"Apologies, Archer," said Marcus from his seat on the far left of the Feline Council. "You were patrolling some of the other domains when their Wildseeker, Loki, came and found us. He led us to Gaius and his clowder. They were still fighting Fenris' pack when my Guardians arrived."

The Savannah Cat looked away. "Was it the entire pack?"

"Yes, Archer," said Marcus. "Gaius and his cats wounded Fenris and killed several of his pack mates. Their Guardian was already down a life. He would have lost the rest of his lives, had we not arrived when we did."

Shaman whimpered.

Archer's jaw dropped. "Fenris is an absolute murderer. How did they survive?"

"Their Guardian is powerful," said Marcus. "I believe he held them off."

"Not quite," said Gaius. "While Ajax certainly fought off Fenris' pack, for a time, our Kitanja, Shaman, held the pack at bay the longest."

"You can't be serious," said Theodore. He looked over at Azimov and Echo, holding up both paws. "You aren't going to let him lie to the Feline Council like that, are you? There's no way that tiny Kitanja held off Fenris and his pack!"

"I know you're tired, Shaman. After what you did, you're probably exhausted," said Gaius. He smiled reassuringly at the Kitanja. "Can you cast Purrtection again? We don't need a large spell, or a strong spell. We just need to see your magic."

Shaman crawled a few steps away from Loki on wobbly legs. "I'll try," he whispered.

"I mean, look at that kitten. He can barely walk!" shouted Theodore. "We've lost many noble cats to Fenris and his pack. Pretending that a tiny Kitanja held them at bay is an insult to their memories!"

Shouts of protest rang out across the assembly. Theodore seemed to be winning them over, and Gaius didn't like it. Cats were crowding around Shaman. Loki hissed, trying to make them back off, but he was a terrible hisser. Gaius moved closer to Shaman, but he didn't want to get too close. The fact that Shaman moved away from Loki before agreeing to try his spell was significant. It was probably harder to protect multiple cats with it.

"Get away from my Kitanja!" shouted Gaius at the top of his lungs. A few cats ignored him, but most shuffled back a step or two. He was a loud and commanding kitty when he wanted to be.

"I can't do it. I'm so tired," breathed Shaman. He was about to cry. "Where's Ajax? I want my dad."

Gaius took a deep breath. He didn't want to lie to Shaman. He didn't want to hurt him, scare him, or manipulate him, but he didn't see another way out of this. Gaius needed Shaman to demonstrate his power. Otherwise, the Feline Council would make a mockery of Gaius. No cat would ever believe him again. He'd lose his ability to protect Shaman and his clowder. "I'm sorry, Shaman, but please understand. Ajax is in danger. You need to prove you're a Conjurepurr. If you can't do that, they'll hurt Ajax. They'll hurt your dad!" Gaius hated himself more and more as each word spilled from his mouth.

"What?" asked Shaman, his voice suddenly stronger. "No," he panted. "They can't hurt Ajax!"

Gradually, a translucent bubble of crystalline azure light formed around Shaman. The mass of angry cats surrounding him backed away. Most of them looked confused, but some of their tails bushed. With each passing moment, the shimmering light grew more and more intense, until it was a solid dome of shining blue light.

"Whiskers of the Great Void Kitty!" cried Archer.

"Good job, Shaman," said Gaius, before he slowly, dramatically, raised a paw above his head. "What you're witnessing is a Purrtection spell," shouted Gaius to the assembly. "Observe." He popped his claws and struck Shaman's barrier of blue energy. A line of brilliant sparks rained down from where his claws made contact with the forcefield.

"What kind of strange magic is this?" said Theodore, shaking his head.

"It's Conjurepurr magic," said Gaius. "But don't take my word for it. You're the Scholar. Why don't you ask your brethren about it?"

Theodore closed his eyes for several moments before meeting Gaius' gaze. His seething anger wasn't subtle. Gaius expected most of the assembled cats noticed. "There is, indeed, a historical record of Purrtection spells." Theodore sighed and shook his head. "The field your Kitanja built… It matches the description."

"Wait, what does that mean?" asked Azimov, the Abyssinian.

"It means that this Kitanja is a Conjurepurr, likely the first in ages, but there's much more," shouted Gaius. He had everyone's attention. He wasn't about to squander his opportunity. "The attacks started the moment he arrived at my home. That Elder Nightmare wasn't after me, Loki, or Ajax. It was after the Conjurepurr. And so was Fenris!" Gaius wanted to mention what Fenris told him, but he heeded Marcus' advice. "This Kitanja is a gift, perhaps from the Great Void Kitty herself. We'd be fools not to cherish him."

"Very well, Cah'ten Ra Gaius," said Azimov, glowering. The fur around his ears rose, and he swished his tail behind him violently. "I don't know what you expect this Feline Council to do for you, but we will hear your request."

"Good job, Shaman. I'm pretty sure you can drop your spell," said Loki. The field of shimmering blue light immediately faded away, and Shaman curled into a tiny ball.

Gaius grinned. Honestly, he didn't expect the Feline Council to do much for him, but he intended to make his demands, nonetheless. Marcus seemed like an honorable cat. Perhaps other members of the council would step up and do the right thing. Even if most of the council was useless to him, there were many other cats in attendance.

They would hear his words, and carry his requests to their clowders, all across the Catsland. Some way, somehow, Gaius knew it would make a difference.

22.
THE NEVER ENDING ROAD HOME

Shaman yawned as he struggled to keep up with Gaius and Loki as they padded down the twisting path. An endless parade of cats wanted to meet him after the Cah'ten Moot, and despite his exhaustion, Gaius insisted he go through with the ordeal. It left him so tired, he could barely keep his eyes open.

Most of the cats just wanted to touch him and wish him luck, but a few wanted him to demonstrate his powers. A couple even asked for his blessing. It was a heady but odd experience. He wasn't used to being worshipped by other cats. Gaius frequently warned him not to get used to it.

The only uncomfortable moment came when Theodore and Echo asked to inspect him. There were clinical and cold in their measurements. They treated him more like a piece of meat than anything else. Shaman was left with the distinct impression that neither of those cats liked him.

"Hold up, guys. Someone's coming," said Loki.

They were on a dark, winding trail. Shaman believed they were within the dense woods lining the edge of Cah'ten Moot. After speaking with that regal looking Savannah Cat, Archer, Loki led them onto the trails. Shaman didn't understand why, but Gaius seemed to support the decision, and he trusted Gaius.

Branches up ahead rustled as Marcus and a colorful, shorthaired cat emerged from the foliage. Ajax followed along behind them. He looked much better than before. All his horrible wounds were healed. He was still missing fur in a few places, but compared to the last time Shaman saw him, it was night and day.

"Dad!" shouted Shaman as he raced to meet the enormous Guardian.

"Heya, little guy," said Ajax. "I'm happy to see you too."

Shaman brushed his face across Ajax's shoulder, nuzzling aggressively. He didn't care if the other cats were watching. Ajax was the most important cat in the world to him. The fact that he was doing better made Shaman's heart sing.

"There, there, little guy," said Ajax in between heavy purrs. "I'm here. I'll always be here for you."

Marcus cleared his throat. "Archer and his team are scouting your paths home. He doesn't expect Fenris to give up easily. It shouldn't take his Wildseekers long to track the pack of coyotes. Archer said he'd meet us here once he knew more."

"Have you considered waiting him out?" asked the colorful, shorthaired cat. "Fenris rarely hunts during the day."

Gaius frowned. "I don't think we can wait that long. We've been in the Dreaming for quite some time already."

Shaman didn't understand the problem. Was their time in the Dreaming limited? "I don't understand."

"Remember when we talked about what happens to us in the real world while we're in the dreaming?" asked Ajax.

Shaman nodded.

"Right now, all four of us are asleep. We've been asleep for a long time."

Shaman didn't see an issue with that. "So what?"

"If we stay in the Dreaming too long, the hoomans will become concerned," said Ajax.

Gaius cleared his throat. "It wouldn't be an issue if only a few of us were in the Dreaming. Hoomans tend to overlook a sleeping cat when they have other cats to interact with." Gaius met Shaman's gaze. "But with all of us sleeping, they'll grow concerned. When they can't wake us, they might panic and take us to one of their hooman pet hospitals."

Shaman thought about the rules governing entering and leaving the Dreaming, and it suddenly made sense. They needed to find their sleeping bodies in order to exit the Dreaming. If the hoomans took them somewhere else, they might get trapped, or worse. "What would happen to us?"

"I know a path to the hospital the hoomans are likeliest to use, but it's a really dangerous journey. I don't recommend it," said Loki.

"I don't recommend it either," said Gaius with a sigh. "As long as we make it home in the next couple of hours, we should be fine."

Shaman didn't think Gaius sounded confident. He was about to question his Cah'ten Ra when he heard rustling down the trail. Based on the way their ears swiveled, tracking the sound, all the other cats heard it too.

"Who goes there?" growled Marcus.

Archer, the Savannah Cat, emerged from the dark foliage. "My, my, aren't we touchy tonight?" said Archer. His eyes sparkled and his tone was playful.

"Sorry, friend," said Marcus, shaking his head. "After what happened to these cats, trust is in short supply."

"Well, I hope you still trust me. We've known each other since we were little Kitanja. Well, since I was a little Kitanja. You were never little," said Archer.

"Of course, I trust you," said Marcus with a sigh. "It's the rest of the cats I worry about."

Archer nodded and approached. When he spoke, his voice was soft. "There is no question in my mind that someone on the Feline Council set you up, Gaius. Please take my word for it. It wasn't me, and it wasn't Marcus."

Gaius nodded. "I'm positive it wasn't Marcus. If he wanted us dead, he would have ambushed Loki out in the Wilds. Without the Guardians' help, Fenris would have finished us. As for you…" Gaius looked down at his paw for a moment. "If Marcus vouches for you, that's good enough for me."

"Right on," said Ajax.

"You played things perfectly tonight at the Moot," said Savannah. "You presented the facts clearly, but you carefully buried your allegations. Most importantly, you proved your claims. Every cat who attended tonight believes your clowder fought an Elder Nightmare. And everyone believes your Kitanja is a Conjurepurr."

"Thanks, but why do I feel like I just leapt from the frying pan into the fire?"

"You kind of did," said Marcus with a chuckle. "Word of this Moot will spread throughout the Catsland. While no one expects the Uhl Cah'ten Ra to defend your Oaken Grove, he can't ignore your second request so easily."

Shaman did his best to pay attention to the conversation, but the politics was a bit over his head. Gaius asked the council to find and contact other Conjurepurrs. That must be what they were talking about.

"Azimov will have to at least try to find another Conjurepurr," said Savannah. "If he can't, he'll need a pretty good excuse. If he didn't have a Scholar on his council, that would be one thing, but he has Theodore."

Gaius closed his eyes and took a deep breath. "At least, I did something right, finally."

"Hey, now," said Loki. "You're not always the nicest cat, but you're doing the best you can. You've been dealing with a lot of big decisions lately. You should really talk to someone about that. Maybe it's time to see a therapist."

"I have time, right now, if you'd like to talk," said the colorful shorthaired cat. Shaman liked her. She seemed nice.

"She's fantastic," said Ajax. "I've never felt better."

"As much as I'd love to take you up on your generous offer, I'm afraid we don't have time," said Gaius, before quickly adding, "Not tonight, at least."

"About that," said Archer, his tail drooping. "I don't have good news for you."

Gaius licked a paw and rubbed across his temple. "I didn't expect you would."

"I sent my team of Wildseekers to investigate both the Verdant Path and the Wilds. It seems that Fenris split his pack. They are watching both those paths back to the Oaken Grove."

"If he split his forces, he'll be weaker," said Ajax. "Can you escort us, Marcus? With three more Guardians, I bet Fenris won't even try."

"I'm sorry, Brother," said Marcus, looking away. "Because of the revelations of tonight, the Uhl Cah'ten Ra has called for a Guardianship across the entire Catsland. He won't let me leave his side long enough to escort you."

Shaman raised a paw, confused. He didn't know what any of that meant. He opened his mouth to ask a question, but Ajax spoke before he could.

"Azimov called for a Guardianship?" growled Ajax. "Let me guess, he tried to draft me, didn't he?"

Marcus nodded. "I told him to go toss his litter! He can institute his draft, but as the lead Guardian in the Catsland, I get to choose who gets called to serve."

"I don't understand," cried Shaman. He was purring. He felt a subtle power resonating in his throat. "Explain it to me!"

Marcus immediately faced Shaman. "In times of war, the Uhl Cah'ten Ra can call for a Guardianship across his Catsland. He is allowed to draft one of every three Guardians into his service. They must serve as his army. He tried to draft Ajax, but I denied him."

"Careful, Shaman," said Gaius soothingly. "These cats are allies. You needn't compel them."

"What just happened?" asked Marcus.

"I felt it too," said Archer.

"Purrsuasion spell," said Loki with a snicker. "He uses it on the hoomans to make them go out and buy us meaty treats. It's really quite handy."

Both Archer and Marus retreated a step. The fur on their backs stood up, and the tips of their tails twitched.

"Sorry, I didn't mean to do it. Sometimes, it just happens," said Shaman. "Thank you for the explanation. I think I understand now."

"So, back to the matter at hand," said Gaius. "You said Fenris is watching both the Wilds and the Verdant Path. Correct me if I'm wrong, but those domains connect to one another in several places."

"Yeah, they do," said Loki.

"So, if we use either domain to get home, Fenris will notice and bring his entire pack against us. Correct?"

Archer nodded. "That's how I see it."

Gaius sighed. "That doesn't leave us many options."

"Not many good ones," grumbled Ajax.

Waves of fatigue crashed against Shaman. Using that small Purrsuasion spell took the last of his energy. He tried to fight it, but there was no holding back his yawn. His legs buckled mid-yawn, and he fell over on his side. Deciding it was comfortable, he curled up in a little ball.

"It looks like your Kitanja needs a nap," said Marcus.

"Regrettably, there'll be no napping for the rest of us. Not until we're home," said Gaius. "The next part of our journey will be dangerous. We really only have one option."

Shaman wondered what it would be like to go on a safe journey. It seemed like the entire world was full of dangers. He wanted nothing more than to curl up in a field of soft grass and fragrant flowers, letting the sun warm his belly while he napped.

"You're talking about the Never Ending Road, aren't you? I've never been through there, Gaius. You understand that, right?" said Loki. "I know the basic rules. All Wildseekers do, but the Never Ending Road is a dangerous place. The things in there will kill us without a second thought."

"I'm aware of only three ways home. If Fenris is blocking both the Wilds and the Verdant Path, we have no other choice."

"What if Fenris figures it out and comes after us?" asked Loki.

"My team will keep an eye on him," said Archer. "If push comes to shove, we'll delay him long enough for you to get a healthy head start."

"That's all we can ask for," said Gaius.

Ajax leaned down and gently nuzzled Shaman. "I know you're exhausted, kid. If you don't mind, I'm going to put you on my back so I can protect you."

Shaman opened his eyes, yawned, and nodded. "Are we going to be okay, Dad?" he asked.

"I don't know, little guy," said the Guardian. "But I'll do everything in my power to keep you safe."

Shaman closed his eyes. He felt Ajax's tail gently encircle his body before lifting him. A moment later, Shaman felt himself deposited on Ajax's back. There were conversations going on all around him, but he ignored them. He nuzzled into his dad's soft fur and drifted off to sleep.

23.
CLANCY, THE COUNTRY RACOON

Loki carefully stepped out onto the smooth, molded stone. It stretched out in front of him like an endless road. He figured that's how this domain got its name. This wasn't the first time he encountered concrete. Heck, in the real world, he enjoyed rolling around on it. In the Dreaming, concrete was something entirely different.

It was cold and unblemished. Pillars climbed from the edges of it, supporting second, and in some places, third levels. Unlike the real world, where concrete had boundaries, here the concrete overflowed the edges of the road, seamlessly stretching into buildings, parking structures, and who knew what else.

Everything here was grey. There were no patches of green grass. There were no colorful trees. Loki saw nothing but cold grey stone and dingy grey machines. He hated this place. It was some kind of twisted nightmare world the hoomans dreamed up. It was no place for a group of cats, yet here they were.

Blinding white lights hung from sporadically spaced poles, but Loki didn't think they did much to illuminate the area. Everything was equally grey, even where no poles were present. Besides the lights, several boxes were mounted on each pole. Lenses sprouted from some boxes and wires hung from others.

"We need to move quickly," said Gaius. "I don't want the hoomans panicking when they can't wake us."

Loki did his best to ignore Gaius. The sooner he escaped the Never Ending Road, the better, but he certainly would not rush it. He took a step forward and carefully studied the poles. Some lenses rotated, tracking his motion. One of them began to glow with an angry red light.

Drawing on his supernatural speed, Loki sprung to the side, and he was glad he did. A sweltering beam of molten light struck the concrete where Loki was standing just a second ago, leaving a smoking hole. Loki glanced back at the pole-mounted lens with the glowing red light. It was no longer lit, and a slender stream of smoke rose from it. He didn't think it was likely to fire another beam.

"On second thought, please take your time. We should be careful," said Gaius.

Loki wasn't seeking Gaius' advice on the matter. He knew it was the Cah'ten Ra's way of admitting he was wrong, but he couldn't afford to think about it until they were out of danger. He was pretty sure that red beam would have ripped a life out of any of the cats, even Ajax, despite his Spirit Armor. "Everyone follow me, but match my pawsteps," he said. "Step only where I step. No deviations."

"No argument from me," said Ajax.

Anxiously watching the poles, Loki carefully pressed forward, step after dangerous step. He barely made it twenty feet before a different box fired a deadly red beam at him. Once again, he relied on his Wildseeker speed to leap to safety. He doubted the other cats would have been capable of it.

Studying the smooth concrete, he noticed a faint, nearly invisible line. He followed the line, expecting it to highlight a pressure plate or something he was stepping on, but it didn't do that. It was simply a foot long line. He backed away from it, hoping he could spot it from a distance, but no such luck. He needed to be nearly on the line to spot it.

"Something's coming," said Gaius.

Off in the distance, an enormous machine rolled towards them. Loki watched intently as it drew closer. It looked to be supported by nine gigantic wheels. Three on each side, and three in the center, supporting its belly. Several segmented arms sprouted from the top of it. Loki wasn't sure, but he thought he saw fingered claws at the end of each. Long tubes were mounted along the sides of it. The machine occupied the entire road, stretching from one side to the other.

Loki heard about machines like the one approaching. They were incredibly dangerous. The tubes on the sides launched metal balls that exploded in deadly fireballs, and the arms would grab anything within reach. "We need to get off this road!" shouted Loki.

"How about that building, ahead and to the left?" asked Ajax.

It wasn't too far, but there was no way they would make it without running. It meant risking getting hit by one of the deadly red beams, but Loki decided it was worth the risk. "That should work. Follow me. Run!"

Loki raced across the street, hoping not to trigger more of the sweltering death rays. He bet he could run fast enough to make them miss, but he kept his pace slow, not wanting to leave the other cats behind. Ajax already lost a life on this journey. Loki didn't want to be responsible for his friend losing another.

The building was formed from the same unblemished concrete as the street. In many ways, it was like the street made a sharp turn and started climbing high into the sky. A few open windows and one open door were the only noticeable features on the ground floor. High above, lights and more of those boxes, with the rotating lenses, dangled from the building.

Seeing no other option, Loki leapt through the open door. A dark, cluttered room greeted him. Stacks of twisted metal boxes lined the walls. His hoomans owned a few boxes like those. They called them filing cabinets, but the ones here climbed all the way to the ceiling, and were warped and bent to the point of being unopenable.

Loki took a few steps forward, clearing space for Gaius and Ajax to enter the room. He wondered if Shaman woke up yet. The Kitanja fell asleep the moment Ajax placed him on his back, but at some point, all the commotion was bound to wake him. Then again, Loki wasn't sure he wanted Shaman awake for this. The poor Kitanja already experienced enough horrors for a lifetime.

Ajax entered the room, bathing everything in a golden light. A moment later, the Guardian charged past Loki. Despite his enormous size, Ajax could really move when he wanted to. He slammed into a pair of the tall filing cabinets, thrusting his paw in between. He swished his tail in agitation as he fished around, before yanking an angry racoon out from between the twisted metal cabinets.

The racoon was larger than Gaius, but much smaller than Ajax. Based on the clothing, Loki assumed the racoon was male. He was wearing faded blue overalls and a tattered sombrero. That surprised Loki. He wasn't used to seeing raccoons dressed like that. Normally, they wore suits and ties in the Dreaming.

"Now wait a damn minute," cried the raccoon. "Unhand me, you brute!"

Throttling the raccoon, Ajax lifted the poor creature above his head before slamming him to the floor. The raccoon coughed when he hit the ground, and his sombrero flew off his head. "What do you want me to do with him, Gaius?"

"I vote you let him go," wheezed the raccoon.

Gaius slowly approached the pinned raccoon. He studied the creature for a moment. "Where are the others? Raccoons normally travel in packs."

The raccoon coughed and gagged. "There ain't no others. Please… can't breathe…"

"Let him breathe, Ajax."

The Guardian stopped throttling the raccoon. He placed his paw on the pitiful creature's chest, his claws fully extended. Loki felt sorry for the raccoon. If he was truly alone, there had to be a reason for it. Did he get cast out of his community?

"Thanks," sighed the raccoon. "My name is Clancy, by the way."

"Alright, Clancy," said Gaius. "Where is the rest of your pack?"

"Ain't got no pack. I'm a country 'coon." Clancy frowned. "Country raccoon, rather. My cousin brought me to one of them fancy diversification meetings a few months back. They said 'coon was a bad word, so I been trying to stop using it. After all, it don't cost nothing to be polite."

Country raccoon rang a bell with Loki. City raccoons were far more common. They were the ones that lived in highly organized packs, but there were others who preferred solitary living, near farms or out in the woods. "I remember hearing something about country raccoons. I think he's telling the truth."

Gaius looked at Loki and nodded. "What brings you into the city, Clancy? Seems like an odd place for a country raccoon."

"Seems like an odd place for a pack of cats, too, if ya don't mind me saying." Clancy flashed a nervous smile. "But since yer askin', I came into town to meet with my cousin. Taking another shot at convincing him to join me out in the countryside."

"Why were you hiding in this building?"

"I was waiting for the harvester to pass on by," said the raccoon.

"How often do those roll through?" asked Loki. It seemed Clancy knew more about the region than the rest of them. "And do other dangerous machines use the road?"

The raccoon coughed dramatically. "If we be fixin' to have a conversation, don't ya'll think it would go better if you, I dunno…" Clancy nodded towards Ajax, "got this monster off my chest?"

Gaius sighed. "Let him up, Ajax."

"Not a good idea, but if you say so." Ajax removed his paw from the raccoon's chest and backed away.

"Much obliged," said the raccoon. Once he was back on his feet, he retrieved his fallen sombrero and re-situated it atop his head. "Now, as for the harvesters, I reckon they come by every half hour or so."

The random squeaks and the deep rumbling of enormous wheels told Loki the harvester was nearby. It would pass by in the next few moments. "It won't hear us talking, will it?"

Clancy shook his head. "It's got cameras and stuff, but I think it only patrols the road. The cleaners on the second level are the same way. Even when they get their sights set on you, they'll leave you alone the second you set foot inside a building."

That was promising. The other Wildseekers often described the machines of the Never Ending Road as cruel and heartless. To Loki, they sounded like really dangerous versions of those robot vacuums the hoomans brought home. They patrolled an area, sucking up anything they stumbled across. Nothing more, nothing less.

"What about the top level?" asked Gaius. "I saw a third level to that road outside."

"You don't want to go up there," said Clancy, shaking his head. "Whirly-gigs patrol the top. They ain't like the harvesters and the cleaners. They fly above everything. Once one sees you, yer a goner."

"So, which level do you recommend we travel?" asked Loki. "It's kind of slow going on the first level, what with those fiery beams and all."

"Yeah." Clancy nodded. "Them lasers are a pain in the patoot, but hey, I thought we was fixin' to have a conversation. From where I come from, conversations go both ways. Right now, this is feeling more like an interrogation, if ya'll catch my drift."

"Very well. My name is Gaius. Ask your questions."

"Pleased to meet you, Gaius," said the raccoon. "Now, what in tarnation are you cats doing in the city, in the Dreaming, no less?"

"This happens to be the safest route home for us."

Clancy made a noise that sounded like a mix between a giggle and a squeak. Loki guessed he was laughing. "Did I hear you correctly? Did you say the safest route?" asked the raccoon. "The Never Ending Road ain't never the safest route to nowhere." Clancy cocked his head to the side and scratched his chin. "Wait… Did I say that right? I'm thinking I used one of them pesky double negatives in there."

"I understood what you were trying to say," said Gaius. "And if you must know, Fenris is hunting us. He's watching the other paths. The Never Ending Road was the one path we knew he wouldn't be patrolling."

"Fenris, you say?" said Clancy. "That's that ornery coyote that ranges through these parts, right?"

Gaius nodded.

"I've heard of him."

"So, which level do you think is the safest?" asked Loki. He felt the conversation went on long enough. They couldn't afford to waste time. He glanced over at Gaius. He didn't look annoyed or offended by Loki's impatience.

Clancy massaged his whiskers. "Well, I reckon the ground level is the safest, but awfully slow to navigate." He pointed to a pile of scrap metal in the corner. "If you hold a pole out in front of you and walk slowly, you can trigger all the lasers safely, but with the harvesters going back and forth, it'll take you a while."

"We need to get home soon," said Loki. He remembered Clancy saying the top level wasn't safe. "What about the second level? Can we safely move through there?"

"It's a lot faster than the main level, but those cleaners will chew you up fast if they catch you?"

Loki didn't think anything here could catch him. "How fast do they move?"

"I've seen them move pretty quick. Maybe as fast as a trotting dog. The problem is there are lots of them."

"You said they stopped chasing as soon as you entered a building, right?" asked Loki. He was formulating a plan to get them through there quickly.

"That's right," said Clancy with a nod. "Most of these buildings have doors to the second floor. You never have to go more than fifty yards or so to find one."

Loki grinned at Gaius. "I think I can get us through there pretty fast."

Gaius nodded. "You don't happen to be going that direction, Clancy?"

The raccoon looked down at his hands. "If it's all the same to you, I prefer to travel alone."

Ajax took a step toward the raccoon and growled.

"But, seeing as you cats are new here," said Clancy, glancing nervously at Ajax. "It'd only be right and proper of me to help guide you on your journey."

24.
BIG CITY RACCOONS

Ajax studied the next room and sighed. The second level was dominated by wide, open concrete rooms, supported by evenly spaced pillars. Most of the rooms they passed through featured scattered piles of debris, but this one was much tidier.

It was probably because of the cleaner machines. Two or three cleaner robots patrolled most rooms, but eight of the odd machines patrolled this one. The cleaners rolled around on two main wheels, with a smaller wheel trailing behind them for stability. They were dingy and grey, like everything else in the Never Ending Road. The front of each cleaner feature a rapidly spinning drum with oddly spaced metal teeth.

"There sure are a lot of them," said Loki. "I think I can still do it, but let me plan it out."

Navigating the previous rooms was simple. Loki ran around the room while everyone else remained in the hallway. Once all the cleaners were chasing him, Loki drew them to one side of the room, allowing Clancy and the cats to pass through on the vacant side.

"Why are there so many, Clancy?" asked Gaius.

"This is one of the main checkpoints," said Clancy. "Lots of hallways branch out beyond this room. Once we make it through here, we won't see cleaners for a little while."

Ajax didn't trust the raccoon. He was leaving out details. Clancy provided them a lot of valuable information, there was no doubt about it, but Ajax worried they were being too trusting. What if Clancy was leading them into a trap?

"Okay, I think I have the timing worked out," said Loki.

"Which side are you leading them to?" asked Gaius.

"The right, just like last time, but wait for my signal before entering the room. I think it will take time to gather them all."

Ajax used his tail to gently stroke Shaman's fur while he watched Loki prepare for his run. He wasn't overly worried about the Kitanja's deep sleep. After all, Shaman cast more spells than he ever did before. The little guy probably needed to cuddle with some stolen items before waking up. Still, feeling the sleeping Kitanja's deep breathing reassured Ajax.

"Wish me luck," said Loki. A moment later, he darted into the next room. The three closest cleaner machines abruptly converged on him. The others slowly rolled to a stop and swiveled to face him. Ajax wasn't sure Loki was ready to deal with so many of the deadly cleaner robots. There wasn't a lot of space to work with. If even one of the machines caught up with him, Loki was in serious trouble.

Loki dashed to the left and waited as more of the deadly robots surrounded him. There was still room for him to move, but he was getting close to the wall. Surprisingly, the Wildseeker held his ground. It was like he was daring the machines to charge him.

In unison, five of the eight cleaners rolled toward Loki. Ajax didn't think there was any place to retreat to, but Loki didn't look scared. If anything, he looked like he was having fun. At the last possible second, Loki vanished from sight. He appeared an instant later, just a few feet behind the deadly cleaner bots. Ajax knew Loki could teleport over short distances, but seeing him actually do it always surprised him.

Clancy whistled through his teeth. "Boy, that cat's a fast one, ain't he?"

"He's the quickest cat I've ever seen," said Gaius.

Loki spun around, backing away from the cleaner machines. The five that tried to run him over crashed into each other, sending showers of sparks high in the air. Ajax thought they would spin around and continue their pursuit, but it was like they couldn't figure out where Loki went. "Hey, dummies!" shouted Loki. "Turn around. I'm behind you!"

The machines spun and advanced on Loki. The three that didn't charge him a moment ago were also approaching. Finally, all eight were chasing. Loki continued backing away, maintaining a comfortable distance from the deadly robots as he led them to the far corner of the room.

"Everyone get ready," said Gaius.

Since they were planning on running along the left wall, Ajax positioned himself to the right of the group. He didn't think Gaius or Clancy would survive an encounter with the cleaner machines. If anyone needed to take a hit, it should be him.

"Alright, guys!" shouted Loki.

Gaius and Clancy charged into the room, keeping close to the left wall. Ajax kept pace, staying just to the right of them. He glanced over at Loki and was happy to see that all eight machines were still chasing the Wildseeker. He was leading them down the right wall. A few of them were fanning out, but they weren't fast enough to have any hope of catching Loki.

The dark hallway on the far side of the room narrowed shortly after they entered it. Ajax waited by the doorway until Loki dashed past him. Fortunately, the cleaner machines behaved the way they did in all the previous rooms. They gave up pursuit the moment all the cats were safely through the door.

"Excellent job, Loki," said Gaius.

"Thanks. I really do outdo myself sometimes, don't I?"

Ajax chuckled and shook his head. As much as he wanted to make fun of Loki's lack of modesty, he couldn't deny the cat's skill. Without Loki, the cleaner machines would have posed a much larger threat.

Clancy cleared his throat. "This hallway continues for quite a way. If you cats take the second left, and then the first right you come across, that should get y'all pretty close to where you're going, if I'm not mistaken."

"What, you're not coming with us?" asked Gaius.

"I reckon not," said Clancy. "It's not that I don't want to," he quickly added. "It's just that we'll cross within spitting range of my cousin. His company of raccoons lives somewhere in this maze of hallways."

"Company of raccoons?" asked Ajax. "I thought a group of raccoons was called a gaze."

Clancy took off his hat and scratched behind his ears. "Normally, it is, but these city raccoons ain't right in the head. Wearing suits and ties is one thing, but it don't stop there. Now, they spend so much times in their offices, holding meetings and that sort of nonsense that they've done decided to call themselves a company."

"Are we in any danger?" asked Gaius.

"No, I wouldn't think so."

Ajax didn't like how Clancy qualified his answer. He didn't trust the raccoon's body language either. "I don't like this, Gaius."

"Neither do I," said Gaius. "How about this, Clancy? Stay with us until we're safely past your cousin and his associates. Then we'll part ways."

Clancy glanced at Ajax and pursed his lips. He was clearly unhappy with the proposal, but eventually he nodded. "Follow me. It won't take us too long."

Ajax and Gaius closely followed Clancy as he led them through the long, dark hallway. They walked for nearly a minute before reaching the first four-way intersection. The hallway to the left was nearly pitch-black. The passageway to the right was much better lit.

Clancy pointed at each hallway. "The one to the left is a dead end. It used to lead to the top level, but it collapsed a long time ago." He was speaking loudly. Ajax wasn't sure why. "The one to the right leads to a bunch of rooms. My cousin lives down that way."

Ajax peered to the right and noticed flickering shadows. Something was moving down there. Maybe several things. "We need to go," he growled.

"Well, shucks," said Clancy. "Looks like it might be too late for that. Seems my cousin and his friends are heading this way."

A trio or raccoons came into view at the end of the hallway on the right. Ajax was certain more were behind them. Deciding there was no time to spare, he knocked Clancy to the side and pushed Gaius into the far hallway. Loki effortlessly darted ahead. Ajax followed, spinning around once he was safely through the intersection.

"Well, howdy, y'all," called Clancy. He was in the well-lit hallway, with his back to the intersection. Ajax figured that was Clancy's intention the entire time. He didn't think the raccoon ever planned to escort them farther than this intersection.

"Clancy? Is that you?" called one raccoon from down the hall.

"Glad to see you, cousin. It sure has been a spell, hasn't it?"

"I thought we talked about your clothing the last time you visited," said the other raccoon. He was getting closer. "We wear professional attire in the office, at all times. It's important to dress for success."

"Dag nabbit, I knew I forgot something," said Clancy.

"It's okay, for now, but going forward, please remember," said Clancy's cousin. "A button-down, some slacks, and a tie is all we're asking for."

"How unprofessional!" said a different voice. "We'll definitely need to circle back and discuss this at our next development meeting."

Ajax gradually backed away from the intersection. He didn't know how many raccoons were gathering around the bend, and he didn't want to find out.

"So, what brings you here, cousin?"

"Aw, nothin' much. I thought we might spend some time together," said Clancy.

"Let me check my schedule." There was a brief pause in the conversation. "I can pencil you in for five PM, tonight, or I have an opening at seven AM, tomorrow morning."

"I guess I can wait a few hours. Let's meet this evening."

"Sorry about the delay, but we're incredibly busy," said Clancy's cousin. "Third quarter results are in, and our year-over-year edible garbage collection is up three percent. It's quite an accomplishment."

"Truly, a group effort," said a different voice. "Wonderful collaboration."

"We really leaned in on this one," said another voice.

"Teamwork makes the dream work," said yet another raccoon.

Ajax continued to back away from the intersection quietly. He didn't know if Clancy gave them honest directions, or if he was sending them into a trap, but he figured anything was better than listening to the raccoons talk.

Gradually, the conversation faded. If Clancy wanted to turn against them, he could have done so easily. Ajax wasn't sure if the city raccoons were all that dangerous. He figured it depended on how many of them there were. Even weak creatures could overwhelm him if there were enough of them.

"Do we trust his directions?" whispered Loki.

"I think so," said Gaius. "He helped us get this far, after all."

"I guess," said Loki. "He didn't turn us in to those creepy city raccoons either, come to think of it."

"Well, we'll find out soon enough," said Ajax with a sigh. "We take the next left, and then a right."

"With any luck, it'll get us close to the Verdant Path. We need to get out of here," said Gaius.

"What about Fenris?" asked Ajax. He wasn't ready to face the coyotes a second time. Frankly, he'd be happy if he never crossed paths with them ever again. He barely survived the first encounter. Maybe the Gor'ahska strengthened him enough to face off with the pack, but he wasn't about to risk it. For all he knew, the Gor'ahska was purely symbolic.

"As long as we enter the Verdant Path close to the Oaken Grove, I don't think there'll be a problem," said Gaius. Ajax didn't think he sounded confident. "Even if Fenris chases us home, once we reach our sleeping bodies, we'll be safe."

Assuming the hoomans aren't driving us to the animal doctors as we speak, thought Ajax. He decided not to voice his concern to the others. It was out of their paws. The best thing to do was press on and hope for the best.

25.
HOMECOMING

Loki popped his head out of the stairwell and quickly scanned the area. They were back on the first level. Fortunately, a harvester recently rolled past their position. He saw it driving off into the distance. If Clancy's estimate about the frequency of harvesters was trustworthy, Loki guessed it would be twenty minutes before they saw another.

"Is it safe?" asked Gaius.

"I'm not sure," said Loki. There were several poles nearby, and each featured several of those boxes with the rotating lenses. Loki wished he grabbed a piece of metal debris, like Clancy suggested, but he forgot. He didn't think it was worth going back up to the second level to search for one. "Wait here. I'll find out."

Accessing his enhanced speed, Loki sprinted across the street. He wasn't sure he was fast enough to outrun the lasers, but he thought it was worth the risk. He didn't even bother looking up as he ran. Loki doubted it would make a difference.

The first explosion startled him. It happened right behind him. He didn't take the time to look back and see what it was, but he was pretty sure it was a laser. Pouring every last drop of speed into his legs, Loki ran for the far side of the street. Two more lasers fired at him, but he was fast enough to narrowly avoid both.

Once safely on the other side of the road, he turned and shouted to the other cats. "Come across. The boxes can't fire again right away."

He wasn't entirely certain of that, but he thought it was a reasonable guess.

Both Ajax and Gaius stepped out onto the street. They nervously stared up at the boxes on the poles as they passed beneath them. Fortunately, Loki's guess was correct. Nothing fired lasers at Gaius or Ajax. The boxes were still smoking from their recent shots.

"Well done," said Gaius as he joined Loki on the far side of the street. Ajax arrived a few seconds later.

"Is that the way out?" asked Loki. A green light flicked off in the distance. It was definitely out of place in the drab greyness of the Never Ending Road.

Gaius studied the light for a moment. "I'm not positive, but I think so. Dozens of domains connect with the Never Ending Road. Even if it doesn't lead to the Verdant Path, it might deliver us somewhere close to home."

"Just so I'm clear, that green light is our destination, right?" asked Loki. In the past, Gaius gave vague directions and blamed the other cats when things didn't work out. Loki wanted to be sure the instructions were clear.

"Yes," said Gaius. "Lead us to the green light. I'll make a final decision once we're close enough to see it clearly."

"Okee Doky." Loki didn't wait for further discussion. He turned and started walking towards the flickering green light in the distance. He found that, by staying along the far edge of the road, he encountered less of the deadly lasers. Loki needed to avoid a few, but it wasn't too difficult.

Gradually, the distant light took shape. It was definitely a doorway leading to someplace green, which encouraged Loki. Except for the Forest of Shadows and the Wilds, all the domains near the Oaken Grove were relatively safe.

Loki sighed and shook his head. Was any place safe? An Elder Nightmare attacked the Oaken Grove. Something was directing the monsters within the Forest of Shadows, and Fenris was outright hunting them. Loki decided to stop thinking of places as safe, and instead label some places simply less dangerous than others.

"That looks promising," said Ajax.

"I agree," said Gaius. "Still, I want to get a little closer before I make the final call."

"What are you worried about?" asked Ajax. "If that door leads to a dangerous place, we can just retreat into the Never Ending Road, can't we?"

"It doesn't always work that way," said Gaius.

"He's right," said Loki. One-way paths between domains were quite common. Most times, a path going the other direction could be found nearby, but there were no guarantees. Things worked differently in various places throughout the Dreaming. Some domains, like the Forest of Shadows, for instance, didn't require paths at all. Creatures freely flowed in and out of that domain.

"That wasn't the answer I was hoping for," grumbled Ajax.

No one said anything else about it. Loki was pretty sure Gaius already decided. They were leaving the Never Ending Road. Even if the green doorway led to a dangerous domain, it was probably better than this place, with all its laser beams and deadly machines.

They walked in silence for several minutes before finally coming close enough to get a good look at their destination. The doorway was essentially a large disc, sitting alongside the road. Loki guessed it was big enough for six or more cats to step through it at the same time.

Peering through the disc, Loki noticed swaying branches covered with thick foliage. The moon and a vibrant sky shone through behind the leaves. It was like Loki was lying on his back, looking up through the branches of an enormous tree. He suspected this was a one-way door into the Verdant Path. He didn't know if it would deliver them close to home, but he was hopeful.

"What do you think, Loki?" asked Gaius.

Loki wasn't sure he should answer. He didn't want Gaius casting the blame on him if he was wrong. "I think it leads into the Verdant Path. I'm just not sure where it will drop us."

Gaius nodded as he approached the two-dimensional doorway out of the Never Ending Road. He looked back at the other cats and grinned before leaping through the doorway. Caught off guard, Loki rushed forward. If anyone should have gone through first, it should have been him or Ajax. What if there were coyotes waiting to ambush him on the other side?

Peering through the doorway, Loki saw Gaius' belly. He was looking down in Loki's direction, but not right at him. It supported Loki's guess that this was a one-way doorway. Gaius was probably just staring at random patches of grass, trying to figure out where the doorway might be. Finally, Gaius grinned and waved.

"I think it's safe," said Loki. "He wants us to come through."

"Alright, let's go," said Ajax as he stepped through the doorway. Loki followed an instant later.

They appeared in a dense patch of trees. An assortment of colorful stars peppered the night sky. The bright purple moon was obscured by the glowing foliage overhead, but Loki knew it was there. Its purple light bathed tree trunks and branches everywhere he looked.

While the trees were overgrown, the grass and groundcover were all neatly manicured. Rows of glowing hostas and ferns bordered a pathway of stone pavers that stretched as far as the eye could see. Warm, milky, golden light shone from the pavers, blending with the hostas' collage of soft greens and the yellowish oranges of the ferns.

"We're in the Verdant Path," said Gaius.

"Yup," said Loki. "We're actually pretty close to home."

Gaius smiled. "Lead the way."

Loki cheerfully trotted down the trail. He deliberately avoided thinking about all the places Fenris, and his pack, might be hiding. Loki didn't even want to consider the possibility of some ancient bug, or squid monster waiting for them beneath the earth, or up in the trees.

He wanted to go home. He wanted to curl up on his pillow, above Maureen's head, and hold her paws. Loki wanted overflowing plates of food, mountains of catnip, and a nap in a warm patch of sunlight. Loki knew their work was important, but after facing so many terrors, he thought it might be nice to be a simple Housen. He didn't want to live out his days as a house cat, but he thought he might enjoy it, at least for a little while.

Loki caught a whiff of something acrid lingering in the air as they navigated a narrow stretch of the trail. They were passing the Forest of Shadows on their left as they approached the Oaken Grove. He recognized the smell from before. It was there when the terrorlings attacked.

"There's that smell again," said Ajax.

"We're almost home," said Loki as he picked up the pace. He knew they needed to investigate the smell, but it would need to wait until later. They couldn't afford to be outside of their bodies much longer. Besides, Shaman was still sleeping.

Loki breathed a sigh of relief as he crossed into the Oaken Grove. Even if he decided it wasn't truly safe anymore, it was still his home. The familiarity was enough to bring him comfort, and with how difficult things were lately, he wasn't about to second guess it.

Pressing his nose against the side of the house, Loki passed through the wall, entering the building. Ajax and Gaius appeared a few seconds later. There were on the first floor, near the catnip table.

"Damnit," growled Ajax. "Me and the Kitanja bedded down near the catnip. Our bodies aren't there!"

Gaius sighed. "Let's not panic yet. Maybe they just moved you upstairs to the bedroom. That's where Loki and I bedded down."

The cats quickly padded through the house until they entered the large bedroom on the second floor. Both the hoomans were there. They were talking. Fortunately, all the sleeping cats were there too. Gaius was right. The hoomans moved their bodies.

"I really don't want to take them to the vet, but they've been asleep for hours," said Jeff. "This is strange."

"They're cats, honey," said Maureen. "Besides, Justin is holding paws with me. Sure, he refused to wake up, but maybe they hit the catnip too hard."

"All of them?"

Maureen laughed. "They've been teaching the Chairman how to get high. It's adorable."

Loki gently slipped into his sleeping body. It felt wonderful to be back home again. He slowly stretched his claws, pressing them into his hooman's hand. She tried to pull away, but he grabbed her hand, pulling it closer. She resisted for a moment, but eventually relented, letting him pull her hand close enough to rest his head on it.

"I think they're finally waking up, hun," said Maureen.

Gaius rose to his feet and stretched deeply.

"Genghis!" said Jeff. "You're finally awake!" He reached over and grabbed the cat, holding him close. "I was worried about you."

Ajax yawned and slowly climbed to his feet. Putting his head down, he crossed the bed and pressed his forehead against Jeff's arm. The hooman obediently scritched the big brown cat for a moment before laying down on his back.

Gaius settled in on Jeff's chest, while Ajax nestled up against him. Loki loved moments like this. He wished Shaman were awake to join the cuddle-pile, but that wasn't an option right now. One of the cats would discreetly nudge a stolen item between Shaman's paws later. Hopefully, that would be enough to wake him.

Right now, all that mattered were purrs and cuddling.

26.
THE MORNING AFTER

Shaman cradled the soft leather pouch beneath his cheek. He didn't want to wake up, but every time he tried to drift back to sleep, the touch and smell of the leather pouch captured his interest. He knew it was something one of the other cats stole and slipped beneath him. What was in the leather pouch?

Deciding there would be no sleep until the mystery was solved, Shaman opened his eyes. It took him a few moments to gather his bearings. He was in the main bedroom, sleeping near the edge of the bed. Based on the light filtering into the room, it was day. It was dark when they went into the Dreaming, wasn't it? It seemed so long ago.

He was all alone in the big bedroom. There was music filtering up from below. If the hooman was playing with the wooden box, it was morning. The other hooman was probably sitting in the other room, staring at her screens.

It also meant he slept through breakfast! What did he do to deserve that? Why didn't the other cats wake him up? It was so unfair, but maybe they left him some of the tastier morsels. If not, he could always force the hooman to feed him brisket.

Armed with a plan, Shaman climbed to his feet. He peered down at the leather pouch resting on the bedspread and thought about what it might be. Even with the prospect of food waiting for him, he couldn't shake his curiosity. He needed to solve this mystery. Breakfast would come after that.

The pouch was open on one end. Shaman slipped his paw inside and immediately felt something hard. He gently curled his claws until he felt them catch on a something. Pulling his paw free from the pouch, he produced a strange set of solid bars and tiny windows. What was it?

He played with it on the bed for a few moments. Some bars seemed to fold. Eventually, he worked them open, and it suddenly made sense. Both hoomans wore strange windows over their eyes. That's what he was playing with. What an amazing treasure!

Shaman carefully folded his prize and slipped it back into its leather case. He thought this object was important to the hoomans. It probably helped them see. Somehow, that made it more precious to him. He liked his hoomans. He didn't want to hurt them, but he couldn't deny the excitement of stealing something important to them.

Grabbing his treasure between his teeth, Shaman leapt from the bed. Getting breakfast was critically important, but so was finding a safe place to stash his prize. Before leaving the bedroom, he peered around the corner. There were no hoomans in the hallway. The coast was clear.

Shaman sprinted across the hallway. He turned his head to the side as passed the open office door. He didn't want Maureen seeing what he held in his mouth. Shaman slowed down as he approached the top of the stairs. Maureen didn't yell at him, so she clearly didn't see. Now he just needed Jeff to start another song before making his next move.

The music started, and Shaman bounded down the stairs. It was challenging to do so with the leather case in his mouth, but he managed. Gaius, who was sitting on the counter next to a plate of food, nodded at him, but Shaman didn't have time for conversation. He was on a mission.

As soon as he reached the first floor, he took a hard right and sprinted toward the basement stairs. Music was blasting from the large wooden box, so Jeff didn't notice him. Shaman was home free! He took his time descending the basement stairs. He didn't want the leather case to hurt his teeth.

Once in the basement, Shaman padded over to the old couch in the corner. The hoomans rarely went near it, making it the perfect hiding place for his precious treasure. He carefully slid the case beneath the couch.

"You know, Maureen will probably want those back," said Gaius from behind him.

His cheeks burning, Shaman spun around. "Want what back?" he asked.

Gaius grinned. "The reading glasses you just stashed under the couch."

"She can't have them," said Shaman, shaking his head. "They're mine now!"

Gaius sat on his haunches and cleaned a paw. "Alright," he said after he finished. "She'll have to buy a new pair. Simple as that."

"Really?" said Shaman. He didn't think Gaius would let him keep the precious object.

"Our hoomans are very important, but never forgot, cats come first," said Gaius. "We've figured out that you need stolen items to recover your power. If Maureen's glasses were no better at satisfying your needs than a hair tie, you'd give them back, but based on how you ran off with them, they're obviously important to you."

Shaman thought about what Gaius said and nodded.

"I think you've selected an excellent place to stash your prizes, by the way. I'll remember to look here for items when we have trouble waking you."

"I'm sorry I keep falling asleep," said Shaman. "I can't help it."

Gaius jumped up on the couch and sat down, beckoning Shaman to join him. "If we're going to talk, we might as well be comfortable. We're cats, after all. We shouldn't be sitting on dirty concrete floors.

Shaman jumped up on the couch and sat down, facing Gaius.

"Let's discuss both statements, one at a time, okay?"

Shaman didn't understand what Gaius was getting at, but he nodded anyway.

"Why are you sorry about falling asleep?" asked Gaius. "It's not like you intended to do it. You're a Conjurepurr, and apparently that's something Conjurepurrs do." Gaius leaned in and gently nuzzled Shaman. "Are you sorry you're a Conjurepurr?"

"No, I enjoy being a Conjurepurr."

"If falling asleep is part of being a Conjurepurr, and you're not sorry about being a Conjurepurr, you shouldn't be sorry about falling asleep," said Gaius, his tone confident. "It's just part of who you are. Does that make sense?"

"Kind of."

"Let me give you a different example." Gaius ran a paw along his whiskers. "Ajax is a Guardian, and Guardians are generally big cats. Should Ajax be sorry about being bigger than the rest of us?"

"Of course not," said Shaman. "It's not like it's Ajax's fault that he's a big cat."

"Exactly!" said Gaius. "Just like it's not your fault you have difficulty staying awake. You're a Conjurepurr, and Conjurepurrs seem to fall asleep a lot."

"Okay, that makes sense," said Shaman.

"Good," said Gaius. "Now let's move on to the second thing you said."

Shaman looked down at his paws. What did he say again? "Um… I kind of forgot."

"You said you couldn't help it."

"Oh," said Shaman. "Well, of course, I can't help it. Otherwise I'd stay awake."

Gaius gently shook his head. "Remember, Shaman, you're just a Kitanja. You've only been with us a short time, and look at how much you've learned. Look how far you've come."

Shaman beamed, enjoying the praise. He waited, hoping the older cat would continue to shower him with compliments.

"You might not know how to stay awake right now, but let's give things a little time. We've just started discovering your abilities. There's so much to learn."

"Okay, that makes sense."

"Good," said Gaius with a curt nod. "Now, I can't promise anything, but I'm trying to find another Conjurepurr to teach you."

"I know. At the Moot, you asked that mean cat to search for one. The one who was in charge."

"I doubt Azimov will spend much time searching for a Conjurepurr, but I've asked someone else to search for one. A spirit, actually. If there is a Conjurepurr out there, she'll find it."

"Thank you!" said Shaman. It meant a lot to him that the other cats were looking out for him. When he arrived at the house, he felt unaccepted and alone, but it didn't take long for him to become a member of the family.

"Speaking of the Cah'ten Moot, there is something else I want to discuss with you." Gaius looked down and took a deep breath. "It might not be easy to hear, but I think we need to talk about it."

"Okay. What is it?"

"I lied to you," said Gaius, meeting Shaman's gaze. "It was during the Moot."

Shaman didn't understand what Gaius was saying. Everything was a blur, but he didn't recall having many conversations during the Moot.

"Remember when I asked you to cast a Purrtection spell?"

Shaman nodded.

"I told you they'd hurt Ajax if you didn't do it. I told you they'd hurt your dad."

Shaman's heart raced. "I remember."

"That was a lie, Shaman," said Gaius. "No one was going to hurt Ajax. He was never in any danger."

Suddenly, all those feelings of acceptance and being a part of a family came crashing down. Families looked out for one another. Families didn't lie to one another. "Why?" breathed Shaman. He wasn't sure why he bothered asking. Could he trust Gaius to answer him honestly?

"Because I needed you to prove you were a Conjurepurr, but you were so exhausted," said Gaius. "I knew you'd do anything for Ajax, so I lied and said he was in danger. I know it doesn't make it right, but I did it to motivate you."

The fur along Shaman's back rose, and his eyes narrowed. "You didn't have to do that. You could have told me the truth!"

"Maybe," said Gaius with a shrug. "Maybe, if I simply asked, you would have been able to cast that spell, but honestly, I doubt it. You could barely stand, Shaman."

"That doesn't make any sense!" shouted Shaman. "I was strong enough. Everyone saw me cast the spell. You didn't need to lie to me."

"It's not that simple, Kitanja," said Gaius. "Sometimes, we need motivation to do great things. In my mind, your love for Ajax helped you succeed."

Shaman jumped down from the couch. He didn't know what to think. Maybe Gaius was right. Maybe the fear of something happening to Ajax gave him strength, but he wasn't ready to believe it. He wasn't ready to forgive Gaius. Not just yet.

"I'm sorry I lied to you, Shaman," said Gaius. "If you want to discuss this again, sometime in the future, I'm always willing. Hopefully, you can forgive me."

Shaman met Gaius' gaze for a moment before nodding. He needed to think things through, but his hunger was becoming distracting. Right now, he needed breakfast. He'd think about it later, with a full belly.

Perhaps after a nap.

27.
CREEPY CRAWLIES

Ajax stretched, enjoying the sensation of grass between his toes. The ground beneath him was soft and cool, and the afternoon sun was soothing and warm. With Autumn on the way, the air would get chilly soon. He needed to pounce on every opportunity to nap outside while the weather was still warm.

Truth be told, it wasn't the weather that worried Ajax. He lost a pair of lives in just a handful of days, and by all rights, he got lucky. He could have easily lost four or more lives during those battles. Ajax understood life was finite. It wasn't uncommon for Guardians to die young. It was part of the job, but if his time was drawing to a close, he wanted to enjoy every moment to the fullest.

For all he knew, this might be the last time he slept outside beneath the sun. So far, it was a glorious day.

The hoomans let Ajax and Loki out shortly after sunrise. Gaius stayed inside, likely to work with the Kitanja, should he wake. Before Shaman, the hoomans used to leave the door open so the cats could come and go as they pleased, but they didn't do that anymore. Shaman couldn't be outside without a leash. He was too small.

Other than a few visits to check on him, the hoomans left Ajax alone all morning. Loki hopped the fence shortly after going outside. That was a few hours ago. He said he wanted to check on a few things around the neighborhood, which was fairly normal. It wasn't uncommon for Loki to spend hours at a time wandering through the woods and the neighbors' backyards.

Ajax knew how to hop the flimsy wire fence the hooman built to keep him inside the yard, but he didn't see a reason to. Gaius was the same way. The hoomans worried whenever their cats were out of sight. It was fine for Loki to jump the fence. He was a Wildseeker, after all, but the rest of the cats needed to stay in the yard. Ajax planned on discussing it with Shaman in the next few weeks. Hopefully, the Conjurepurr would see things the same way.

Then again, it was hard to find time to speak with Shaman. Every time the Conjurepurr relied on his powers, he became exhausted. Shaman spent the last few days either sleeping or desperately fighting for survival. There didn't seem to be any middle ground for the little Kitanja.

Gaius seemed to think things would improve. Hopefully, he was right. As much as Ajax enjoyed naps, he thought what was happening to the Kitanja was unfair. Shaman was just a kitten. His life was supposed to be filled with a parade of fun new experiences. Instead, the Kitanja's life was a blend of horrifying monsters, and deep slumber. There wasn't any space in between.

Rustling leaves and the ping of the flimsy wire fence attracted Ajax's attention. Loki was climbing back into the yard. Normally, he only climbed near one of the larger support poles, but this time, he was climbing an unsupported section of the fence. Deciding the behavior was odd enough to investigate, Ajax meandered toward Loki.

"Whew, that was close," panted Loki, before flopping over the fence in a chaotic collection of twisting limbs. Being a cat, he landed on his feet, of course.

"What was close?" asked Ajax. He noticed a small brown speck on Loki's forehead, just beneath his right ear.

"I think I ran through a nest of creepy crawlies, or something," said Loki. "I was racing through the trees, keeping tabs on the turkeys. You know, there's quite a big crop of baby turkeys this year. They're really cute. Anyway, while I was following them, I passed under a tight web of branches. That's when I suddenly felt them crawling all over me."

"Were you exploring someplace new?"

"Nope. I run under those branches all the time," said Loki, shaking his head. The brown speck beneath Loki's ear moved when he shook his head. He must have caught sight of it out of the corner of his eye, because he asked. "Hey, is there something on my forehead?"

Ajax didn't particularly care for bugs. He was a big cat, built for dealing with big things. Still, Loki was asking for help. It wasn't right to turn his back on another cat without a good reason. He slowly approached Loki until he was close enough to identify what was going on. "Yup. There's a tick on your forehead."

Loki shuddered. "Is it already dug in?"

Ajax nodded.

"Is it big?"

Once again, Ajax nodded.

"That doesn't make sense," mumbled Loki. "How did it grow so fast? You didn't notice it on my face this morning, before we went outside, did you?"

"It wasn't on your face this morning. I definitely would have noticed." Of all the bugs in the world, ticks bothered Ajax the most. He noticed another speck of brownish tan, this time on the back of Loki's left ear. "Do me a favor, Loki, and turn around."

"That doesn't sound good," said Loki, his tiny tail suddenly bushed. He slowly turned, providing Ajax a good view of his back. One engorged tick hung from Loki's ear. He spotted another between the Wildseeker's shoulder blades. Based on the lay of Loki's fur, Ajax suspected there were a few more nestled close to the skin.

"Sorry, buddy, but it's not good," said Ajax.

"Whiskers!" Loki faced Ajax. "You think you can claw them out?"

Ajax probably could, but he wasn't sure it was a good idea. Gaius warned him never to do that, though Ajax couldn't remember why. It had something to do with Banes. "Let's see what Gaius has to say about this. I think we better get back inside."

"Alright," said Loki with a dramatic sigh before he trotted over to the backdoor. Ajax followed. One of the hoomans must have been watching, because the door slid open before the cats reached it.

"Justin!" cheered Maureen from beside the open door. "Welcome back from your walkabout. Do you want a meaty treat?"

Loki ran past her and climbed the stairs to the second level, meowing the entire time. Despite really wanting a meaty treat, Ajax decided it was best if he stayed with his friend. The ticks clearly disturbed Loki, and who could blame him? They were really creepy.

"Well, I guess no one wants treats," called Maureen from beside the door.

Ajax didn't bother to look back. He ran up the stairs after his friend. Loki was already speaking with Gaius by the time Ajax made it to the second-floor hallway. Shaman was there also, which was refreshing. It meant the glasses Gaius stashed under the Kitanja worked to wake him.

"Slow down, Loki," said Gaius, holding up a paw. "What's wrong?"

"They're all over me!" said Loki. His tail was still bushed. He wasn't handling it well.

"What's all over you?" said Gaius.

"What's that on his face?" asked Shaman.

"Ticks!" shouted Loki.

Ajax approached the rest of the cats, but stayed a few feet behind Loki. He didn't want to make the poor cat any more nervous than he was. "He's got three or four ticks on his back, maybe more. What's strange is they're all full-sized. I thought that took a few days."

"Right, it normally takes days for a tick to puff up," said Gaius.

"Can someone just get them off me?" cried Loki. He sat on his haunches and began scratching the side of his neck with his back foot.

"Stop! If you claw them, you'll kill them," hissed Gaius.

"I'm trying to kill them!" howled Loki.

"If you do that, you'll make it worse," said Gaius. "These ticks have likely injected Banes inside you, but if you kill them, they'll send even worse Banes into you as they die."

Ajax stepped forward, placing a paw on Loki's leg. "Calm down, buddy. We'll get those ticks off you."

Loki struggled at first, trying to kick at his neck despite Ajax's paw being on his leg, but Ajax leaned in, gently pressing more and more of his weight against Loki. Eventually, the terrified cat stopped trying to claw himself.

"Let me take a closer look," said Gaius. "I have a sinking suspicious these are no ordinary ticks." Gaius sat down and gazed at Loki. Ajax knew the Cah'ten Ra was checking for spirits. Gaius took several deep breaths before shaking his head. "Each of those ticks is possessed by no less than seven Banes. I've never seen anything like it."

"Is that bad?" asked Shaman. He peered at Ajax. "That's bad, right?"

"Yeah, I think so." Ajax didn't understand the significance of seven or more Banes inside each tick, but he didn't need to. Banes were bad. That meant more Banes were worse.

"What's going to happen to me?" asked Loki. The poor cat sounded terrified.

"We have to get these ticks off of you immediately. Once that's done, I'll need to pull their Banes out of you. The good news is, once we do all that, you should be fine," said Gaius reassuringly.

Ajax studied the tick protruding from the back of Loki's ear. As much as he didn't want to touch the disgusting thing, he didn't think there was much choice. "I guess we might as well get started."

"No," snapped Gaius. "This isn't something we should do. Remember, we don't have thumbs. This is a job for our hoomans."

Ajax sighed in relief. He wanted no part of removing ticks from Loki. "Maureen is downstairs. You want me to go fetch her?"

Gaius shook his head. "Jeff is in the bedroom, napping. Go wake him up. His fingers are deft and strong. He's ideal for this task."

"On it," said Ajax as he padded past the other cats toward the bedroom. Given his size, waking a hooman was never an issue for Ajax. All he needed to do was sit on Jeff's back or chest and the hooman would wake up..

As Ajax entered the bedroom and jumped up on the bed, he decided to take a gentler approach. He needed Jeff to remove an army of ticks from Loki, after all. He might as well wake the poor man as pleasantly as possible. Carefully walking across the bed, Ajax sat down next to the hooman's pillow. Once in position, he leaned in and nuzzled Jeff's face. For good measure, he fired up a deep rumbling purr.

Jeff reached out and scritched Ajax's neck, but he didn't open his eyes.

Licking was the next step.

28.
GLOOM, BLOOMS, AND DOOM

Gaius rubbed a paw across his itching eyes. He removed several Banes from Loki without much of a struggle, but these last two were proving difficult. He likened it to grabbing a minnow from a shallow pond. When there were many minnows, it was easy to grab one. Now that there were only two, there was no shortage of places for them to hide.

"We can always try again tomorrow," said Loki.

Gaius sighed and shook his head. He understood Loki's impatience. The poor cat endured quite an ordeal. Jeff removed seven ticks from Loki. Each left an angry wound in its wake. Gaius didn't get it. None of those ticks should have been able to burrow and engorge as quickly as they did. The Banes obviously played a part, but the how and why of it was beyond Gaius' understanding.

"You look tired, and I thought you wanted to visit the Hunter this afternoon," said Loki.

Gaius looked up at the ceiling and willed his vision out of the Endless Tide, back into the real world. He hated to admit it, but Loki was right. "We'll work on removing the last two tomorrow. I don't like leaving Banes inside you, Loki."

"I don't like Banes inside me either, but you've been working on me for over an hour," said Loki. "Don't get me wrong, I really appreciate it." Loki used his back leg to scratch one of his tick wounds.

"Anyway, what I'm trying to say is thanks. Thanks for helping me out, Gaius."

"Don't mention it." As much as Gaius coveted the other cats' respect and obedience, he wasn't all that comfortable with gratitude and compliments. It was something he wanted to change about himself. It was important for cats to excel at receiving praise. As the Cah'ten Ra, he needed to provide an example for the others. If he couldn't display a properly aloof attitude, how could he expect the rest of the cats to?

"Okay," said Loki. "Should we head downstairs and find the others?"

"Sure," said Gaius as he jumped down from the soft couch and padded over to the stairs. The hoomans provided the cats with a large house, featuring several comfortable couches and many plush chairs. It was one of the main reasons Gaius was highly protective of his hoomans.

Gaius descended the stairs slowly. Loki must have been impatient, because he raced ahead. Either way, Gaius intended to take his sweet time. Pulling Banes out of cats was incredibly taxing, and he was far more exhausted than he was letting on. The last thing he wanted to do was tumble down the stairs like a clumsy kitten.

After descending to the relative safety of the kitchen floor, Gaius noticed the rest of the cats gathered by the large shiny box the hoomans used to store their food. A plate covered in steaming meat sat in between them. Gaius sniffed the air, savoring the rich smell.

Brisket.

The Kitanja must have forced one of the hoomans to give him brisket. As much as Gaius considered himself above participating in something so uncouth as eating hooman table scraps, he couldn't deny his hunger. A hearty meal would do him some good, especially if he planned on meeting with the Hunter. Besides, since the food was on a plate, he wasn't sure it qualified as table scraps. "Please, save some for me."

Loki and Shaman kept eating, but Ajax looked up. The big brown cat nodded and backed away from the plate, giving Gaius his spot.

Letting his hunger get the best of him, Gaius trotted over to the plate of food. It would have been more dignified to saunter to the plate, feigning indifference, but perfect was the enemy of the good.

"Shaman made the hooman put out a full plate," said Ajax with a grin. "He even forced him to heat it up for us. I gotta say, it's pretty nice having a Conjurepurr around the house."

Gaius pressed his face down to the plate, carefully planning out his first few bites before digging in. Both Shaman and Loki were messily eating, but Gaius was better than that. He was almost dainty in the way he plucked his first morsel from the plate. The meat was warm, but not too hot. It was just the way he liked it. He loved how the rich juices coated his tongue as he slowly chewed.

The cats ate in silence for several minutes. The amount of meat on the plate surprised Gaius. There was no way one cat could eat all of it, not even Ajax. If Shaman used his Purrsuasion spell on the hooman, he was considerate enough to compel a large enough portion for all of them. It spoke well of the Kitanja.

After Gaius ate his fill, he backed away from the plate and patiently waited while Loki finished up. Shaman kept eating, but that didn't surprise Gaius. He was a growing Kitanja. It took a lot of food to fill his kitten battery.

"Good job, Shaman," said Loki, licking his chops. "That Purrsuasion spell is really quite handy."

Shaman nodded, but didn't stop eating. Gaius let the Kitanja wolf down several more bites before speaking. "I know none of us are ready yet, but we need to go back into the Dreaming this afternoon." Gaius paused to let the other cats grumble and complain, but they held their tongues. "I hope to keep our visit brief. We'll be leaving the Oaken Grove, but only to visit the Hunter's Glade."

Shaman stopped eating and looked up at the other cats. "I'm sorry I brought you all so much trouble. I didn't mean to. I'm just a kitten."

Loki started to say something, but Gaius held up a paw to quiet him. "Never apologize for who you are, Shaman," said Gaius. "You're a cat, and a Truepaw at that. Nothing in this world is above us. No one can judge us. It is we who pass judgement on everyone else."

"Aren't you laying it on a little thick?" mumbled Ajax.

Gaius ignored him and continued. "But you're just not a cat, Shaman. You're a Conjurpurr. All these things that happened since you arrived, they aren't your fault. For reasons only Grimalkin, the Great Void Kitty, herself understands, you were born with a tremendous gift. Yes, power often comes with the heavy burden of responsibility, but we won't let you shoulder it alone. You're a member of our clowder. You're part of our family, and we will face these challenges together."

"Great speech," said Loki.

Gaius didn't know if Loki was mocking him, but he didn't care enough to investigate. His goal was to reach Shaman, and based on the expression on the Kitanja's face, he did. "Now, finish eating. We need to enter the Dreaming soon. I want us in and out before nightfall."

· · · · ·

Gaius opened his eyes and slowly drank in his surroundings. He was in the Dreaming, perhaps a dozen feet from the back door. Ajax was waiting for Shaman to cross over, which didn't surprise Gaius. The Kitanja wasn't nearly as practiced as the rest of them at entering and leaving the Dreaming. Loki was standing by the door, looking out into the yard. His posture seemed nervous.

Padding over to the door, Gaius peered into the backyard, following Loki's gaze. It didn't take him long to spot the changes. A section of the grass was stained. Instead of glowing various shades of green, it glowed scintillating silver, but the discoloration didn't end with the grass.

A large stretch of hostas glowed with nearly blinding golden light. Yellows and browns weren't uncommon colors within the patch of hostas, but this section of golden light was something different. It burned hot and bright, with an intensity that overshadowed everything nearby.

"What is it?" breathed Loki.

"I'm not sure."

"What are you guys looking at?" said Ajax as he approached.

"Neat colors," said Shaman. Gaius didn't need to look to know that Shaman was riding on Ajax's back, protected by the Guardian's Spirit Armor.

"Those new colors," said Ajax. "It looks like they appeared where the Elder Nightmare finally died. One part of it was on the grass, and the rest was in the hostas."

Gaius wasn't certain. Much of the battle with the Elder Nightmare was a blur to him, but Ajax was probably right. With the length of the monster's tentacles, it never needed to stray far from the center of the yard, but it might have stepped into the hostas toward the end of its life.

"Do you want me to scout?" asked Loki.

"Please, if you don't mind." Gaius wished he answered the question differently. He was the Cah'ten Ra. It wasn't fair for him to give wishy-washy answers like that. It's not like Loki was going to turn him down. Gaius was hiding behind softly phrased commands so he could rationalize away his responsibility if something went wrong. That was something hoomans did. He was a cat. He needed to be better than that.

"I'll be right back," said Loki as he stepped through the silver-veined glass of the back door and out into the yard. He sprinted to the far side of the yard before turning and running along the perimeter.

"That cat is crazy fast," said Ajax.

Gaius didn't feel a need to respond. Instead, he carefully watched, following Loki's journey around the Oaken Grove. He breathed a sigh of relief when Loki turned the corner and started heading back toward the shimmering glass door where the other cats waited.

"Seems safe to me, guys," called Loki, skidding to a halt.

Pressing his nose against the strange glass, Gaius left the house and entered the Oaken Grove. He padded over to the retaining wall with its colorful, glowing rocks and deftly leapt into the hostas. He wanted to get a closer look at the special golden ones.

Gaius felt no heat, but rather a tingling sensation, as he approached the golden hostas. He found it oddly unnerving. The intensity and coloration of their glowing foliage reminded him of dancing flames. His eyes told him the hostas were molten, but his other senses said otherwise.

"Kinda strange, huh?" said Loki from right behind him.

Gaius' tail partially bushed. "Don't startle me like that!"

"Sorry," mumbled Loki. "I guess I am pretty sneaky."

Precariously reaching with a paw, Gaius brushed the leaves of one of the golden hostas. Despite its molten appearance, it was cool to the touch. The tingling sensation inside Gaius swelled, but not unpleasantly. He felt energized. The extreme fatigue from removing Loki's Banes melted away. It was as if he just awoke from a long nap.

"How did it feel?" asked Ajax from off to Gaius' left.

"It felt amazing."

"Should we touch it?" asked Loki.

Gaius didn't see any reason for them not to. "Yes, by all means."

Loki reached out, stroking one of the golden leaves. "Oh, wow," he breathed. "When I sprinted around the yard, I drew upon my Wildseeker abilities to run faster. That energy I spent… It's back. It's like I never even cast a spell."

Ajax stepped forward, entering the patch of golden hostas. The Guardian's recklessness surprised Gaius. What if it was safe to touch one of the hostas, but dangerous to walk through them? Fortunately, Ajax didn't seem harmed.

"Reach down and touch one, Shaman," said Ajax. "They won't hurt you."

Shaman reached to the side until he brushed his paw against some leaves. Gaius guessed Ajax stepped into the patch to allow Shaman a chance to touch one of the hostas. Otherwise, it would have been difficult for the Kitanja to do so without leaving the safety of Ajax's back.

Tendrils of vibrant blue light sprung into existence, stretching between Shaman's paw and several of the golden hostas. The tendrils danced like liquid lightning. Initially, Gaius worried the tendrils were dangerous, and that they might hurt the Kitanja, but his fear quickly faded.

"Wow! This is great!" cheered Shaman.

Gradually shifting his sight into the Endless Tide, Gaius studied the spiritual world. It connected to both the real world and the Dreaming, though in different ways. Several spirits were gathered, forming a loose ring that stretched around the patch of golden hostas and the strip of silvery grass. It was clear they were interested in the anomalies, but were unwilling or unable to come approach them.

The golden hostas and the silver grass looked different in the Endless Tide. Color barely existed within the spirit world. The hostas and the grass were as grey as everything else, but they shimmered. From time to time, patches of light burst out of the hostas and grass, as if bubbling up out of a fountain, or shooting out of one of the strange devices the hoomans used to spread water over their grass.

Gaius let his vision return to the Dreaming. "The Hunter told us there would be Blooms. He said some of the power from the slain Elder Nightmare would bubble up within our domain. I think that's what the golden hostas and the silver grass are."

"Hopefully, these Blooms are a new permanent feature within the Oaken Grove," said Ajax. "My Spirit Armor feels stronger than ever. It's like these hostas are somehow supercharging it."

"Let's all step away from these Blooms for now," said Gaius. While he didn't understand the Blooms, he was taught throughout his life that all power was finite. Perhaps the power of the Blooms would outlast all the cats, but he saw little value in wasting it. "The Hunter is the one who told us about them. We should go speak with him."

"Sure, no problem," said Ajax as he walked out of the patch of golden hostas and worked his way across the yard. As expected, Loki raced ahead. He briefly paused, looking back at the other cats, when he reached the doorway into the Hunter's Glade. Then he stepped through it, disappearing from view.

It didn't take Ajax, Shaman, and Gaius long to reach the doorway. With Loki already across, no one paused before stepping through the doorway. If something was dangerous or wrong in the neighboring domain, Loki would have warned them by now.

Gaius quickly scanned the glade. Not seeing anything out of the ordinary, he focused on the enormous pool of shimmering turquoise in the center. The Hunter, as usual, was standing in the pool, behind the cascading waterfall. Loki was already near the pool, though not close enough to touch it.

"Greetings, noble Cah'ten Ra," called the Hunter. "Today, you and your clowder are once again my welcome guests. No harm will come to you."

Following the custom, Gaius said, "Thank you, great Hunter. We appreciate your hospitality."

The hunter stepped out from behind the waterfall, revealing his strange body. Gaius was comfortable around the Hunter, but he was still often surprised by the dog's body, human torso, and owl's head. "I've noticed a few less chipmunks in my wall, but there are still many to remove."

Gaius bowed his head. "Other matters required our attention, but we have not forgotten our debt to you. We will honor our commitment and resume our hunt as soon as we are able."

"It's all good," said the Hunter, adjusting his droopy tan hat. "I've run into a few complications trying to keep up my end of the bargain, truth be told."

"Tell me more," said Gaius.

"It seems that Fenris and his coyotes have started hunting this region again," said the Hunter. "It's safe during the day, but come nightfall, the Forest of Shadows isn't safe."

Ajax shot Gaius a quizzical glance. He probably wanted to talk about their recent fight with Fenris. Gaius nodded at the big brown cat, giving him permission.

"Fenris came after us the other night," said Ajax. "We were crossing through the Wilds when he attacked. We got away, but he's still after us."

The Hunter nodded. "Well, that explains it. Fortunately, for you cats, I've spent the past day or so rebuilding all my traps. I even took the liberty of placing a few around your Oaken Grove. With any luck. They'll deter Fenris and his pack."

"Are you using the same traps you did last year?" asked Loki.

The Hunter turned to the Wildseeker and nodded. "All the snares are in the same spots they were last year. I added a few deadfall traps, and a pair of pits, but those are around my domain. I don't think you'll have any trouble avoiding them, Loki."

"Okay, just double checking."

Gaius changed the subject. He wasn't sure how much he wanted to share about Fenris with the Hunter. "The Blooms you spoke about appeared. Some of the hostas changed colors. Touching them revitalizes us. Do you know how long they'll last?"

The Hunter grinned. "My Blooms are still going strong. If anything, they're stronger now than when they first appeared."

"Hopefully, ours will do the same," said Gaius.

"I expect yours will do better," said the Hunter. "Mine came from hunting Old Ones. Sure, they were powerful, but they don't come close to matching an Elder Nightmare."

Gaius smiled. He didn't want to get his hopes up, but if the clowder could use the new Blooms in the Oaken Grove to replenish themselves, they'd be able to accomplish so much more. Just being able to replenish Shaman without him needing to sleep with stolen treasures would be a game changer.

"So, not to change the subject, but did you have time to search for whatever is hiding in the Forest of Shadows?" asked Loki.

"I searched for a couple of hours, but I found nothing," said the Hunter. "My instinct tells me, whatever it is, it's hiding off to the west."

"Well, that's a start," said Loki.

"One other thing," said the Hunter. "I noticed a lot fewer terrorlings tracks than normal in the region. Now, maybe Fenris has got them spooked, but it also might mean that something is gathering them."

Gaius considered all the ways the terrorlings were involved with the Elder Nightmare. Something was definitely coordinating them. He didn't think Fenris was responsible for the changes to their behavior.

"There's a few hours of light left. I wonder if I should take a quick scouting run through the Forest of Shadows. What do you think, Gaius?" said Loki.

Something about Loki's eagerness troubled Gaius. He was a fine Wildseeker, but he rarely volunteered for risky missions. Gaius wondered if touching the Blooms gave Loki a newfound confidence. "Only if you promise to be back before dark."

"Okay," said Loki. "I wasn't planning on being gone long."

"This is just a scouting mission, nothing more. I don't want you taking any chances out there, understood?"

"Understood," said Loki with a nod.

"Alright, then get moving," said Gaius. He watched Loki dart off toward the twisted trees that marked the path into the Forest of Shadows. Once Loki disappeared from sight, he returned his attention to the Hunter. There wasn't much more to discuss, but he thought it was important to maintain cordial and polite relations with their powerful neighbor.

29.
OH, THAT TICKLES

Loki didn't think it would take him long to scout. He had a pretty good idea of where to look. The Dreaming and the real world often mirrored one another. In the real world, strange things happened to him when he passed under a certain web of branches. He bet that was the place he needed to investigate in the Dreaming.

Despite it being two hours before sunset, the Forest of Shadows was dark, but that didn't surprise him. The Forest of Shadows was always dark. That's how it got its name. Fortunately, Loki was a Wildseeker. His already excellent feline night vision was enhanced by his Wildseeker abilities. The light of the moon, filtered through the dense leaves overhead, was all Loki needed to see clearly.

Cutting through the woods, Loki pressed deeper into the Forest of Shadows. He was running parallel to the Oaken Grove, but he wanted to distance himself from the trail. The Hunter warned him about his newly built traps. Tomorrow, when there was plenty of time, he'd carefully scout the area and find all the traps. Right now, it was easier to travel paths the Hunter wouldn't have sabotaged.

The faintest whiff of sour milk hung in the air. It meant terrorlings were still in the region, but Loki didn't think they were close. He paused and took a moment to taste the air with his tongue. He ignored the sour milk and focused on the acrid scent he encountered before.

That was what he really needed to watch out for. Satisfied that the acrid smell was absent, he resumed his journey.

Loki hummed as he trotted through the dense underbrush. It was a dangerous mission, but for some reason, he felt confident about it. He knew exactly where to go. He wasn't sure what he'd discover once he got there, but he was eager to find out. It struck him as a bit odd. This wasn't how he approached dangerous scouting missions in the past.

A large group of Dreaming turkeys grazed off to his right. They were gathered at the top of a hill, just outside the Forest of Shadows. That hill was part of a neighboring domain. Loki visited it from time to time, mostly to keep an eye on the turkeys. Sure, they looked scary with their overly toothy beaks, but Loki didn't think they were dangerous. Truth be told, he wanted to ride one someday.

Focusing on the task ahead of him, Loki returned his attention to the Forest of Shadows. He wasn't too far from that nest of branches where the ticks got him. He was surprised by how eager he was to return to it. If it was dangerous in the real world, it was likely deadly in the Dreaming. Why wasn't he nervous about it?

Passing through a dense patch of trees, Loki spotted his destination. It was shrouded in impenetrable greyness. It wasn't that it was dark, and it wasn't obscured by branches, foliage, or anything else that might block his sight. It was just shadowy and grey. He considered backing off and studying the strange place, but some things were best done quickly.

Kind of like when the hooman removed all those ticks. He didn't dawdle about it. He got a firm grip on their heads and ripped them free.

The air grew musty and wet as Loki approached the strange formation of suspended branches. They stretched out like evenly spaced spokes on a wheel, with crossing branches connecting each spoke. If he were to draw it out, he expected it would look a lot like a spiderweb.

Loki felt something brush against his fur as he stepped beneath the suspended canopy, but it didn't concern him. In fact, nothing concerned him. The sticky substance adhering to his fur, or that fact that he was slowing down, despite his best efforts, did not bother him. He wasn't annoyed by the clinging webs tangling his whiskers, or the strange hissing noise coming from above him.

Something wasn't right. Loki closed his eyes and shook his head, trying to clear the cobwebs from his mind. Why did he just charge into a dangerous place? This strange configuration of branches couldn't have been naturally occurring. This was something's lair. Why did he casually, even carelessly, enter it?

Loki tried to back up, but his legs were held fast. Looking around, he realized thick webs tangled all four of his limbs. His face was stuck against a sheet of webbing as well. He managed to turn his head to look above him, and his heart leapt. He wasn't alone, and the creature peering at him looked anything but friendly!

"My, my, my, such a tasty morsel, and so easily caught in my web. Drawn like a moth to the flame," hissed the enormous bug monster. Loki couldn't see all of it, but he guessed each of its main legs stretched a dozen or more feet from its bulbous body. It looked a lot like a giant spider, but its face resembled that of a beaver, complete with buck teeth. Several tentacles, tipped with bony syringes, dangled beneath it.

"Whiskers," cried Loki. "Who are you? Let me go!"

"Why would I do that?" teased the creature. "But, to answer your question, I am known by many names, most of which you couldn't pronounce, little cat. For now, you can call me Tickles. I think it's only appropriate." The creature snaked one of its syringe tipped tentacles down and poked Loki. The syringe stung as it bit into his neck.

"Ouch!"

"There, there, little cat," said Tickles. "This will only hurt for a few moments. Soon, you'll become lightheaded. You won't even feel it as I feed on you. By the way, how many lives do you have left? I hope you don't mind me asking."

"Nine."

"How marvelous!" said Tickles. "Ordinarily, I'd take me time and feed on a cat like you for weeks, but my Mistress is sure to come claim you." The enormous creature crept closer, causing the branches overhead to creak.

Loki noticed a shimmering tunnel of webs extending behind the monster. It didn't quite align with what he saw before wandering into its lair. Was the tunnel some kind of doorway to another dimension? Whatever it was, Loki didn't want to find out.

"I'm rather surprised my little trap worked," said the monster. "My Mistress warned me of a powerful Spiritchaser among you. I expected him to extract all my Banes from you. Lucky for me, he missed one or two."

Loki remembered Gaius struggling to remove the last few Banes from him. They must have been what led him into Tickles trap. How could he be so foolish? He should have known something was wrong. Wildseekers were trained to be incredibly cautious, yet the Banes forced him to all but abandon caution.

"You better let me go!" growled Loki, pushing aside a sudden wave of lightheadedness. "My friends will come looking for me. You won't stand a chance against them."

Tickles laughed. It was an eerie, almost creaky sound. "They won't find us, my tasty little morsel. This place I've lured you to, it exists in a special place. On the outside, it's nothing more than a tangled clump of branches, shrouded in shadows. Inside, it's far more spacious. In fact, if my Mistress leaves you with me, perhaps I'll take you deeper into my web."

"Who's this Mistress person you keep talking about?" Loki didn't expect Tickles to answer, but he needed to keep talking. The longer he remained engaged, the longer he'd maintain consciousness. Eventually, he knew he'd pass out from blood loss. Out of the corner of his eye, he saw the syringe-tipped tentacle pulsing as it drank his blood.

"Oh, come on now. You don't really expect me to answer that, do you?" said Tickles. "I'm not some foolish villain in a stupid story, eager to gloat and regale you tales of my ingenious plans."

"Well, you seem pretty clever to me."

"Oh, you don't know the half of it, little cat," said the monster. "You'd be amazed by all the creatures I've hunted over the centuries. You're far from the first victim to stumble into my web."

Tickles seemed pretty confident, and Loki thought she had valid reasons to feel that way. After all, her plan worked perfectly on him. If she served someone else, that creature had to be incredibly powerful. "If you're centuries old, your Mistress must be super old."

"She is ancient."

Loki wondered if Tickles was giving him a clue. He knew the oldest, most powerful beings were known as Ancients. "So, why is your Mistress going to claim me? If she's powerful enough to rule you, surely she doesn't need anything from a little Wildseeker like me."

"Why don't you just go to sleep, little one? It will all be over soon enough," said Tickles.

Loki shook his head. "Nope. Not tired."

Tickles sighed. "I guess there is little harm in chatting. You won't be awake much longer, and once you fall asleep, I doubt you'll ever open your eyes again."

Loki suppressed a shudder. The monster's prediction hammered home the desperation of his situation. He was young, with a full nine lives ahead of him. There were so many things he wanted to do, and now he wasn't going to get a chance to do any of them. He was destined to die in some tick-spider's web, or worse.

"My Mistress is very interested in your clowder of cats," said Tickles. "Most particularly, she covets the Conjurepurr. The kitten who recently arrived."

Loki struggled to keep his eyes open. "Is she the one who summoned the Elder Nightmare?"

"Of course," said Tickles with a nod of her strange beaver head. "I'm merely an Old One. I wouldn't dream of trying to call an Elder Nightmare." Tickles bent her legs, bringing her face closer. "I must say, she was absolutely furious with you cats for killing her pet."

"She commands the terrorlings, doesn't she?" Loki's vision darkened dangerously.

"Terrorlings are weak-minded, simple creatures. I suspect any Ancient could easily tame armies of those sniveling simpletons."

Deep regrets swirled around Loki's fading mind. He wished he was nicer to Ajax for how patient and kind the Guardian was with him when he was just a Kitanja, and he probably shouldn't have hissed at Shaman as much as he did.

More than anything, he wished he lived his life more courageously. Why didn't he try to talk to that cute girl-kitty, the Guardian with the gorgeous tail? Feyluff was a nice kitty. She probably would have spent time with him. Instead, he was going to lose all nine lives without ever cuddling with a girl-kitty. It wasn't fair.

Loki let out a shuddering sigh.

"There, there, little one," said Tickles. "If I have anything to say about it, you'll fall asleep and never wake. There'll be no pain."

His head spinning, Loki closed his eyes.

"Then again, if my Mistress claims you, it might not be painless. In fact, I suspect, after what you cats did to her pet, it will be rather excruciating."

Loki should have been terrified by Tickles words, but he was struggling to stay awake. It was difficult to put thoughts together. As he drifted to sleep, the only thing he could think about was his profound sadness.

30.
FEYLUFF'S GIFT

Ajax paced in front of the door. He couldn't shake the sinking feeling that Loki was in trouble. The cats chatted with the Hunter for nearly a half an hour after Loki departed on his mission. Just before Ajax left the Dreaming, his Spirit Armor flashed pink, and an overwhelming sense of dread washed over him.

He was probably just being silly and worrying for no good reason. Sundown wasn't for another thirty minutes. Loki was likely already done with his mission. If Ajax were to guess, Loki was in a neighboring domain, spying on the Dreaming Turkeys. He sure loved those turkeys. He'd sneak back home a few minutes before sundown.

Then again, why did Ajax's Spirit Armor flash pink? Feyluff's Spirit Armor was tinted pink, and she took part in the Gor'ahska. If Ajax understood the ritual correctly, his Spirit Armor absorbed some aspects of Feyluff's. Was it possible that Feyluff's Spirit Armor warned her when her friends were in danger? If it did, maybe his tried to warn him that Loki was in danger.

"It's okay, Dad, he'll be alright," said Shaman. "I bet he'll be back any minute."

As much as Ajax appreciated the Kitanja's attempts to calm his nerves, he couldn't shake his sense that something was terribly wrong. "No, I don't think so. He's in danger. I know it."

Shaman's tucked his tail between his legs. "What do we do?"

Ajax considered racing back into the Dreaming and searching for his friend. Maybe his Spirit Armor would lead him to Loki. If it was alerting him of the danger, it wasn't too much of a stretch to believe it could locate Loki. Ajax sighed and shook his head. What if his Spirit Armor couldn't track Loki? Ajax would have no chance of finding him. "Gaius!" he shouted at the top of his lungs. "Gaius, I need you now!"

Shaman covered his ears with his paws. "You're really loud, Dad."

Ajax probably could have gone and searched for Gaius, but he thought yelling would get the job done more quickly, and he was right. A few moments later, Gaius trotted into the room.

"What is it?" asked Gaius.

"Loki should be back by now," said Ajax. "He's in trouble. I know it."

Gaius peered out the window. "It's still light. I told him to be back before dark. There's still time."

Ajax expected that kind of answer. On a certain level, he understood the Cah'ten Ra's point. Loki loved exploring. If he knew he didn't need to be back before sunset, it would be incredibly strange of him to come home with a half hour to spare. "I don't know, Gaius. Something happened with my Spirit Armor. It flashed pink, and I felt like something was horribly wrong."

Shaman took a seat facing the two cats. He kept quiet, but he looked like he was alertly following the conversation. Ajax was grateful for it.

"Has your armor ever flashed pink before?" asked Gaius. "Has it flashed any other colors, for that matter? Every time I've seen it, it has been gold."

"This is the first time, but I took part in a ritual with the other Guardians at the Cah'ten Moot," said Ajax. He wished he took the time to question the other Guardians about their Spirit Armor when they were together, but everything was so rushed. "My Spirit Armor may have gained some abilities of the other Guardians."

Gaius stared intently at Ajax. "Okay, so you're thinking that flash of pink was related to these new abilities. Do you know what the other Guardians' Spirit Armors can do?"

Ajax looked away. He felt stupid. Of course, Gaius was going to ask that question. "I'm sorry. I don't."

"Alright, we'll have to make a point of asking at the next moot," said Gaius with a sigh. "Hmmm… Let me think about this." Gaius casually flopped to the floor. "The Hunter hadn't discovered anything about the new threat in the Forest of Shadows, so Loki suggested a scouting run. I told him to be back before nightfall, and he raced off. Perhaps a half hour later we left the Hunter's Glade. Sometime shortly after that, I presume, your armor flashed pink, and you got the sense Loki was in danger. Am I missing anything?"

Ajax ran the sequence of events through his mind. "That sounds about right. I think it's kind of strange that he volunteered, don't you?"

Gaius nodded. "I found it a bit odd, but with everything going on, I thought perhaps he was taking his scouting duties more seriously."

"I don't think so," said Ajax, shaking his head. "If you were going to ask me what was more likely, my Spirit Armor warning me about danger, or Loki getting serious and volunteering for dangerous missions, I'm betting on my Spirit Armor."

Gaius climbed to his feet. "Now that you put it that way, I think you might be right."

"What about what happened earlier?" asked Shaman.

Ajax peered at the Kitanja for a moment, confused, and then it dawned on him. "Are you talking about the ticks from earlier in the day?"

"Yes," said Shaman. "Gaius said they had icky Banes in them."

"Whiskers!" cursed Gaius. Ajax wasn't used to the Cah'ten Ra cursing. "I knew I shouldn't have waited. How could I make such a Kitanja's mistake?"

"Wait, what did I do?" asked Shaman nervously. "Did I do something wrong?"

"I don't think you did anything wrong," said Ajax reassuringly as he studied Gaius' expression. The Cah'ten Ra's tail was flicking with agitation, and there was tension throughout his face. "What happened, Gaius?"

"Each of those ticks injected several Banes into Loki," said Gaius, looking down at his paws. "I removed as many as I could, but two of them proved hard to catch." Gaius took a deep breath and met Ajax's gaze. "Loki told me to take a break. He asked me to remove the rest in the morning, and I listened to him."

"Whiskers," mumbled Ajax.

"I was just so tired," continued Gaius. "I don't think there was any way I could have pulled them out of Loki without resting, but still, I shouldn't have let him out of my sight. Not until I got rid of those Banes."

"What's going on?" asked Shaman. "I don't understand."

Ajax started to answer, but Gaius cut him off.

"Remember when we spoke about Banes, Shaman?"

Shaman nodded.

"They can inflict many ailments on their hosts. They can make a victim sick, or sad, or forgetful." He took a deep breath. "They can also make their victims do certain things, or behave in certain ways."

"I think I get it."

"What he's saying, little buddy, is that the Banes tricked Loki," said Ajax. "They may have led him into a trap."

"What do we do?" asked Shaman, panic raising the pitch of his voice. "How do we get him back?"

"We're running out of daylight," said Ajax. "If we're going to look for him, we better get started."

Gaius shook his head. "No."

"What do you mean, no?" said Ajax. He angrily swished his tail. There was no way he was abandoning his friend.

"I need you to enter the Dreaming," said Gaius, his tone stern. "Take Shaman with you. Wait for me by our new Blooms. I have a few things I need to take care of."

"We don't have time to pussyfoot around," growled Ajax.

"Just do as I say!" screamed Gaius.

Ajax heard the Cah'ten Ra raise his voice before, but never like that. There was something frantic and desperate in his tone. He didn't know if it should reassure him or scare him.

"Running through the Forest of Shadows in the darkness of night, with no idea where we're going, will get us all killed. You have to know that," continued Gaius, his voice still loud, but under control. "I need to call some spirits to help us. It's the only way we'll find Loki."

Ajax took a deep breath before nodding. Gaius was right, of course. "Come on, Shaman. Let's get you some catnip. We're going back into the Dreaming."

31.
INVOKING THE MUSE

Gaius waited until the other cats curled up and drifted to sleep before forcing his vision into the Endless Tide. The Procession was there, as always, but he wasn't interested in any of them. He needed a powerful spirit to help him. He considered trying to reach out to the Celestine, but he didn't really know how. Celestines came and go as they wished. They weren't known for responding to summons.

Having few other options, Gaius softly meowed the song Melody taught him. He wished there was another way, but he didn't see one. Melody was a Muse. She wasn't one of the nine Muses from mythology. Gaius doubted they existed anymore. It was more likely that they all fragmented into several weaker spirits.

As Gaius meowed Melody's simple melody, he gradually felt his energy diminish. It meant his song reached her ears, and she was responding to his call. With how often he found her haunting this house, he suspected she was close. She liked to visit in the mornings when Jeff practiced the piano.

"Greetings, Gaius," called Melody from off in the distance. She was as beautiful as ever, with her porcelain white face, and long twisting coils of raven hair that wrapped around her body, only covering the places modesty demanded she cover. "To what do I owe this meeting?"

Normally Gaius would downplay the intensity of his need in order to strike a better bargain, but he didn't have time for that. "I need your help, Melody."

"My, my, so direct," hummed the Muse as she approached. "It's rare for a cat to be forthright with a request. Is my second favorite kitty in a hurry?"

"Actually, yes," said Gaius. "It's about your favorite kitty. He's missing, and we need to find him."

Melody cocked her head to one side. "Loki is missing?"

Gaius nodded.

"And you're asking me to find him?"

Gaius nodded again.

"How long has he been gone?" asked Melody. "Do you have any idea where he might be? Do you think he is in danger?" She raised her pitch by a perfect third with each subsequent question.

"He hasn't been gone long," said Gaius. "Less than two hours, and we think he is west of us, in the Forest of Shadows." Gaius paused a moment. "We think he is close. We also believe he is in great danger."

Melody sighed beautifully. Everything she did was beautiful. Gaius thought she was probably a cat in another life. "If he's in danger, let's make this quick. I so adore his gorgeous soprano meows."

"All I'm asking is that you find him and guide us to him, nothing more."

"No combat, whatsoever?"

Gaius shook his head. "None. I'll be calling other spirits to handle that part."

"Good," said Melody with a nod. "I rather loathe violence."

"Name your price, Muse."

"Oh, I think you know what I want," said Melody. A few dissonant tones crept into her otherwise musical voice. "Your hooman has lost his way. He isn't practicing nearly enough. Let me help him. Let me light the fires of maddening obsession within his heart. His art desperately craves it. He plays Chopin so beautifully, but what is Chopin with tragic loss, and overwhelming melancholy?"

Gaius knew she wanted to haunt his hooman. He chased her off more times than he could count. Gaius let Melody haunt Jeff for a few months after Kelly died. Jeff was playing some of his saddest pieces, and he thought the touch of the Muse would help him grieve. For the most part, Gaius thought it did.

But letting her mess with him right now was out of the question. Jeff was struggling to keep up with all his responsibilities. Shackling him with obsessive devotion to some impossible piece of music might push him over the edge. "I don't think that's a good idea."

"Then you better have something else to offer me," said the Muse.

"I'll get the hooman to practice more," said Gaius. He wasn't sure how he was going to accomplish it, but he'd think of something.

"What are you going to do, sit on the piano bench and meow until he practices?"

That wasn't a bad idea. "If that's what it takes."

A dangerous smile spread across Melody's lips. "If you're so confident in your ability to make him practice, then I propose a wager."

"What kind of wager?" Gaius didn't like where this was going.

"Starting tomorrow, and for a period of two months, make him practice no less than two hours each day," said the Muse. "If you fail, I'll make him practice."

Gaius shook his head. Jeff wasn't practicing every day, and he rarely played for more than an hour. Melody's terms were impossible to meet. "I'll get him to practice ten hours each week. He has many responsibilities that demand his time. Ten hours is the best I can do."

"Music should be his priority," said the Muse. "Work, family, and the rest of it should come second."

"What you're asking isn't possible," said Gaius. "I stand by my offer. Ten hours each week, for the next eight weeks."

"Make it twelve weeks, and we have a deal."

Gaius didn't think it was sustainable. Jeff went through periods where he played often, or very little. Maintaining a heavy practice load for twelve weeks was going to be a challenge, but Loki desperately needed Melody's help. Gaius would have to make it work. "Agreed. We have a deal."

"Excellent," said Melody with a nod. "Once I've found your Loki, I'll return and lead you to him."

"I'll wait for you in the Oaken Grove."

Melody didn't waste any time. She turned and raced away, quickly disappearing from sight. Some spirits in the Endless Tide were faster than others, but Melody was the fastest Gaius ever met. It was one of the reasons he called on her. He thought she had the best chance of finding Loki before sunset.

There were more spirits to summon, but Gaius thought the next part was best handled in the Dreaming. He didn't know how much energy it would take, but if the Blooms worked like he expected they would, energy wouldn't be an issue.

Padding over to the large cabinet along the wall, Gaius flattened out on his belly. He stretched his paw beneath the cabinet and fished around until he gripped something solid. When he retracted his paw, he was holding a tiny blue sphere. It immediately began to glow. Fortunately, none of the other cats found the Calling Stone Kiyo gave to him. It would have been just his luck for one of the other cats to have run off with it.

Curling into a tight ball, Gaius closed his eyes and drifted to sleep.

When he opened his eyes again, he was in the Dreaming. Quickly climbing to his feet, Gaius raced over to the glass door with the silver veins. He pressed his nose against it. He waited until he felt it yield before stepping out into the Oaken Grove.

Ajax and Shaman were standing next to the bright golden hostas. The Guardian's Spirit Armor was more intense than ever. At first, he thought it was just reflecting some of the light of the Blooms, but as he approached the Guardian, he realized that Ajax's Spirit Armor burned even brighter than the hostas. Hopefully, the blooms somehow supercharged it.

"Are we ready to go?" asked Ajax.

"Not yet."

"It will be dark soon."

"I know, but we still need to wait." said Gaius. "I have a spirit looking for him now. She'll lead us to him."

"Do we have a plan for after we find him?" asked Ajax. "We'll probably have to fight to free him."

Gaius smiled. "I'm working on that right now, my friend." He jumped up into the hostas and approached the golden patch he thought of as Blooms. He brushed some of the leaves with his paw, savoring the swell of the energy rushing into him.

Holding the Calling Stone in the palm of one paw, Gaius closed his eyes and summoned a rumbling purr. The energy rushing through him flowed down his arm and into the Calling Stone. Despite the tiny blue sphere remaining cool to the touch, Gaius felt the heat of the energy escaping the Calling Stone.

"Wow!" gasped Shaman.

Opening his eyes, Gaius was astonished by the intensity of the light blasting forth from the Calling Stone. He heard about such stones, but he never used one before. The pulsing, frosty blue light from his Calling Stone painted the entire area in shades of blue. Gradually, Gaius felt the energy coursing through him wane. The light from the Calling Stone dimmed at the same time until he finally decided his summoning spell was done.

"Well, look at that. I'm seeing something new every day," said Ajax. "Now what?"

"To be honest, I'm not sure. Let me think about it for a minute," said Gaius.

Ajax sat down in front of Gaius, staring at him with his molten gold eyes. He casually tapped a paw against the ground. Even sitting, he towered over Gaius. Ajax was anything but subtle. His impatience was, quite literally, on display.

The cautious approach would be to wait for Kiyo and Tokugawa to respond to Gaius' spell, but he didn't know how long that might be. He assumed that as long as he brought the Calling Stone with him, they'd be able to find him wherever he went. "We need to wait for the Muse to lead us to Loki, but once she's here, we're going. We don't need to wait for the other spirits to respond to my calling. They'll find me once they're in the region."

"A Calling Stone," said Melody, her words soft and musical. "I'm impressed, Gaius."

"Have you found him?" asked Gaius.

The Muse nodded.

"Is he in danger?" asked Ajax, springing to his feet.

The Muse nodded again.

Ajax looked like he was ready to charge into the Forest of Shadows, but Gaius thought a few seconds of discussion wouldn't hurt them. "Is there anything we need to know before we go? What are we going to find out there?"

Melody regarded Gaius for a long moment before speaking. "The being that has him is an Old One, and a powerful one at that. It was difficult for me to find her lair. You were wise to contact me, cat. You would never have found her without my aid."

Gaius dreaded asking the next question, but he needed to. "Is Loki still alive?"

"Yes," said Melody with a nod. "She is feeding on him."

"Oh no," whimpered Shaman.

"If she wanted to kill him, she could have easily done so," said the Muse. "The fact that she is taking her time and feeding on him is a good thing."

"Is there anything else you can tell us?" asked Gaius.

"You'll have to enter her lair to fight her," said Melody. "Be careful when you do. Your enemy is much like a giant, but very clever spider. I'm certain there'll be traps."

"I hate bugs," muttered Ajax with a shudder.

"Thank you for your aid, Melody," said Gaius. "Please lead the way."

32.
TICKLE TORTURE

Ajax followed the Muse through the Forest of Shadows, his Spirit Armor flashing gold each time he broke through branches or slammed into a tree trunk. He quickly realized the spirit could race through the region unhindered. The only thing slowing her down was the cats. Since Ajax's Spirit Armor protected Shaman and him from damage, he decided plowing a path through the woods would make things easier for Gaius, speeding up the journey for all the cats.

Even though the spirit said having the monster feed on Loki was better than the alternative, thinking about it made Ajax's skin crawl. Cats belonged at the top of the food chain. The thought of something feeding on a cat was just wrong. It wasn't acceptable for ticks or fleas to dine on cats, and it definitely wasn't okay for creepy monsters to do it!

The faint smell of sour milk tickled Ajax's nose as he wound his way through the dark forest. He was happy the Muse was leading them. He didn't think they were far from the Oaken Grove, but he already felt terribly lost. Once Loki was safe, Ajax needed him to show him how to navigate the domains that bordered the Oaken Grove.

The Muse held up one hand and pointed with the other. Ajax looked where she was pointing, but he saw nothing out of the ordinary. To him, it looked like a clump of trees, shrouded by the ever-present darkness within the Forest of Shadows.

"Your friend is in there," said the Muse.

Ajax padded a few steps closer to the clump of trees she was talking about. "I don't see anything."

"You won't," said the Muse. "It's hard to explain. You won't understand until you get closer, but trust me, Loki is in there."

Ajax looked back at Gaius, hoping for some kind of direction. The Cah'ten Ra was peering at that strange blue sphere he used back in the Oaken Grove. "We ready to do this?" asked Ajax.

"I hoped the spirits would have arrived by now, but I don't think we can wait," said Gaius. "Loki needs us. Let's go."

"Follow me," said Ajax as he cautiously approached the clump of trees. He was about to stop and ask the Muse if she was absolutely certain, when everything shifted around him. One moment, he was out in the Forest of Shadows. In the next, he was in a strange ravine, with a tangled web of branches above him. The air was musty and wet, and he got the distinct impression he was being watched.

"There!" shouted Gaius. "He's there, in the web."

Ajax looked around, but saw nothing. He noticed the glistening webs all around him. Fortunately, they couldn't adhere to his Spirit Armor. He didn't expect Gaius to be so lucky.

"Above us, Dad," said Shaman insistently.

Ajax looked up and his blood ran cold. Loki was suspended in an enormous web, wrapped in a cocoon of glistening white silk. His face was exposed. He was breathing shallowly, clearly unconscious. A monstrous, angry wound on his neck peeked out from just beneath the edge of the web cocoon.

A shimmering tunnel of spiderwebs stretched out behind Loki. What Ajax didn't see was the spider. He reasoned that a web as enormous as this one needed to be spun by an equally enormous spider. Why couldn't he spot it? Surely, something that large couldn't hide.

"Dad, look out!" shouted Shaman.

Ajax spun around just in time to see the gigantic spider materialize out of thin air. How did it do that? It was right behind him! On closer inspection, it wasn't quite a spider. Several wicked spiked tentacles dangled beneath it, and a goofy beaver head sat where a normal spider's head should be.

The creature sprung forward, slamming its bulk into Ajax. His Spirit Armor flared blindingly gold as it dissipated the attack, but the sheer weight of the beast was enough to knock Ajax back into a net of sticky webs. Fortunately, the spiderwebs couldn't adhere to his Spirit Armor.

Leaping forward, Ajax lashed out. The golden energy surrounding his claws lengthened and smoldered as he struck. The monster sprung back with surprising quickness for its size, but it wasn't quite fast enough. Ajax tore a smoking gash across its body, right beneath its ugly beaver face.

"Now, now, fight fair," said the Monster. "If I'm not using fire, you shouldn't get to either."

Ajax considered breathing fire, but he didn't know if the webs were flammable. He didn't want to risk burning Loki. For now, he'd rely on his smoldering claws and the searing strands of his mane. "Don't like fire, do you?" he said as he advanced on the gigantic spider.

"Oh, it doesn't bother me much, but nothing you do is likely to hurt me," said the monster. "My name is Tickles, by the way. I'm pleased to meet you."

Ajax caught a flash of white out of the corner of his eye. He guessed Gaius was searching for a way to free Loki. With a roar, Ajax sprung forward, swinging both claws. Tickles was prepared this time. She rocked back on her swollen abdomen and parried Ajax's claws with a pair of her chitinous legs.

Tickles rocked forward and slammed several of her legs against Ajax. His Spirit Armor hissed and sparked as it absorbed the blow, but it held strong. "My, such a tough kitty," she said. Tickles lashed out with her legs again, this time lancing them over the top of Ajax. Gaius cried out from behind him. "Not so fast, tiny cat. You must be the Spiritchaser I was warned about."

Ajax backed away, turning to get a better view of the room. Gaius was stuck to the web. There was a growing red spot on his fur from where Tickles likely struck him, but the wound didn't look lethal. Disturbingly, Ajax couldn't spot an exit anywhere. Thick sheets of webbing blocked every path out of this chamber. When did that happen?

"And if that one is the Spiritchaser, then the kitten on your back must be the Conjurepurr," said Tickles. "Surrender him, and you can take your wounded and go. He's all my Mistress wants."

"We've been getting that offer a lot lately, but the answer is still the same. Not a chance," said Ajax. He shifted to his right, trying to position himself between Tickles and his entangled friends.

"Such a pity, but no matter. I'll enjoy feasting on each of you cats, one by one," said Tickles. "I think I'll let you live the longest, Guardian. I want you to suffer while you watch each of your friends wither and die."

Roaring, Ajax leapt again, but the spider was ready for him. Sweeping several of her legs in an arc, Tickles knocked Ajax to the side, sending him tumbling to the ground. His Spirit Armor burned blindingly as it absorbed the impact.

Tickles didn't wait for Ajax to regain his footing. She pounced, driving a chaotic sea of legs and tentacles down at him. Ajax hoped his Spirit Armor would deflect all the attacks, but fortunately, he didn't need to find out.

A shimmering barrier of blue light sprung into existence, blocking all of Tickle's attacks. Showers of scintillating sparks exploded from each impact, but the defensive forcefield easily weathered the damage. Ajax witnessed Shaman's Purrtection spell take hits from an Elder Nightmare. He didn't think Tickles was nearly as powerful.

"I thought I told you to fight fair!" hissed Tickles.

Shaman's forcefield effectively pinned Tickles in one corner of the chamber, giving Ajax access to his entangled friends. "Keep her pinned back there as long as you can, little buddy," said Ajax as he started freeing Gaius.

The webbing was oily, thick, and as tough as steel. It hissed and popped as Ajax's smoldering claws tore into it, but it didn't burn. It took several strikes to cut through even a few strands of the nasty stuff. Fortunately, Gaius wasn't badly entangled. A few more cuts and the Cah'ten Ra would be free.

A constant stream of tiny explosions rang out from behind Ajax. Tickles was likely slamming her legs against Shaman's Purrtection spell. The repeated impacts were comforting. They told Ajax exactly where the monster was, and that he and the other cats were still protected.

The explosions abruptly stopped.

"Dad!" cried Shaman. "She disappeared, Dad."

Ajax struck through the last webs holding Gaius before spinning around. Tickles was nowhere to be seen. He wondered if she retreated, but he knew that was too good to be true. Ajax caught the faintest flicker of motion at the edge of his vision. He turned just in time to see the enormous spider monster materialize out of thin air, just like she did earlier in the encounter.

"Surprise! It's suddenly, spider!" shouted Tickles.

Ajax's Spirit Armor crackled and burned, bathing the room with golden light as the monstrous spider crashed into him. Somehow, she appeared inside Shaman's protective forcefield. Her tremendous weight was enough to knock Ajax flat. Beneath her, he was protected from her legs, but he wasn't protected from her army of syringe-tipped tentacles.

"Shaman," shouted Gaius. "Drop your Purrtection spell."

Ajax didn't have a good view of everything, but he was pretty sure Shaman dropped his spell. Pinned beneath the spider, Ajax feared for what might happen to the other cats. Loki was unconscious, trapped within her web. While Gaius was free, his form in the Dreaming was barely larger than a house cat. He didn't stand a chance against a massive monstrosity like Tickles.

Ajax tried to get his feet back beneath him, but Tickles was too heavy. Fortunately, the tentacles lining her underbelly were much weaker than her armored legs. His Spirit Armor was doing an admirable job protecting him from them, but eventually they'd break through.

"Tickle, tickle, tickle," taunted the spider as she struck Ajax's Spirit Armor, over and over, with her sharpened tentacles.

He needed to find a way out from beneath the monstrous creature, sooner rather than later.

33.
TICKLE FIGHT

Gaius backed away from the terrifying beaver-faced spider monster, careful not to touch any of the sticky webs. Fortunately, Tickle's battle with Ajax prevented her from focusing on the other cats. Gaius didn't doubt she could kill Loki in an instant. The Wildseeker was completely helpless. Gaius also didn't doubt, if she ignored Ajax and focused on him, he wouldn't last more than a few seconds.

Even if they somehow defeated Tickles, Gaius didn't know how to escape her lair. Was it some kind of pocket dimension? Tickles seemed able to control her surroundings in ways that stretched reality. Pocket dimensions weren't unheard of in the Dreaming, but Gaius never heard of one functioning like this.

Shifting his vision into the Endless Tide, Gaius took a moment to study his surroundings. He knew it left him vulnerable, but he didn't think it mattered. If Tickles turned on him, he was done for. Paying attention wouldn't save him, at least not for long. With no place to run, and webs all around him, Gaius didn't stand a chance.

The view from the spirit realm horrified Gaius. All throughout the web, tortured souls silently screamed, struggling to free themselves from the ever-present spectral webs. Gaius guessed he was seeing all of Tickle's past victims. The fact that they were still struggling, even though it was hopeless, terrified him. In Gaius' experience, most spirits eventually gave up and accepted their fate. Something was motivating these souls to keep fighting, and Gaius guessed whatever it was, it wasn't pleasant.

Carefully scanning the perimeter of the pocket domain, Gaius finally found what he thought might be the exit. It didn't look much different from the rest of the place, but Gaius spotted the spirit world's ever-present Procession of shuffling ghosts through a translucent section of the wall.

In the real world, Tickles shrieked and howled. Gaius took a mental note of exactly which part of the wall led to freedom before shifting his vision out of the Endless Tide. Roiling gouts of flame blasted out from between Tickles' legs. Ajax must have breathed fire, and Tickles definitely wasn't enjoying it.

The enormous spider skittered ahead, releasing Ajax from her pinning weight. Finally free, Ajax sprung to the side. His golden Spirit Armor wasn't nearly as bright as it was before, but it was still there. Without it, none of the cats stood a chance.

Tickles spun around, facing Ajax. "How dare you, foul cat!" she hissed. Streams of smoke rose from her body. Gaius noticed several places where her chitinous carapace was blistered and burned. "Just for that, I'm going to kill your friend!"

The spider dashed toward her web, her forelegs lancing down at Loki's unconscious body. Gaius tried to race toward Loki, not that he could do anything to protect him. Still, he felt he was at fault. He never should have left those Banes inside Loki. If anyone deserved to lose a life, it was him.

"No!" cried Shaman from Ajax's back.

A small sphere of blindingly blue light snapped into existence around Loki. Tickle's legs crashed against it, producing showers of sparks, but the forcefield held strong. "How dare you!" screamed Tickles as she spun around to face the cats.

A different tiny sphere of blue light began to glow. In all the confusion, Gaius forgot he was still holding his Calling Stone. Hopefully, the light meant that Kiyo and Tokugawa were close. What else could it mean?

"I'm done playing with you cats," hissed the enormous spider. "This domain is mine, and mine alone. Everything within it answers to me!"

Suddenly, webs erupted from several tiny bumps, scattered across the floor. They looked like miniature volcanos, belching out clouds of sticky white silk, and streams of liquid that resembled curdled milk. Gaius tried to dodge the nasty stuff, but there was too much of it. He quickly grew entangled.

Ajax seemed to fare better. His Spirit Armor proved difficult, if not impossible, for the webs to adhere to. Unfortunately, there was so much of the foul stuff, Ajax struggled to move through it. "Now, that's just nasty," growled Ajax as he backed away from Tickles.

"The exit is a few feet behind me," said Gaius. "I'm pointing my tail at it. I'm afraid that's about the best I can do, but help is on the way."

"You're wrong, foolish cat," said Tickles. "No one will find you in here. No one is coming to save you."

"Really?" said Gaius. "What makes you so sure? We found you easily enough." He wanted to keep her talking. He needed to buy time for Kiyo and Tokugawa to find him.

"That's because I let you find me," said the enormous spider. "I knew you'd try to rescue your friend, so I left the door open, just a sliver, but it's closed now."

Gaius hoped the Calling Stone was strong enough to lead the ancient spirits to him. He suspected it was, but it's not like he ever used one before. If it didn't work, they were probably dead. He didn't see a way for them to win the fight without help.

Tickles raced forward, slamming her legs down at Ajax. The Guardian rose to meet her attack, and when he did, several slender strands of molten gold, woven throughout his mane, lashed out at Tickles exposed underbelly.

Ajax roared, and Tickles howled as the two combatants slammed into each other. With his Spirit Armor beginning to flicker, it was obvious Ajax suffered worse from the exchange, but Tickles didn't escape unscathed. Several new blisters appeared across her already smoking underbelly.

The tiny blue sphere in Gaius' paw flared to life, bathing the whole chamber in pale blue light. A chill wind blew through his fur. With the webs holding him fast, he couldn't twist around to look, but he was pretty sure Kiyo and Tokugawa were approaching.

"What is that you're holding?" asked Tickles. She didn't sound so sure of herself anymore. "Is that a Calling Stone?" she screeched. "How dare you bring that foul thing into my home!"

The enormous spider skittered toward Gaius, but Ajax moved to block her. He was panting, and his Spirit Armor was fading fast. Hopefully, the heroic Guardian wouldn't need to protect them much longer.

Tickles and Ajax slammed into each other, but Gaius wasn't focused on that battle anymore. To either side of him, the wind swirled, sending clouds of webs spinning like tiny tornados. Gradually, two spirits manifested next to him. Thank the Great Void Kitty! They found him in time.

"We meet again, Spiritchaser Gaius," said Tokugawa, drawing his glowing katana.

"Your payment is fair for the task in front of us," said Kiyo, nodding towards Tickles. "We will battle this Old One for you, but understand, the next time you need to summon us, the price will climb."

Kiyo's words did not surprise Gaius. This time, it didn't really cost him anything to summon the ancient ghosts. They syphoned a tremendous amount of energy from him, but the Blooms replenished it. Powerful spirits, like these, were often costly to work with. It wouldn't surprise him if they demanded much more should he need to summon them again.

"Curse you, Spiritchaser!" screamed Tickles. "I should have killed you first. I'll never make that mistake again."

"You're assuming you survive to face us again. I wouldn't make that bet," said Gaius.

Tokugawa turned, and in one smooth motion, cut Gaius free from the webs binding him. "Noble Guardian, hold her off for a little while longer," shouted Tokugawa as he drifted toward where Loki was imprisoned in the web.

"I'll try," coughed Ajax. His Spirit Armor rippled and flashed as all the golden light flowed to the front, where it formed a vibrant shield of energy.

With new threats facing her, Tickles retreated a step. She seemed unsure of whom to attack. Turning toward the web, it looked like she planned to intercept Tokugawa, but Ajax shifted to the side, blocking her path to the ancient ghost.

A shining arrow of silver light slammed into Tickles, drilling a hole in the enormous spider's chitinous carapace. Putrid yellow fluid leaked from the fresh wound. A second silvery arrow slammed into the spider an instant later, creating a second hole in her carapace.

"It should only take me a few moments to free your friend," called Tokugawa. His glowing blade seemed barely hindered by Tickles webs. He was cutting all around the vibrant blue forcefield protecting Loki. Gaius hoped the forcefield could be moved, otherwise Shaman would need to drop it before they could rescue Loki.

"Watch yourselves, cats," said Tickles as she began to shimmer and fade. "I will hunt you until the end of time." A moment after speaking, Tickles faded from view. She appeared, an instant later, a few dozen feet deeper down her tunnel of webs.

Tokugawa sliced through the last few cords, anchoring Loki to the web, causing the Wildseeker, and the blue forcefield surrounding him, to tumble to the ground. "Your friend is free. Do you want us to pursue the Old One?"

Gaius considered sending the spirits after Tickles, but he doubted they would catch her. If what Tickles said about her control over her domain was true, she probably had access to several hiding places. "Do you think you can kill her?"

"Doubtful," said Tokugawa. "I suspect Kiyo has a chance, but this Old One shifts in and out of phase. She'll likely evade us."

As much as Gaius wanted the vile spider dead, his priority was the safety of his clowder. "If you're giving me a choice, I would prefer you accompany us back home to our domain. Is that acceptable to you?"

Tokugawa looked at Kiyo. She nodded. "Yes, that is acceptable to us."

Gradually, the bubble of blue light protecting Loki faded away. He was still wrapped in a cocoon of webs. "Ajax, do you think you can carry Loki?"

"It will be slow going, but yes. I can carry him."

"Tokugawa, would you be kind enough to free Loki from his cocoon?"

The ancient ghost nodded. It took longer than Gaius expected, but he guessed Tokugawa was being incredibly careful not to injure poor Loki. Eventually, Tokugawa worked his glowing blade through all the webs, freeing the Wildseeker from his cocoon.

Loki looked horrible. The gaping wound on his neck must have been from one of Tickles syringe-tipped tentacles, but it wasn't his only wound. There was a second, similar wound on his thigh.

"Everyone follow me," said Gaius. "We're getting the hell out of here."

34.
THE HOWLING NIGHT

Shaman dug his claws into Ajax's thick mane. He was used to effortlessly riding, protected by the Guardian's Spirit Armor, but Ajax wasn't able to maintain his defensive magic after the fight with Tickles. Having Loki draped over Ajax's shoulders didn't help matters either. There wasn't a lot of space.

Given the situation, Shaman thought he would be better off running alongside Ajax, but Gaius said it was completely out of the question. Shaman didn't understand what the problem was, but he wasn't about to challenge the Cah'ten Ra, especially given recent events.

It wasn't lost on Shaman that Gaius summoned the spirit that led them to Loki. He also summoned the pair of spirits that scared Tickles off. Maybe Gaius made a mistake leaving those Banes inside Loki, but as far as Shaman was concerned, the Cah'ten Ra saved the day.

Then again, Ajax impressed him as well. The Guardian went toe to toe with that scary spider creature. None of the other cats could have taken a single hit from that monstrosity, but Ajax took countless blows. He was the only reason any of them survived.

Shaman wondered when he would be the one to save the day. Sure, he used a Purrtection spell to save Loki, but it seemed like his magic just delayed things. Nothing he did damaged his enemies. Were his powers limited to magical shields?

He knew he was capable of more. On several occasions, he manipulated the hooman, making him feed the cats brisket. Just the other day, he created light. Still, he seemed so weak compared to the others. Why was everything after him? There had to be a reason. Maybe he was capable of greater magic, and he just didn't know how to do it yet. Shaman hoped that was the case.

Ajax grunted as he stumbled through a patch of thickets. "I know this place is called the Forest of Shadows for a reason, but it's way too dark."

"We'll be home soon enough," said Gaius.

"Are you sure?" grumbled Ajax. "It would have been nice if that spirit of yours waited around to lead us back home."

"I paid her handsomely to lead us to Loki," said Gaius. "I couldn't afford to pay her more."

"What about these other spirits, the ones escorting us? Do they know the way?"

Shaman glanced at the pair of spirits. They were facing out into the darkness, weapons drawn. If they heard Ajax, they were ignoring him.

"Kiyo and Tokugawa aren't guides," said Gaius. "They are here to protect us should we encounter something on our journey home."

If darkness was the problem, Shaman thought he could help. Purring deeply, He conjured a dim blue light. The illumination grew with each successive blast of purrs. It didn't take long for Shaman's magic to cover the entire area with cool blue light.

The spirit with the glowing sword spun around. "What's happening? Why is there light?"

"It's too dark. I keep slamming into trees and stumps. My little buddy took care of that problem for me with a little Purrception spell."

"Fool!" snapped the angry spirit. "Everything in the region can probably see us now."

"Calm down," said Gaius. "Everyone, take a moment to get a sense of your surroundings. Shaman, please cancel your spell. We need to continue stumbling through the darkness, but not for much longer. Based on how long we've been traveling, we're close to home."

A howl rang out across the night. A moment later, a second howl sounded in the distance. Several other howls immediately followed.

"See what you've done?" said Tokugawa.

Shaman's light quickly faded, but it seemed like it was too late. The damage was already done. Shaman looked down at his paws and sighed. He thought he was being helpful, but he only made things worse. These cats were leading wonderful lives before he showed up on their doorstep. Now, everything was terrible, and it was all his fault.

"Everyone stay close together. We move as a group," said Gaius.

"Based on the howls, it sounds like the pack is spread out," said Ajax. "After our last encounter, Fenris will gather his numbers before moving against us. We have time."

"Let's not waste it," said Gaius as he trotted ahead. Riding on Ajax's back made it difficult to see, but Shaman got the impression they were traveling faster than before. The spirit named Tokugawa moved closer to the group, probably to protect them. The other spirit drifted back until she was ten feet behind the group.

They moved in that fashion for several minutes, crossing a variety of terrains. Ajax stumbled into stumps frequently. Shaman heard several naughty words come out of the Guardian's mouth. He whispered a few of the more colorful terms to himself. He planned to use them later.

"Whiskers!" cursed Gaius. "They've found us."

Off to the side, Shaman noticed an enormous dog stepping out from behind a tree. Its eyes pulsed with frozen blue light, and one of his rear legs looks to be made of ice and snow. A pair of smaller dogs came into view behind it. Their eyes were molten and fiery. Glancing the other direction, Shaman noticed another pair of dogs gazing at them from atop a fallen log. With how limited their visibility was in the Forest of Shadows, there was no way to truly know how many of Fenris' coyotes were out there.

"Cast another Purrception spell, little buddy," said Ajax.

"But the spirit will get angry with me, Dad."

"Just do it."

Once again, Shaman purred deeply. This time, the illumination grew quickly. He didn't know if he was improving at casting the spell, or if his fear was driving his magic to respond quickly, but Shaman wasn't about to question it. It only took a few seconds to flood the area with shimmering blue light. In addition to the five coyotes Shaman previously spotted, he saw another four, and more howls were echoing across the dark forest.

"Well, this ain't good," mumbled Ajax.

"We need to get back to the Oaken Grove," said Gaius. "If we can reach the Blooms, you can replenish your Spirit Armor."

"You cats keep moving," said Tokugawa. "We'll hold off the coyotes as long as we can."

"You heard him!" said Gaius.

Shaman considered leaping from Ajax back. If the coyotes were after him, and he alone, maybe if he surrendered, they'd spare the rest of the cats. He was just about to jump to the ground when the first silvery arrow raced across the night, striking a coyote squarely in the chest.

Ajax lurched forward, causing Shaman to hold on tight. Jumping off the Guardian now was out of the question. He was moving too fast. The spirit with the sword drifted along beside the cats as they stumbled through the forest, seemingly daring Fenris and his pack to charge.

Fenris followed the cats, but kept his distance. More coyotes gathered near him as they traveled. The pack was definitely getting larger. Silvery arrows occasionally lanced across the dark forest, but with the coyotes maintaining their distance, most shots missed their marks.

"I will offer you this deal one more time, cats," called Fenris, his voice echoing eerily. "Give up the Conjurepurr and the rest of you may go in peace. He is all we want."

"Dad," whispered Shaman. As much as he loved Ajax, and enjoyed the time he spent with all the cats, he thought it was time to stop being selfish. If his sacrifice would save the rest of them, he thought it was the right thing to do. "Maybe it's time. Maybe I should go."

"Don't say that," said Ajax.

"But you're all going to die, Dad," said Shaman. "Let me save you."

"We fought too hard to get this far. There's no way we're giving up on you now!"

"Our answer hasn't changed, Fenris," called Gaius. "No deal."

"Then you leave me no choice," said Fenris. "Take them!"

Gaius spun around to face Shaman. "Earlier, when you used your Purrtection spell to protect Loki, it moved with him. Tokugawa cut him free from the web, and both Loki and the forcefield fell to the ground."

Shaman nodded. He didn't understand what Gaius was asking him.

"If you build a forcefield around us, and we keep moving, will it move with us?" asked Gaius.

"I don't know," said Shaman. His heart pounded as panic raced through his mind. Here they were, on the verge of death, and he didn't even know how his own powers worked.

"Well, we're going to find out," said Gaius with a reassuring smile. "Tokugawa and Kiyo, I hope you choose to hunt these coyotes, but I release you from my service. I don't want to risk either of you falling. Not to them."

Tokugawa looked over his shoulder and nodded to Gaius. As he did, a pair of silvery arrows raced across the dark night. Shaman guessed that was Kiyo's way of saying she planned to fight.

"Cast your spell, Shaman."

Waves of fatigue washed over the Conjurepurr as he frantically purred. After casting so many spells, he was bordering on exhaustion, but he needed to fight through it. All he wanted was a chance to save his friends. Now that he had that chance, he wasn't going to screw it up.

A shimmering bubble of bright blue light sprung up around the cats. Through the translucent bubble, Shaman noticed the coyotes charge, and Tokugawa's glowing sword dancing in the darkness. As much as he wanted to pay attention to the battle, he found it hard to focus.

He nearly toppled to the ground when Ajax started moving. To his delight, his Purrtection spell moved along with Ajax, but pinpricks of pain raced up and down his spine after each step. To make matters worse, the pain wasn't fully fading. It was building inside him with each step.

"It hurts, Dad."

"It's okay, Son," said Ajax. "You can do it. I believe in you."

Showers of blue sparks exploded from the Purrtection spell as coyotes sprung, slamming into it with their bodies, and striking at it with their claws and teeth. The explosions were coming from every direction. There were so many coyotes, a few even leapt on top of the defensive forcefield. They began attacking it from above.

Step after step, the pain swelled inside Shaman. What started as a tingle now felt like burning. Every beat of his terrified heart delivered as much pain as it did blood to his quivering little body. If there were a way to pass out and still maintain his magic, he'd do it in a heartbeat, but he guessed it wasn't possible.

"I believe in you, Son," said Ajax, louder this time.

Shaman clenched his teeth and flexed his paws. He hoped he wasn't hurting Ajax, but tensing his muscles seemed to help ward off the sweltering pain racing through his body. He never experienced being burned, but he imagined this is what it must feel like. All across his skin, his nerves cried out in agony.

"We're almost there!" shouted Gaius. "The Oaken Grove is just a few steps away!"

The coyotes increased the pace of their attacks. Tiny explosions erupted all across Shaman's protective forcefield, forcing several cracks to appear within the barrier. The cracks must have motivated the enemy, because the intensity of their attacks crescendoed.

"Hold on just a little longer!" bellowed Ajax.

Shaman tried to fight back against the blinding pain and crippling exhaustion, but he was drowning in it. His vision faded as he grasped at Ajax's mane, gasping for air. He meowed angrily into the night as the coyotes pressed their attack, expanding every crack in Shaman's Purrtection spell.

And then it shattered, sending shards of blue light in every direction.

Ajax howled as coyotes tore into his fur and muscle. He lurched forward, but Fenris slammed into him, knocking him to the side. Shaman tried to hang on, but the force of the impact sent him tumbling into the grass. Loki bounced to the ground several feet in front of him.

They were in the Oaken Grove, not far from the hostas, but they weren't alone. Everywhere he looked, Shaman saw coyotes trotting out of the Forest of Shadows. How did Fenris gather such a large pack? Shaman noticed a few coyotes stagger and fall as silver arrows slammed into them, fired from deep within the trees, but it seemed too little and too late.

"Shaman, run!" howled Ajax as a pack of coyotes descended on him.

"Get the Conjurepurr!" barked Fenris.

His legs wobbling, Shaman climbed to his feet. Gaius was off to the side, near the golden glowing hostas. He was beckoning Shaman to join him, but the horrifying sight of Ajax staggering with a pack of coyotes climbing all over him paralyzed the Kitanja. He wanted to help his Dad!

"Come to me, Shaman!" shouted Gaius, his voice steady and commanding. "Now!"

A group of sprinting coyotes bore down on Shaman, but he couldn't afford distractions. Something about the intensity of the Cah'ten Ra's command spoke to him. Shaman didn't know what to do. He didn't know how to make everything right, but it sounded like Gaius did.

Stumbling and staggering, Shaman collapsed into the golden hostas. The moment he did, energy raced through his depleted body. A vibrant blue bubble of light sprung up around him, deflecting the leaping coyotes a mere breath before they were on him, but he didn't care about that. Shaman didn't care about protecting himself.

He needed to save Ajax.

"Leave him alone!" meowed Shaman at the top of his lungs. Sweltering energy swelled within him, but it didn't hurt. All around him, the battle ground to a halt. It was like time slowed to a crawl, allowing him to see every detail with absolute clarity.

Six coyotes were tearing at Ajax as he plodded toward the hostas. Somehow, the Guardian was still standing, though Shaman didn't know for how much longer. At the same time, a pair of Coyotes were charging toward Loki's motionless body. They would make short work of the unconscious cat.

Shaman looked to the sky, yelling, "Purrforate!" Eight concentrated beams of blinding blue light exploded from his body. Six struck the coyotes attacking Ajax. The other two struck the coyotes advancing on Loki.

For a moment, nothing happened. Several of the coyotes continued what they were doing, ignoring the strange beams. Others stopped and looked around, confused. Everything changed as the beams finished burning holes through their targets. Agonizing howls filled the night as, one by one, the coyotes realized what happened to them. The beams struck some of them in the shoulders or haunches. They were the lucky ones. They were able to hobble away. The deadly beams struck others in the head, heart, or vital organs. They weren't so lucky.

"Retreat!" howled Fenris. "Retreat!"

Shaman tried to purr. He tried to meow. He wanted to cast another spell, but he couldn't keep his balance. As he fell, he noticed a few of the golden hostas stop glowing and rapidly turn to ash. He wondered if he did that, but he didn't dwell on it.

As he felt his cheek crash against the soft earth, Shaman wasn't bothered by much of anything. In his heart of hearts, he knew he saved Ajax and Loki. Whatever he did, it worked. Maybe he wasn't destined to be a screwup after all.

Closing his eyes, Shaman drifted off to sleep.

35.
HEALING GREEN

Ajax staggered forward, blood pouring from his side. The weight of the coyotes was too much to carry. He knew he'd collapse soon, but he had to keep trying. If he could just reach the Blooms, he'd survive this. With the hostas constantly recharging his Spirit Armor, these coyotes wouldn't stand a chance.

But he wasn't going to make it. Another coyote leapt on his back, and it was just too much. His legs shaking, Ajax collapsed into the softly glowing grass of the Oaken Grove. The hostas were just a few steps away. If only he were a little stronger.

But he wasn't. All that was left for him was to lie there and wait while the coyotes ripped his remaining lives from his body, one by one. Based on what Fenris told them last time, his suffering wouldn't end with death. As a victim of the pack, he was doomed to follow Fenris around for all eternity as some kind of tortured ghost. Ajax thought he'd make an excellent ghost. He was pretty scary, after all. He bet that would translate well in his cursed afterlife.

"Purrforate!" shouted Shaman from somewhere off to the side. Ajax tried to turn his head and look, but he couldn't. There was a coyote chewing on his neck. The world tinted blue, and he felt an intense heat wash over him. It puzzled him. Did one of the stupid coyotes try to burn him? Why would it bother burning him when it could just gnaw away at him?

Then the coyotes began to scream and howl. Blood splattered in the grass all around Ajax, and he felt a tremendous weight lift from his back as the entire pack of coyotes gave up attacking him. What the heck happened?

Fenris howled, "Retreat!" He said it twice, which struck Ajax as a touch odd.

Climbing to his feet on shaky legs, Ajax saw scattered coyotes hobbling as they tried to flee. Others were flopping around in the grass. All of them seemed to have been recently burned. Taking a closer look, he noticed some coyotes had matching wounds on both sides. It was like a bullet bored a hole through them, but Ajax doubted bullets were involved. There was no bang, after all. If he were to guess, those coyotes were hit by a burning beam, similar to what they witnessed in the Never Ending Road.

Then it dawned on him. The blast of heat, and the horribly wounded coyotes, all happened after Shaman shouted 'Purrforate'. The little Kitanja must have cast a spell, and this time a destructive one. Searching the area, Ajax located Shaman. He was lying on his side in a barren spot within the hostas.

Struggling to walk, Ajax approached Shaman. Gaius was there, next to the Kitanja. He didn't look concerned, so Shaman was alright. Ajax, on the other hand, wasn't alright. Blood was flowing from several wounds, and his vision was darkening. The last time this happened, Patches, the Medicat, was there to save him. This time, he feared he would lose a life from blood loss.

Ajax took one last step before tripping and falling forward into the golden hostas. Energy flowed into his body the instant he touched them. He quickly regained enough strength to rebuild his Spirit Armor, but he questioned the value of doing so. It would have been handy a minute ago, when the coyotes were tearing at his flesh. Now he wondered if there was a point to it.

Deciding to error on the side of caution, Ajax rebuilt his Spirit Armor. Just because the coyotes were fleeing didn't mean there wasn't something else out there waiting to kill them. With both Shaman and

Loki down, Ajax Spirit Armor might be necessary to protect one of the other cats. Even though they were unconscious, he could still bind one of them to him.

This time, Ajax's Spirit Armor formed with patches of green interspersed throughout. He never saw it appear like that before. He immediately thought back to the Gor'ahska. Marcus' Spirit Armor was green. Perhaps that's where the splashes of color came from.

A tingling sensation spread across Ajax's body. At first, he thought he lost so much blood, his nerves were misfiring, but when he looked at his mangled flank, he noticed very little blood. If he wasn't mistaken, his wounds were healing.

"What's happening?" asked Gaius, peering intently at Ajax.

"I don't know. This has never happened before."

"Are your wounds healing?"

"I think so," said Ajax, grinning. "I bet it has something to do with the ritual I took part in, the Gor'ahska."

"So, this is a new thing your Spirit Armor can do, like when it flared pink, and you knew Loki was in trouble."

"I think so." Ajax surveyed several of his other wounds, and was pleased to see that they were healing. The more he thought about it, the more convinced he was that his newfound healing abilities were a gift from Marcus.

Spirit Armor came in various forms. Golden Spirit Armor was renowned for the strength of the barrier. It was popular because it absorbed the most damage, without question. Another popular choice, especially among larger cats, was a type of Spirit Armor that only absorbed some of the damage, but rapidly healed the Guardian. The theory was, by letting a portion of the impact through, but continually healing the Guardian, the Spirit Armor could continually operate, weathering endless storms of attacks.

"I think the coyotes are running away," said Gaius.

Ajax scanned the horizon and was pleased to see that all but a handful of coyotes already fled into the Forest of Shadows. Even better,

Ajax noticed a few silver streaks of light lance across his vision. "It seems your spirits are hunting them."

"I knew they would," said Gaius. "Both of them are warriors, through and through. Releasing them gave them the freedom to fight the battle on their own terms. Instead of being bound here, defending us, they're free to retreat and engage whenever they feel the need. It makes them more effective."

Ajax reflected on Gaius' logic. The Cah'ten Ra wasn't wrong. There was a cold calculation beneath it all. He couldn't decide if he admired it, or hated it. Either way, he couldn't argue with the outcome. "What next?"

"We need to find a way to rouse the other cats. They need to find their bodies before they can exit the Dreaming."

Ajax studied Shaman. He didn't seem wounded. He looked to be sleeping peacefully. Slowly padding over to him, Ajax kneeled and nuzzled the Kitanja. Shaman weakly flailed with one paw, trying to push him away. It was positively adorable. Undaunted, Ajax continued to nuzzle Shaman until, eventually, he opened his eyes.

"Did I do it, Dad?"

Ajax nodded. "You saved me, Son."

Shaman grinned. A frantic, almost manic purr followed. "Thanks for believing in me."

Ajax shook his head. "No thanks needed. You earned it, little buddy."

"What happened? Are the coyotes gone?"

"Yes," said Ajax. "Most of them turned tail and ran after you blasted them."

Shaman closed his eyes and rested his head against the soft ground.

"I know you're tired, Son, but you need to get up," said Ajax. "The sooner we're out of the Dreaming, the better."

Shaman sighed, but opened his eyes. Slowly, he rolled over and climbed to his feet. "What about Loki? How do we wake him up?"

"An excellent question," said Gaius.

"Leave that to me," said Ajax. "I think I have an idea."

"That makes one of us," said Gaius.

Ajax padded over to where Loki's body rested on the soft grass. Using his tail, he gently cradled Loki. The Wildseeker was much heavier than Shaman, but Ajax eventually managed to lift him onto his back. Once Loki was in position, Ajax cast his Binding spell, forcing his Spirit Armor to accept Loki.

Hopefully, the healing qualities of his Spirit Armor would work on Loki as well. It made sense to Ajax. The whole point of binding a rider was to extend the benefits of Spirit Armor to another. Sure enough, it worked. Loki coughed and gasped for air.

"What happened?" croaked Loki.

"We rescued you, friend," said Ajax. "We'll talk more about it once we leave the Dreaming. Are you okay to walk?"

"No, not yet," said Loki. "What's happening to me?"

"Apparently, Ajax's Spirit Armor heals him now," said Gaius. "I suspect, since he extended it to protect you, it's healing you as well."

"So, I'm not dead?" asked Loki. "Tickles didn't kill me."

"No, Loki," said Gaius. "We wouldn't let that happen to you."

"But how did you know I was in trouble?"

"Ajax sensed you were in danger," said Gaius.

"I think it's another thing my Spirit Armor does now," said Ajax. "For whatever reason, I thought you were in danger. I convinced Gaius something was wrong, and he did the rest."

"I wouldn't go that far," said Gaius. "I summoned a spirit to lead us to you, and another set of spirits to help us in the battle, but it was a team effort." Gaius paused for a moment. "Truth be told, Shaman is the one who saved you."

"Really?" said Loki. "The Kitanja saved me."

"I think Ajax did the most," said Shaman.

"When the battle was going poorly, Tickles tried to kill you," said Ajax. "Shaman protected you. Then later, when Fenris was after us, he made all the coyotes run away."

Loki shifted on Ajax back. He was a surprisingly heavy kitty in the Dreaming. "Thank you, Gaius, Ajax, and Shaman. It's really nice to know that my kitty-family has my back. I thought I was a goner."

"Don't mention it," said Gaius.

"How about we head back inside, find our bodies, and leave the Dreaming," said Ajax. "I don't know about the rest of you, but I could really go for a plate of brisket right about now."

36.
COUNTING THE COST

Loki held as still as possible as Gaius worked. At least he was pretty sure Gaius was working. It was sometimes hard to tell. Loki didn't understand the Spiritchaser stuff, but if Gaius said he was removing those last two Banes, that was what he was doing.

"There we go," said Gaius. "That's the last one. I finally caught it."

"So, am I Bane free now?"

"Of course not," said Gaius, shaking his head. "None of us are Bane free. There are always some, but I removed the ones Tickles put inside you. Those were the dangerous ones."

"You're telling me," said Loki with a sigh. He wished he were more patient when Gaius was working on him earlier. He should have let the Spiritchaser remove all the Banes.

"For what it's worth, Loki, I'm sorry," said Gaius.

"Why? I'm the one who told you it could wait until the morning."

"I know," said Gaius. "But you didn't know any better. When it comes to Banes, I'm the expert." He paused and looked down at his paws. "I let you down, and I'm sorry for that."

Loki wasn't used to receiving apologies. The hoomans often apologized to him when they didn't want to let him outside, but that wasn't special. Both Jeff and Maureen constantly apologized for trivial reasons, but an apology from Gaius was meaningful to him. "Thanks, Gaius," he said. "Apology accepted."

"Look, I don't know how to ask this, so I'm just going to come out and say it, as awkward as it might be." Gaius met Loki's gaze and took a deep breath. "How many lives did Tickles take from you?"

Loki didn't want to talk about it, but he knew he needed to. He thought Ajax was trying to ask about it earlier, but he changed the subject. Gaius asked directly, though. There was no easy way for Loki to dodge the question. "Two," he said with a sigh. "She drained two lives from me."

Gaius winced. "That's horrible."

"I know," said Loki. "I've been thinking about it quite a lot. I mean, had you guys not found me, she might have taken all my lives. The only reason she didn't was because she was saving me for her Mistress."

"I remember her mentioning her Mistress during the fight," said Gaius. "She said that if we gave up Shaman, the rest of us could leave."

"Everyone wants our Kitanja."

Gaius nodded. "It seems so, but let's not talk about that right now. I want to talk about you. Losing lives is tragic. Are you alright, Loki?"

"We can talk about me in a minute. Right now, I think we need to discuss Tickles." Loki didn't want to annoy Gaius by contradicting him, but he thought it was important. He needed to share what he learned, but he didn't want to do it in front of all the cats. Gaius was the Cah'ten Ra. He needed to know. What Gaius decided to tell the other cats was his decision. Loki didn't want the responsibility.

Gaius sat down, wrapping his tail around his paws. "Alright, Loki." If he was annoyed, he wasn't showing it.

"Tickle's Mistress is the one who summoned the Elder Nightmare. She commanded the terrorlings too," said Loki. "I'm pretty sure that acrid smell me and Ajax noticed came from Tickles Mistress."

Gaius nodded. "That all makes perfect sense. Tickle's lair was foul, but I smelled nothing acrid in there. What else did Tickles tell you?"

"Her Mistress is an Ancient."

Gaius eyes widened, and he took a sharp breath. "You're sure of that?"

Loki nodded. "She admitted it when we were talking about the terrorlings. I asked if her Mistress controlled the terrorlings." Loki paused, trying to remember the exact exchange. "She said something about the terrorlings being so dumb that any Ancient could easily control them."

"You really got her talking, didn't you? I'm quite impressed."

"It wasn't too hard. I think she was just chatting while she waited for me to pass out from the blood loss," said Loki.

"Don't sell yourself short," said Gaius. "Most cats would have been too terrified to carry on a conversation with a monster like that, but you kept your wits. Not only that, you managed to find answers to many of our questions."

Loki beamed with pride. Gaius definitely had a point. He went out there looking for answers, and he found them. "I guess I didn't think about it like that, but you're right. I'm pretty awesome, aren't I?"

"Yes, you are," said Gaius with a chuckle. "But seriously, Loki, how are you holding up?"

Loki took a deep, shuddering breath. "I guess I'm alright. When I was beginning to pass out, I couldn't help but think about all the things I've never done. I mean, I almost lost all my lives without ever having cuddled with a girl-kitty. It felt like such a waste."

"Go on," said Gaius softly.

"I really got to thinking about my lives, and how I was spending them, and I'm just not sure anymore."

"Sure about what?"

"I'm not sure I'm cut out for this," said Loki. He didn't intend to have this conversation, but now that he started it, there was no way to stop it. "Being a Wildseeker, and exploring the Dreaming. Maybe I'd be better off as a Housen."

"Many Housen don't get to go outside," said Gaius. "I've seen how you get when you're cooped up inside during the winter. I don't think being a Housen is for you."

"Maybe I could find hoomans like ours. They let me go outside." Loki knew staying here as a basic house cat was out of the question.

This house hosted one of the nineteen Abyssinial Gateways. Every cat in the house needed to be involved in its defense.

"Would you really consider leaving?" said Gaius. He sounded concerned. "What about Maureen? You've adopted her. She's your hooman now. I know the Dreaming has grown incredibly dangerous, but would you really abandon her?"

Gaius' words stung Loki. As much as he wanted to lash out at the Cah'ten Ra for bringing Maureen into it, he had a point. "I guess not," said Loki with a heavy sigh.

"I didn't think so," said Gaius. "You're a better cat than that."

"I'm just worried about never having time to live my life. There are so many things I've never experienced. Do you think there'll ever be time for fun?"

"Of course, there will be," said Gaius. "We'll just need to make it a priority. We're cats, Loki. We get to make the rules."

"Okay, that sounds a little better." Loki wasn't sure Gaius would follow through on his commitment, but at least they were talking about it. It was a good start.

"There are a few loose strings for me to pounce on, but with a little luck, I think things will improve around here."

"How so?" asked Loki. He struggled to chase the nagging doubts and lingering sadness from his mind. He kept remembering how horrible he felt, in Tickles lair, the moment before he lost consciousness. Maybe some good news was what he needed to hear right now.

"We live in a wonderful home, with good hoomans. And now, with Shaman summoning brisket and other tasty meats for us, it's even better," said Gaius with a grin. "As far as the Dreaming is concerned, Shaman's Conjurepurr powers are developing. On top of that, the Oaken Grove is strengthened by the Blooms that recently appeared. If you ask me, I think we're pretty safe, as long as we don't venture too far from our domain."

"What about the Ancient that's after us?" asked Loki. "If it summoned one Elder Nightmare, who's to say it can't summon another?"

Gaius shrugged. "I don't know. The Ancient is something we might have to face in the coming days."

"If it's after Shaman, and Shaman lives here, I'm guessing we'll have to face it." Loki thought his logic was sound.

"With any luck, I'll find another Conjurepurr to train Shaman. Everyone must be after him for a reason. The sooner we learn what Conjurepurrs are truly capable of, the safer we'll all be."

He appreciated Gaius' attempt to paint a rosy picture of their situation, but Loki wasn't feeling overly reassured. "Thanks for chatting with me Gaius, but I'm pretty tired. If it's all the same to you, I'd like to go upstairs and nap."

"Of course, friend. Go hold paws with your hooman."

Loki left without saying another word. He slowly climbed the steps and padded down the long hall to the hoomans' bedroom. He passed Ajax and Shaman napping in the office, next to a couple of cardboard toys and a small army of sparkle balls. One of them must have gone on a sparkle ball hunt beneath the couch. Loki was pretty careful with his sparkle balls. He could play with one for days without losing it.

Continuing into the bedroom, Loki hopped onto the bed, crawled up next to the headboard, and sat on his favorite pillow. The hoomans cleaned it last week, so it wasn't covered with as much of his fur as he preferred, but it wouldn't take him long to fix that problem. A few more nights of sleeping on it, and it would be covered again.

Maureen stirred, but she didn't wake. She was a deep sleeper. After curling into an appropriately cat-shaped ball, Loki built a deep, throaty purr. Without waking, Maureen reached up and placed her hand next to him on the pillow. Even deeply asleep, she responded to his purr.

Loki smiled and cradled his hooman's hand between his paws. This was his favorite part of the day. A few days ago, he would have said it made everything worth it, but that was before a giant beaver-faced spider-tick sucked two lives out of him. Now, his priorities seemed different. The stakes were higher.

But right now, all those horrors were in the past. He was in his happy place, holding paws with his hooman. Soon, his purrs would line up with Maureen's deep, slumbering breaths. Shortly after that, he'd drift to sleep.

37.
PAYING THE COST

Gaius yawned, deepening his stretch. He didn't want to get up. He was enjoying the sensation of the heated bathroom floor far too much, but there was work to be done. Besides, something in the spirit world was trying to get his attention.

Climbing to his feet, Gaius surveyed the room. Ajax and Shaman were sprawled out on a different rug, both seemingly enjoying the heated floor. With the way they were intertwined, Gaius guessed they wrestled, lost interest in that, started cleaning each other, and then promptly fell asleep. It wasn't an uncommon occurrence for those two.

Padding out into the hallway, Gaius noted the spirits swirling along the ceiling. They were more agitated than usual, but not so much where Gaius was concerned. Honestly, it was in their nature. Spirits that resisted joining the Procession were often despondent and unpredictable. As long as they didn't try to infect his hoomans, he'd tolerate their presence in his home.

Gazing at the ceiling, Gaius gently allowed his vision to drift into the Endless Tide. The Procession was there, as it always was. It was moving briskly today, which Gaius considered a good sign. A slow moving Procession often led to increased spiritual activity.

Off to the side, a flicker of motion caught his eye. Sybil was standing down the hall, gazing at him. Gaius couldn't quite decide if she looked amused or annoyed. On a certain level, he thought she might be capable of both expressions at the same time. Her beautiful silver hair often turned into gleaming chains, and her normally musical voice, at times, became dissonant.

Gaius casually trotted over to her, has tail held high, with the tip bent over. He hoped she found another Conjurepurr. He was eager to learn what was all involved. Gaius doubted Azimov and Theodore would ever deliver any answers. Short of attending a different Catsland's Cah'ten Moot, Gaius didn't have a straightforward way to investigate much farther on his end.

"Greetings, clever cat," said the Celestine. Her voice was soft and musical today, at least so far. "My spirits tell me much has happened in the past few days, and looking at you, I think I can see it in your eyes. You've changed, Gaius."

"Things have been difficult, as of late," said Gaius. He didn't doubt Sybil had spirits spying on him. He wondered if there was a way to identify them. Then again, she might have been tracking Kiyo and Tokugawa. Gaius summoned them, after all.

"Leadership changes all of us, clever cat," said the Celestine. She smiled, and her normally wavering face gradually grew more substantial. "It is a heavy mantle. Those of us who must wear it often bend beneath its weight. I don't envy you the decisions you've been forced to make, and the ones awaiting you in the future, but know that I understand the burden."

"I can't change the past, so let's discuss the future," said Gaius.

"Indeed, clever cat, lets." Sybil ran her hand through her hair. Beyond her fingers, her hair shifted into chains. Gaius saw her do that once before, but it still unnerved him.

"Did you find another Conjurepurr?" Gaius didn't see any value in beating around the bush. His previous negotiation with Sybil was a careful dance, but he didn't think this one would go that direction. If Sybil found the Conjurepurr, Gaius was prepared to go forward with the deal the two discussed during their last meeting.

"My, you've changed," teased the Celestine. "I'm not used to you being so direct."

"If you prefer we take this slowly, then by all means." Gaius sat down and began lazily cleaning a paw.

"To answer your question, clever cat, yes," said Sybil. The intensity of her voice swelled like a choir approaching the climax of a performance. "I found a Conjurepurr. If I'm not mistaken, she's the only other one left."

Gaius didn't like hearing that detail. He was afraid the Celestine might use it to increase her demands. "But you could be mistaken, correct? There could be more."

Sybil nodded. Her hair changed to shimmering chains, but only for an instant.

"Did you know that Tokugawa and Kiyo refer to you as the Chaining one?" asked Gaius. If they weren't negotiating before, they definitely were now. "I only mention it because your hair is changing often today. To be honest, I preferred it when it was a subtle effect."

"Of course, Tokugawa and the others spoke ill of me," said the Celestine. "They were warriors, from an ancient, rougher time. Those two required a harsh Mistress, so that's what I was to them."

"They described you as a predator. They said that once you snuck one chain around me, others would follow."

Sybil pursed her lips and paused, as if considering what he said. "They weren't wrong. Once I get a taste of dominion over you, I will seek to expand it. That is my nature, but is that such a bad thing?"

"Cats are the embodiment of freedom. We are not meant to be tamed," said Gaius defiantly.

"Which makes the prospect of binding you exquisitely irresistible to me."

Gaius glared at the Celestine. "You've admitted your intent, and it's definitely not in my best interests. Why should I bargain with you?"

"Who's to say it isn't in your best interests, clever cat?" Sybil smiled, revealing rows of sharpened teeth. "I am about to deliver you one of the last living Conjurepurrs, and it's only costing you one measly life."

"I happen to have a rather high opinion of my lives."

"How many lives do you think you and your clowder would lose before Shaman learned what he was capable of?" said the Celestine, her voice cool and confident. "That is what we're talking about here, is it not?"

Gaius nodded. "Everything we've faced has been after Shaman, and he alone. There must be a reason for it."

Sybil nodded. "Which is why you need another Conjurepurr. Shaman needs a teacher."

"Have you spoken with this Conjurepurr? Are you able to deliver her to us?" asked Gaius. His heart was racing. He didn't know what answer he wanted to hear.

"Yes, I've spoken with her," said Sybil. "I might be able to deliver her as soon as tomorrow."

Gaius fought to mask his conflicting emotions. He didn't want the Celestine understanding how he felt about all this. "I noticed you used the word might in your answer. If we are bargaining for one of my lives, I expect delivery before payment."

"Of course, clever cat. If you would permit me, I would like to offer a formal, binding proposal."

Gaius took a deep breath and looked down at his paws. Once he agreed, there was no going back. Even if it was only one life, he'd be bound to this Celestine. She made her intentions clear. Once she got a hold of him, she didn't plan on letting him go.

On the other hand, how many more lives would his clowder lose if he backed out of this agreement? Ajax lost lives fighting the Elder Nightmare. Loki just lost a pair of lives to Tickles. The Ancient hunting Shaman wasn't likely to stop. Gaius needed to do everything in his power to prepare his clowder for what was to come, and this agreement with Sybil was the best way for him to do that.

"I will deliver the Conjurepurr to you. I've spoken with her, and she will teach Shaman. In exchange, you will surrender one life to me, Gaius. While I must bind you now, I will not take the life from you until after I make good on my commitment. I will not take the life until after I deliver the Conjurepurr. Do you agree to my terms?"

Gaius swallowed hard. "Yes, Sybil. I agree to your terms."

"Excellent," said the Celestine. She leaned forward, and her hair immediately became a sea of gleaming chains. The chains lengthened, creeping toward him like slithering snakes.

Gaius stepped back, startled, but it only took him a moment to master his fear. Closing his eyes, he waited for the spectral chains to take him. Even though they were in the spirit world, and he was in the real world, he felt them tighten around him.

"There," said Sybil. "It is done."

"Do we want to meet here, in this hallway, after the Conjurepurr arrives?" said Gaius, before adding. "You know, to handle the whole life taking part of this?"

"I think not, clever cat."

Gaius cocked his head, confused. "I don't understand."

"I have no intention of taking one of your lives, at least not right now," said the Celestine. Dissonant notes crept into her voice, making her sound creepy. "I'll wait until you are down to just a few precious lives. That's when I'll come to collect."

A chill ran down Gaius' spine. "That wasn't the arrangement."

Sybil laughed. "Yes, it was. I never told you when I was going to take that life. I merely said it would happen after I delivered the Conjurepurr to you."

"You tricked me," hissed Gaius.

"Oh, don't be so melodramatic," said the Celestine. "I told you exactly what I intended prior to making our deal. You knew I'd try to entangle you. Don't act surprised."

Gaius cheeks burned. He hated feeling used. "What happens if some monster kills me before you can collect?"

"That is a risk I'm willing to take," said Sybil. "You are a clever, careful cat. I'm confident you'll protect yourself," said the Celestine. She smiled, and the chains faded, replaced by elegant silver hair. "Don't worry, Gaius. If I were to guess, I'll most likely trade your life back to you in exchange for several hours of your time, each week. That's what I did with the last Spiritchaser I bound."

"I'm not sure I understand."

"Cats are among the best at removing Banes from people," said Sybil. "Spiritchasers, if they're shown how, can remove Banes from people while in the Dreaming."

Gaius knew it was possible. He tried it once, with Jeff. He couldn't manage to do it, but he heard of other Spiritchasers pulling it off. "Why is that important to you?"

"I feed on the prayers of thousands of believers. Every Celestine does this. That is how we survive," said Sybil. "While I'm sure there are Celestines who blindly ignore the prayers they feed on, I would like to think most of us take them very seriously."

Gaius struggled to follow Sybil's logic. He knew Celestines survived off the devotion of the religious. While he never thought about how that actually worked, he supposed prayers were as good a vehicle for that devotion as anything else.

"Have you ever heard someone talk about the power of prayer, Gaius?"

He nodded. His hoomans weren't religious, but he knew that many believed that when they prayed for things, their prayers were sometimes answered.

"It's real, Gaius," said the Celestine. "When someone is sick, hopeless, sad, or lonely, they often pray about it. They beg a higher power to give them hope and ease their suffering."

Gaius nodded. He understood what she was saying now. In many cases, Banes caused sickness, sadness, and all the rest of it.

"I am that higher power," said Sybil. The dissonance was gone from her voice. Each of her words rang out as a clear chord. "And when I find a worshipper's prayer worthy, I take steps to help, in whatever way I can."

"Can you remove Banes from people?"

Sybil nodded. "I spend much of my time removing Banes, but like I said before, I hear the prayers of thousands. For every prayer I answer, hundreds go unanswered."

Gaius considered the implications of what Sybil was saying. If he were low on lives, and Sybil offered him such an arrangement, he very well might take it. Removing Banes was honorable work. That being said, there was no guarantee she was telling the truth. For all Gaius knew, the Celestine was painting a rosy picture of the future in the hopes of eventually coaxing more lives out of him. "You mentioned binding another Spiritchaser. What happened to that cat?"

"She died," said the Celestine with a shrug. "It was several years ago. I never found out what killed her."

Gaius didn't like how casual Sybil was with her answer. "Does working for you come with special risks? We all have enemies, after all."

Sybil pursed her lips. "Yes, I have enemies, clever cat. Heaven and Hell, angels, and demons, and all that assorted rot." She ran a finger through her hair, but no chains appeared this time. "There is a kernel of truth in all myths, fables, religions, and fairy tales. There are beings, Dark Ones, that oppose the Celestines."

Gaius was familiar with a wealth of malevolent spirits, but Dark Ones was not a term he heard before. "Is it possible one of your enemies took issue with the Spiritchaser removing Banes from your flock?"

"Perhaps, clever cat," said the Celestine. "But I think that's enough discussion for today. I have work to do. I suspect you do as well."

The way Sybil abruptly ended the conversation might be significant. Gaius resolved to prod and explore this topic in future conversations with the Celestine. Now that she controlled one of his lives, it was in his best interest to understand all the dangers. "Very well, Sybil, but before you go, is there anything we need to do to prepare for the Conjurepurr's arrival?"

"She will arrive through the Abyssinial Gateway," said the Celestine. "You will find her in the Dreaming."

Gaius nodded and watched as Sybil waved and gradually faded from view. When she was gone, he gently padded down the steps and into the piano room, contemplating the next challenge ahead of him.

How was he going to get his hooman to practice enough to satisfy the agreement with the Muse?

Based on the light shining through the shades, it was close to sunrise. If Jeff wasn't already awake, he would be soon. He normally practiced his piano shortly after washing in the water chamber and getting dressed.

Gaius considered his options. He often sat on the chair next to Jeff while he played, providing gentle licks and bites of encouragement. That was often effective, but incredibly time-consuming. Gaius was a busy cat. He didn't have time to listen to the piano for an hour or more each day.

Looking around, he spotted a large stuffed rat. It was one of the finely crafted ones. The hoomans generally filled it with catnip, before giving it to the cats to play with. As far as Gaius was concerned, it was an item of great value.

Hooman interactions seemed to revolve around exchanges. They frequently traded items or services with one another. How they valued the things they traded was a mystery. For the life of him, he didn't understand why they placed as much value in decorative pieces of paper as they did, but he didn't think it mattered. No one, cat or hooman, would question the value of a finely crafted catnip rat.

Gently gripping it between his teeth, Gaius picked up the stuffed rat and leapt onto the padded piano bench. He carefully placed it on the key that he felt marked the exact middle of the piano, perfectly centering it within the light fastened on top of the large wooden instrument.

This was the perfect plan! Upon seeing the rat, so expertly placed, the hooman would immediately understand the nature of the exchange. Gaius paid one stuffed catnip rat for a piano performance. If Jeff failed to live up to his end of the transaction, disciplinary nose-bites would definitely follow.

Brilliant! His plan was undeniably brilliant.

38.
THE ETERNAL WAR

Ajax stretched, enjoying the sensation of the warm sun against his belly. Above him, the leaves were just beginning to tinge with gold. The air was crisp and cool, but not cold, and the blue sky was dotted with fluffy white clouds. Ajax loved Autumn.

"Look, Dad, I caught another chipmunk," called Shaman. He was in the hosta patch, near one of the chipmunk burrows. He was wearing his collar and leash, as was normal when he was outside. Both Maureen and Jeff insisted Shaman was too small to roam the yard.

Except for Gaius, the cats were all outside, hunting chipmunks. Ajax wasn't really hunting, but he didn't think he needed to. Loki was over in the neighbor's yard, hunting around the retaining wall, and Shaman was doing an admirable job patrolling the hostas. Ajax figured he could afford a little nap time.

He more than earned it.

Gaius was the only one of them who stayed inside. He was sitting by the piano, encouraging Jeff to practice. Evidently, Gaius struck some kind of bargain with the Muse to get her to lead the cats to Loki. Additional piano practice was part of the arrangement. Ajax didn't understand it, but, then again, he didn't need to. Bargaining with spirits was best left to the Spiritchaser.

"Kill it and catch another one, little guy," said Ajax, suppressing a yawn. With the Banes inside them, the chipmunks were just plain dumb. Shaman already caught three, and Ajax didn't want to think about how many Loki caught. Probably double or triple that.

"Okay, I'm on it," said Shaman. He crouched down, facing a different chipmunk hole. He wiggled his butt a little bit as he prepared to pounce.

Ajax didn't think butt-wiggles were necessary for catching these particular chipmunks, but he found it adorable, nonetheless. He had to admit, no matter how difficult and costly the last few days were, he would do it all over again. Shaman brought tremendous joy to his life. Ajax didn't want to think of a life without the new Kitanja in it.

Shaman suddenly sprung, his face disappearing beneath a hosta. A moment later, he appeared with a chipper dangling from his mouth. He must have caught it by the tail, because that's how he was holding it.

"Dad," he said, dropping the chipmunk. It tried to scamper away, but he easily pinned it to the ground with a paw. "I'm getting really good at this!"

"Yes, you are, Son," said Ajax. He thought about mentioning that these were easy to catch, but decided against it. Chipmunk season was nearly over. Shaman would be almost fully grown by next season. All the cats in the house were capable hunters. Ajax didn't doubt Shaman would grow into a capable hunter in his own right.

Ajax yawned and considered if he wanted to go back to sleep. The sun felt wonderful, but he couldn't afford to get lazy. At a minimum, if he wanted to nap, he should at least patrol the Dreaming. Gaius privately asked him to keep an eye on the Oaken Grove for the next few days. He said to expect a visitor. A friendly one.

The last visitor to the Oaken Grove nearly destroyed them all. Ajax hoped never to face another Elder Nightmare, but after hearing what Loki shared with Gaius, he wasn't confident about the future. If the Ancient who summoned the Elder Nightmare was still out there, and by all accounts, she was, who knew what she would do next?

But it wasn't just the Ancient that worried him. Something was happening within the leadership of the Catsland. Neither Marcus nor Feyluff denied Gaius' allegation that the Uhl Cah'ten Ra sent Fenris after them. That was some foul litter! Cats shouldn't be working against other cats.

If the Uhl Cah'ten Ra was working against them, the fact that he called for a Guardianship was terrifying. Ajax didn't want to think about what Azimov might do with an army of Guardians. Ajax didn't believe any of his brethren would turn against him, but who knew? The thought of being forced to fight other Guardians made his tummy churn. With all that was going on, the last thing cats could afford to do was fight each other.

"I think that's enough hunting for me for this morning," said Loki as he haphazardly flopped over the flimsy garden fence that surrounded the yard. "I killed twelve of those little critters. That's probably a record."

"Good job, Loki," said Ajax as rolled over onto his side.

"How's Shaman doing?"

The Kitanja emerged from beneath a clump of hostas. He was grinning. "I've caught four so far. I even killed three of them!"

"Wait, what happened to the one you didn't kill?" asked Loki.

"Um, he got away," said Shaman, without an ounce of apology in his voice.

"I don't know, Shaman," said Loki. "We're supposed to be killing them. If you let one get away, I think you don't get to count that one."

Shaman shook his head. "It totally counts. I caught four!"

Ajax grinned at the playful banter between the two cats. "Do you mind working with him for a bit, Loki? Maybe you can give him a few pointers."

"Sure, I can do that."

Closing his eyes, Ajax listened as Loki and began teaching Shaman. It was nice hearing those two get along so well, especially after how resistant Loki was to the Kitanja when he first arrived at the house. Then again, Shaman saved Loki's life from Tickles. Sure, they all played a part, but Ajax felt Shaman was the most responsible for saving the Wildseeker.

Ajax gently purred as he drifted off into the Dreaming. The transition was smooth and effortless for him. Even with all the recent attacks on the Oaken Grove, he wasn't worried. It wasn't that he believed their enemies would avoid the region. If anything, Ajax suspected he would encounter increased threats in the coming days. But now, especially with the Blooms present, Ajax felt more confident in his ability to defeat any enemies that dared invade the Oaken Grove.

Quickly scanning the region, Ajax didn't notice any immediate threats. Sniffing the air, he didn't detect any hints of sour milk or the foul acrid scent they were associating with the Ancient. The Oaken Grove seemed safe and secure.

Ajax wasn't far from the stretch of silver grass, or the patch of golden hostas. He counted the hostas again, as he did the last time he visited. Seven of the Blooms remained. Three turned to ash when Shaman cast his deadly Purrforate spell. It was an important lesson for all of them. The power of the Blooms was finite. It was possible to drain them to death.

None of the cats understood the limitations. Gaius thought the Blooms were powerful batteries. The cats could use them to replenish their energy, but if they took too much at one time, they would kill some of their Blooms. That made sense to Ajax. It certainly explained why three withered to ash.

The patch of silver grass was a mystery to all the cats. It didn't seem to have the same energizing properties as the golden hostas. Ajax was certain the grass represented some kind of modification to the Oaken Grove. He simply didn't understand how it worked. He was tempted to take a nap in the glowing silver grass, to see what happened, but he thought better of it.

A crackle, followed by a faint humming, interrupted Ajax's thoughts. Someone or something was accessing the Abyssinial Gateway. Gaius said there was going to be a visitor, but Ajax didn't expect the visitor to arrive through the Gateway. Then again, he didn't know what to expect. He just hoped it wasn't another Elder Nightmare.

Ajax backed away from the Abyssinial Gateway. He waited until he was just at the edge of the Blooms before summoning his Spirit Armor. If something nasty stepped through the Gateway, he wanted to be as close to the Blooms as possible. He considered standing next to where his sleeping body was in the real world. It would allow him to escape quickly if some gigantic monster arrived, but he decided against it.

The creature that appeared was anything but gigantic. Ajax thought tiny was a better description. It was definitely a cat. Based on size and facial features, Ajax was pretty certain the cat was female. Her markings looked a lot like Gaius', but her hair was short. She was probably a Siamese. Even from a distance, Ajax noticed she had far more toes than a normal cat.

"Greetings, honorable Guardian," called the diminutive cat. "My, you are a big one. I'm not used to seeing Asian cats with such size. Are you the only Guardian of this place?"

Ajax wasn't sure he should answer. Then again, he didn't see any harm in it. "Yes. I'm the Guardian of the Oaken Grove, and its clowder."

"Then it is a good thing you are so fat," said the tiny Siamese. "Back when I had a clowder, I had two Guardians."

"I'm not fat, I'm big boned," snapped Ajax.

"If you say so," said the Siamese with an impish grin.

Ajax struggled to read her mood. She spat her words at him in a teasing, almost derisive way, but her eyes sparkled playfully. There was no aggression in her posture. "My name is Ajax. What's your name?"

"You can call me Poppy," said the tiny Siamese with a slight bow. "I see you're standing near the Blooms of Uohr'Koren, the Devourer Beneath the Dark Earth."

Ajax mouth hung open. How did she know the Elder Nightmare's name? Gaius mentioned it to him, and apparently at the Cah'ten Moot, but where did this little cat hear it? Ajax attended most Moots, and he never saw her before. He would have remembered a tiny Siamese with extra toes, that's for certain.

"You look surprised by my knowledge, but don't be," said Poppy. "Your Cah'ten Ra sent a great spirit to find me and request my presence. You should tell him I am here."

Ajax slowly walked to where his body was sleeping in the real world. "Stay there. I'll get him. It shouldn't be long." For good measure, Ajax sniffed the air. Poppy smelled old, but pleasant. There was no acrid odor.

"Good. you should not keep me waiting." The tiny Siamese began to lazily clean a paw. With all her toes, Ajax suspected it would take her a while.

Flopping down in the warm grass, the spirit of Ajax left the Dreaming, rejoining his body in the real world.

39.
POPPY FIELDS

Gaius feigned disinterest as he gazed at the tiny Siamese cat sitting in the middle of the Oaken Grove. She was also feigning indifference, and she was quite good at it. Ajax was fidgeting off to the side. His impatience was distracting. The Guardian clearly didn't understand how important it was for cats to show how little they cared about a subject, regardless of its actual importance.

"Would you two please knock it off," grumbled Ajax.

"Your honorable Guardian is not wrong," said the miniature Siamese cat. "I'm told you paid handsomely to procure my presence. Your casual indifference is clearly an act."

She wasn't wrong. "And you accessed an Abyssinial Gateway to come here," said Gaius, turning it back on the Siamese. "Your indifference is as much theater as my own."

"Perhaps, Gaius," said Poppy. "Perhaps."

Setting aside his pride, Gaius stopped cleaning his paws and gazed at the newcomer. Ever so slowly, she folded her legs beneath her, matching Gaius' posture. "Now that we're past our initial meeting," said Gaius. "There is much to discuss."

"Indeed, Cah'ten Ra," said Poppy. "But tell me, where is your Conjurepurr? I came all this way to see him. Why do you keep him from me?"

"Our Conjurepurr is safe. He's in the real world, for now," said Gaius. "I wanted to talk with you about a few matters before proceeding."

Poppy regarded him cooly. Her facial expression didn't change, but Gaius could tell she was annoyed. "Very well. If you feel the need to interrogate me, please begin."

Gaius nodded. "You came here through the Abyssinial Gateway. Where is your real body? The next closest Gateway is weeks away."

"My body is very far from here, Cah'ten Ra."

"Can you use our Gateway to return to your body?" asked Gaius.

"No. This is a one-way trip."

"Man, that makes me sad," said Ajax. "You better be nice to her."

Gaius looked down at his paws. He didn't want to continue this line of questioning, but he needed to understand. "If your body is far from here, and you have no means to return to it, won't you die?"

"Yes, Gaius," said Poppy. "In the real world, my body will die. I expect it will happen quickly. I'm a very old kitty. It has grown difficult for me to keep sufficient water flowing through me."

"I'm sorry to hear that," said Gaius. He ran a paw through his whiskers as he considered his next words. "How much time do you have? I'm sorry to have to ask."

"You need not apologize. You are asking the right questions, noble Cah'ten Ra," said Poppy. "We teach all cats who aspire to enter the Dreaming, that their sleeping bodies and their Draeh'Ma, their forms within the Dreaming, are inextricably linked. That is only partially true."

Gaius nodded to Poppy, encouraging her to continue.

"If my Draeh'Ma remains in the Dreaming, my body will never wake. Without food, water, and the spark of my personality, it will quickly die," said Poppy.

"What happens when you die?" asked Ajax. He sounded concerned. "We were always taught that if you die in either world, you're a goner."

"That is what you were taught, honorable Guardian, and for most cats, it is true," said the tiny Siamese. She slowly approached Gaius and

Ajax. "If you will permit me to live here, in your Oaken Grove, noble Cah'ten Ra, my Draeh'Ma will live on, long after my body dies."

Gaius wanted to give her permission, but he needed to understand what was at stake first. "How will that work? Will you be here waiting for us every time we venture into the Dreaming?"

"Yes, something like that."

"If cats can survive in the Dreaming, why don't we see more of them?" asked Ajax. "This doesn't make sense."

A surge of energy rushed through Gaius as he inadvertently brushed his tail against one of the Blooms. Suddenly, he understood. "It's the Blooms, isn't it?"

Poppy nodded. "By drawing on the power of your Blooms, I will sustain my Draeh'Ma for months, if not years."

Gaius didn't fully understand how the Blooms functioned, but he knew they were important. He needed to protect them. "What will happen to the Blooms?"

"They will slowly fade." Poppy pointed to the dusty remains of the Blooms Shaman depleted. "They will eventually turn to dust, like those."

Gaius was filled with questions, but he needed to be careful with his phrasing. He didn't want to offend the Siamese Conjurepurr. "How fast will it happen, and is there a way to protect some of the Blooms?"

"I don't know how fast the Blooms will fade. I suspect it will happen slowly." Poppy looked down at her polydactyl feet. "To answer your second question, yes, I can choose to stop feeding on your Blooms."

"What will happen when you do?" Gaius suspected he knew the answer to the question, but he wanted to be absolutely certain.

"I'll die."

"Come on, Gaius," growled Ajax. "This little lady came here on a one-way ticket. Are you really negotiating about how long she gets to live?" Ajax shook his head. "Man, that's some foul litter!"

"While I appreciate your kindness, honorable Guardian, trust your Cah'ten Ra. He must weigh the needs of the present with the needs of the future. He is wise to consider the health of the Blooms."

"Yeah, well, I don't like it," said Ajax.

Poppy approached to within inches of Ajax. "Please understand. I chose to come here. I have lived a long life. Too long, really. My old bones are eager to rest, but my spirit is still strong. I wish to help all Felinity thrive and grow." Poppy reached out and placed her paw on top of one of Ajax's enormous claws. "Even if your Cah'ten Ra grants me but a single week, it is a tremendous gift."

Gaius didn't know if he could trust Poppy. If the Celestine told her how much he paid to bring her here, she knew there was no way he was going to refuse her. That being said, her words seemed genuine. She could have easily turned Ajax against him, but she didn't. "We'll discuss the Blooms at a later date. I think we need to see how quickly they fade before we can make any commitments."

Poppy turned to face him, but she said nothing.

"For now, you can stay, provided you are willing to teach Shaman."

"Of course, I'm willing to teach your young Conjurepurr. That is why I came."

"Do you have any enemies, little lady?" asked Ajax. The abrupt question surprised Gaius.

"Of course, I have enemies, Ajax," said Poppy.

"Do you think any of them will find you here?"

"That is hard to say," said the tiny Siamese. "There are some who might search for me, but I doubt they will be nearly as dangerous as what is already here."

"You know about the Ancient, don't you?" asked Gaius.

Poppy nodded. "The Celestine spoke with me for some time."

"The Ancient was after Shaman," said Gaius. "Everyone seems to be after Shaman. Why is he so important?"

"Because once I'm gone, he will be the last Conjurepurr," said Poppy.

"Are Conjurepurrs that powerful?" asked Ajax. He sounded mystified.

"Powerful isn't the right word. Just like your powers differ greatly from Gaius' Spiritchaser abilities, Shaman will have abilities no other cats share," explained Poppy. "Will he be powerful? Yes, most certainly. Is his power much greater than your own, or that of any other accomplished cat? Probably not."

Gaius understood what Poppy was saying, but he wasn't sure Ajax was following. "Will you please go get Loki and Shaman? I think it's time the rest of the clowder meets Poppy."

Ajax nodded. "Sure. I'll be back in a couple of minutes with the others."

Gaius waited until Ajax left the Dreaming before speaking. "The Celestine told you how much I paid, right?"

Poppy nodded. "At first, I was surprised you paid the price, but after thinking about it, I think I see the wisdom beneath your decision."

"I'm not sure I do," sighed Gaius. "To be honest, I'm not sure about anything anymore."

"We are not put on this earth to get it, noble Cah'ten Ra," said the tiny Siamese. "All across the long history of cats, more often than not, the significant figures were those who found themselves embroiled in events beyond their control."

"I don't know if significant applies, but I'm certainly dealing with events beyond my control."

Poppy laughed. "Your actions have already made you more significant than hundreds of thousands of cats. Don't you see that?"

Gaius sat back on his haunches. "I guess…" He rarely found himself at a loss for words. "I don't know what to say."

"The Conjurepurr landed on your doorstep. Within days, you were forced to fight an Elder Nightmare. You've survived betrayal from your Uhl Cah'ten Ra. You've brokered a dangerous, but significant deal with a Celestine, and through that, you've brought purpose and hope to the last days of an ancient kitty's fading life." Poppy purred. It was a thin, wispy sound, but it carried with it a gentle, genuine warmth. "As far as

I'm concerned, there isn't another cat who could have done better, noble Cah'ten Ra."

Gaius swelled with pride. In the back of his mind, he knew it might be flattery, but in the depths of his heart, he felt Poppy was being honest. He didn't know how long she would be with them, but he hoped the Blooms could sustain her for many months to come. Shaman would certainly learn much from her, but all the cats would benefit from her presence. Poppy lived a long life. There was much to learn from her.

40.
POPPY SEEDS

Shaman sprawled on the soft grass, panting. His afternoon studies often exhausted him, leading to frequent naps, but he didn't mind. There was so much to learn. He worried he would never master all the skills necessary to become an accomplished Conjurepurr. Poppy was an elderly kitty, after all, yet she claimed to have much to learn. How was he supposed to learn it all as just a kitten?

"You're making your shields bigger and stronger than necessary," snapped the tiny Siamese cat. "You needlessly waste energy. That's why you are always tired."

Shaman yawned and climbed to his feet. As much as he wanted to nap, he knew his teacher wouldn't allow it. "But how am I supposed to know? Isn't it dangerous to cast a small Purrtection spell?"

Poppy shook her head. When she spoke, her voice was gentle. "I know it is difficult to gauge, especially for you. The first Purrtection spell you cast was against an Elder Nightmare, of all things. You must understand, most enemies are far weaker."

"But my Purrtection spells always break," said Shaman. "If anything, shouldn't I make them larger?"

Poppy looked to the sky for a moment. She often did so before introducing new subjects. "I want you to think about lifting something heavy. Can you do that for me?"

Shaman nodded. He remembered catching a particularly fat chipmunk. He struggled to hold it above the ground.

"What are you thinking about?" asked Poppy.

"A fat chipmunk."

Poppy smiled. "How many times could you lift it? How long could you hold it in your mouth, or above your head?"

Shaman didn't know why he'd bother holding a chipmunk above his head, but the other questions made sense. "The chipper I'm thinking of, I could hold him for maybe a minute. I don't think I'd want to lift him more than a couple of times."

"Good," said Poppy with a nod. "Now, I want you to think about something much smaller. Since we're talking about chipmunks, think about the smallest one you've ever caught. Even better, think about a mouse."

"Okay. I can do that."

"How many times could you lift that mouse, Shaman? How long could you hold it in your mouth?"

"Who knows? Mice are tiny," said Shaman with a shrug. "Honestly, I enjoy tossing them in the air. If I time it right, I can catch them in my mouth before they hit the ground."

"Now, think about your Purrtection spells," said Poppy. "Making a big shield is like lifting a heavy object. Making a strong shield is similarly heavy. Making a shield that is both big and strong is like lifting something far heavier than the fattest of chipmunks. Making a smaller shield, on the other hand, is like lifting a mouse." Poppy paused. "Contemplate this for a few moments. Please nod when you are done."

Shaman remembered how it felt casting his Purrtection spells. It didn't feel the same as lifting a chipmunk, but he remembered straining to make larger shields. At one point, he created a small shield to protect Loki from Tickles. It was much easier for him to build. Shaman nodded, letting his teacher know he was ready to continue the lesson.

"A weaker shield may shatter more quickly, but you will not struggle to make it. A stronger shield may last longer, but you will grow tired building it," said Poppy. She smiled at Shaman. "The same can be said about larger shields. Creating a shield to protect a single cat is easy. Building a large dome, to protect several cats at once, is exhausting."

Shaman followed her logic, but he didn't think there was ever much of a choice for him. "I understand, but what if I need to protect all of us at once?"

"Instead of building a large dome, make several smaller shields, one for each cat."

Poppy's explanation seemed so simple, but he wasn't sure it was possible. "Can I do that?" he asked. "Can I create more than one shield at a time?"

"Yes, and no," said Poppy patiently. "Each time you cast Purrtection, you will only build a single protective forcefield, but nothing is stopping you from casting the spell several times."

Shaman finally grasped what Poppy was trying to teach him. He grinned and began frantically purring. "Can we practice?"

"Absolutely, but we'll need more cats. Let me call the others."

Poppy used a special spell to speak with other cats. She called it Whispurr. There were several versions of the spell. Shaman didn't know how to cast any of them yet. Poppy said they were too advanced for him, at least right now. The version she was using allowed her to send her words to cats, across any distance, and even between worlds.

"I told Gaius to gather the others and join us. I suspect they'll be here shortly."

"What other kinds of spells can we cast?" asked Shaman. "I mean, I've been thinking really hard about other words with purr in them, and I'm running out of ideas."

"Why are you limiting your thinking in such a strange fashion?" asked the tiny Siamese.

"Aren't all our spells purr-puns?"

"Whatever made you think that?"

Shaman swished his tail in agitation. "Well, I used a Purrtection spell to make shields. I used a Purrception spell to make light. I used Purrsuasion to get others to do what I wanted, and I created deadly beams with a Purrforate spell. On top of that, you just used a Whispurr spell to communicate with Gaius. I don't know about you, but I'm kind of seeing a pattern here."

Poppy giggled. "It's all a joke. Long ago, a few mischievous Conjurepurrs started creating purr-puns for some of our more obvious spells. I think they wanted to see if they could trick the other cats into believing our magic functioned that way. It turns out, their trick worked."

"You mean Gaius was right, all along?" said Shaman. "Our abilities aren't based on purr-puns?"

"Yes, but you can never tell him."

"Wait, I'm supposed to lie to him and the other cats about it?" Shaman didn't think he could pull it off. He wasn't a good liar.

"It's an important, almost sacred part of being a Conjurepurr," said Poppy.

"But what if I can't think of a purr-pun to describe one of my spells?"

"They don't have to be good purr-puns," said Poppy. "In fact, using terrible puns is part of the fun. You'd be surprised by what some cats will believe."

"Okay, this is a lot harder than you're making it out to be," said Shaman. "What happens if I make a big explosion or something?"

"Purrsplosion spell."

"What, that doesn't make any sense?"

Poppy grinned. "They'll believe you."

"Okay, what if I create puddles of water?"

"Purrification," said Poppy without missing a beat.

"Huh? What does that have to do with making water?"

"You made exceptionally clean water."

"Wait, is that something we can even do?" asked Shaman. "Can we make water?"

"I don't know," said Poppy with a shrug. "At least now, you'll have a pun ready to go if you figure out how to do it."

Shaman sighed. "It's hard enough learning how to cast these spells. If I'm going to need to come up with new puns to describe new magic, I might just stick to the basics."

"No, never limit yourself," said Poppy, shaking her head. "I'll work with you on developing new puns, but that is a lesson for another time." She nodded toward the hostas. "The other cats have arrived. It's time to practice your Purrtection spells."

Shaman considered trotting over to the Blooms to recharge, but decided against it. He was supposed to be learning to use his magic more efficiently, after all. Besides, if the Blooms were sustaining Poppy, he didn't want to drain any precious energy from them, if it could be helped. He enjoyed spending time with Poppy. He wanted her to live within the Oaken Grove forever.

"So, what are we working on today?" asked Gaius, as he trotted toward them. Ajax and Loki were following closely behind him.

"Shaman needs to work on his Purrtection spell," said Poppy.

"Really? He seems pretty good at that one," said Ajax.

"He can learn to be more efficient," said Poppy. "For this exercise, I need Gaius and Loki to join us, here in the grass. Ajax, on my signal, you charge us."

The cats quickly moved into position and started practicing. It took Shaman a few attempts to get the hang of casting multiple Purrtection spells. He found that his concentration waned with each additional spell he cast. At one point, one of his Purrtection spells faded when he went to build an additional shield.

Over time, Shaman learned to maintain several shields at once. He relied on little tricks to remind him of the many shields he was controlling. Something as simple as glancing at his existing shields before creating a new one went a long way toward managing his magic.

Learning to calibrate the shields proved even more difficult for Shaman. Fortunately, Ajax was the perfect partner for this part of the exercise. The enormous Guardian delivered quite an impact when charging. Poppy's instructions were for Shaman to create multiple shields, each capable of safely absorbing a single charge from Ajax.

Loki suffered a few bumps and bruises when one of Shaman's shields failed to deflect Ajax's charge, but the rest of the shields held up. The major struggle for Shaman was building shields that faltered after a single blow. He was so used to desperately pouring everything he could into his Purrtection spells, relaxing and trusting smaller shields was tremendously difficult for him.

The cats worked for more than an hour. Shaman needed to use a Bloom to recharge once during that time, but by the end of the practice session, he felt he was making solid progress. The other cats seemed to enjoy his progress, as well. They cheered for him when his shields worked as intended. By the end, even Loki joined the celebrations.

Eventually, Poppy called a halt to the exercise. She gathered all the cats together before speaking. "Today's lesson went well. Shaman is quite skilled with his Purrtection spell. If he keeps working on it, his skills in this area of magic will easily surpass mine."

"Hey, do you hear that, little guy?" said Ajax.

The compliment surprised shaman. Poppy could do things he never dreamed of. The thought of being as good as her, or even better than her, at anything was hard for him to grasp. "Thanks," he managed after a few moments.

"Excellent," said Gaius. "What will he learn next?"

Shaman didn't care for Gaius' frequent attempts to manage his training. It didn't work like that. When working with Poppy, they often stumbled upon topics they wanted to discuss. Nothing was regimented, and that's how he liked it.

"It is hard to say, Cah'ten Ra," said the tiny Siamese. "We will do many training sessions, like this one, to continue to develop his Purrtection spell. With the threats you're facing, Purrtection is of the utmost importance."

"I understand, but what about his other spells?"

"All in due time, Cah'ten Ra." Poppy took a moment to clean a paw before continuing. "We mustn't rush him. For now, the best course is to perfect the spells he already knows. These are the spells he will excel at throughout his life. As we continue to improve his existing magic, we will dabble in new magic, until we find other spells that speak to him."

"Does that mean we need to practice that Purrforate spell of his?" asked Ajax. "Because that doesn't look fun to me."

"Yes, honorable Guardian, we will practice that spell, but not anytime soon. Shaman must develop greater control before he risks casting that again."

"What about Telepurrtation?" asked Loki. "I know that's a really neat one."

Poppy nodded. "It is, as you say, quite neat. It is also quite difficult. Shaman and I will approach that spell slowly. It is risky for a Kitanja to play with that type of magic."

"I'm not trying to be pushy," said Gaius. "I just want to make sure Shaman learns as much as possible in the time we have. As I'm sure you're aware, we lost a Bloom last night."

Shaman dreaded this part of the conversation, but he knew it was coming. Losing one of the Blooms hammered home the reality that Poppy's time was finite. Hopefully, the Bloom that died was weakened earlier by his Purrforate spell. It was next to the others that died, after all.

"I hear your concerns, noble Cah'ten Ra, but Shaman's training can't be rushed," snapped Poppy. She looked down at her paws and sighed. When she spoke again, her tone was much lighter. "Please understand, teaching Shaman is my life's work. I know how deeply important it is to you, Gaius. I know how much you sacrificed to bring me here, but please…" She paused and met Gaius' gaze. "Nothing in life is more important to me. You must trust me. Please allow me to train the Kitanja as I see fit."

Gaius remained quiet for several breaths. "Of course, Poppy. I understand."

"Thank you," she said, bowing. "Now, speaking of training, have you reconsidered your position on his Purrsuasion spell?"

"Sorry, but no," said Gaius. "He's welcome to use it on the hoomans, but cats are about consent. I don't want him practicing it on other cats."

"I disagree, but I will respect your wishes," said Poppy. "If practicing Purrsuasion is out of the question, I have another suggestion."

Shaman was hearing some of this for the first time. He knew Gaius and Poppy occasionally spoke in private, but he never thought that they discussed his training. He didn't know how he felt about it. As much as he trusted Poppy's teachings, it felt nice that Gaius was heavily invested in his studies.

"What do you suggest?"

"I find the Whispurr spell incredibly useful, but it has some notable limitations," said Poppy.

"What kind of limitations?"

"Shaman knows very few cats right now. While it is incredibly difficult, it is not impossible to speak with new cats using the Whispurr spell. With your permission, I would like to introduce him to some of my friends and allies."

"I don't understand the limitations of your magic," said Gaius. "Frankly, it amazes me that you can speak to me when you are here, in the Dreaming, and I'm in the real world. Are you saying you can teach Shaman to contact cats he's never even met?"

"It will take Shaman many hours, if not days, to learn to do so, but yes, that is what I'm saying."

"What contacts do you have?" asked Gaius, his eyes wide.

"I am an old kitty," said Poppy. "Over the years, I have met many cats, of all Callings, some of which might greatly interest you. I know a very powerful Spiritchaser, for instance. More importantly, I know many Scholars. I suspect you'll require their research in the weeks and months to come."

Gaius nodded. "Yes, absolutely. Please teach him to do this."

Shaman wasn't sure he wanted to learn to speak with strange cats, scattered all around the world, but it didn't seem like he was being given any choice in the matter. If both Poppy and Gaius thought the Whispurr spell was important for him to learn, who was he to argue?

When he stopped and really thought about it, Shaman couldn't complain about much of anything. He lived in a wonderful home, with caring and protective cats. Even the hoomans seemed decent. Sure, his life was filled with terrible danger, but if he wanted a boring life, he would have become a Housen.

Shaman enjoyed being important. He thrived on the attention the other cats showered on him. He loved the concept of being the last Conjurepurr, and he didn't mind spending every last ounce of his energy becoming the best Conjurepurr he could be. It was his true purpose. He was very fortunate to discover it so early in his life.

Shaman had eight lives left. He planned to use each and every one of them to the fullest.

41.
THE DREAMS OF CATS

Jeff looked down at Genghis and Justin. Both cats were resting on the bed. Genghis was curled into a perfectly round ball of cat, while Justin was stretched out, lying on his back. Both cats were asleep. Watching them curl and flex their paws while they slept never ceased to amuse him.

"I wonder what they're thinking about?" said Maureen. She was lying in bed, half under the covers.

Jeff didn't realize she was awake. He must have made too much noise when he crept into bed. Dinner wouldn't be ready for another half an hour. He didn't plan to wake her before then. "It's hard to say. I bet they're dreaming about hunting chippers."

"I wish they would stop dreaming about it, and go downstairs and hunt the one they brought into the house yesterday," said Maureen with a yawn. "I heard the damn thing cheep twice during my shift last night."

Jeff didn't mind the fact that the cats brought chipmunks inside. He knew Maureen didn't really care, either. He preferred them not to, but the only way he could stop them was by keeping the backdoor closed while they were outside. Jeff liked to leave it open a crack, so they could come and go as they pleased.

"Here you go, Justin," said Maureen as she placed her hand next to him. "Do you want to hold paws?" Perhaps he heard her, or perhaps it was instinctual, but Justin slowly reached over and cupped her hand between his paws.

"That's painfully cute," said Jeff, shaking his head.

"I know. What can I say? Justin gets me."

"Chairman is getting huge," said Jeff. There were so many things he wanted to talk about, but he was exhausted. Work wasn't getting any easier. Sometimes, it was just simpler to talk about the cats.

"That's because you keep feeding him."

"Wait, you don't feed him?"

Maureen snickered. "I don't hand feed him shrimp every morning."

"Alex and Justin get shrimp, daily," said Jeff. "Do you expect me to deny Chairman his share? Besides, I didn't see you stop him from running off with that crab leg the other night."

"That was too damn funny," she said in between laughs. "He leapt up onto the table like a little ninja, grabbed it, and took off running. Funniest shit I've seen a cat do."

"He needs to learn to wait for us to crack the shells for him," said Jeff, but he couldn't deny the humor of the situation. Watching that cat run off with a crab leg was hilarious.

"Where is the Chairman?"

"He's in the bathroom, with Alex." Jeff saw them on his way into the bedroom. As usual, they were curled up together as a single, giant, pile of cat.

"Alex is the best cat dad ever."

"I know," said Jeff. "I sent you pictures of how he allowed Justin to climb all over him, back when Justin was just a kitten. He's so patient with them."

"Patience seems to be a thing around here," said Maureen. "You're pretty patient yourself, you know. I'm lucky to be here. Thanks for putting up with my craziness."

Jeff knew her words were sincere, but he struggled to hear them, nonetheless. On most days, he didn't like himself. He knew it wasn't rational. He watched brutal depression slowly wither a person away until there was nothing left. Jeff understood how it worked, but that didn't change the way he felt. "Thanks," he said after too long of a pause. "You're pretty patient yourself."

Genghis yawned, climbed to his feet, and gracefully stretched. Jeff expected him to crawl up onto his chest. It was what Genghis normally did. Unfortunately, Genghis often tried to knead exposed flesh, ignoring the blanket. It was painful., but it was worth it. Jeff enjoyed spending time with his cat. Now that Thor was gone, Genghis was the oldest.

Maureen sang quietly. "The rumbles and the snorts, the rumbles and the snorts, all hail lord bunny-fur, the rumbles and the snorts." It was a silly song, but they both enjoyed it. It was based on Lord Rumblesnort Bunny-Fur, one of Genghis' many nicknames.

Jeff smoothed out the blanket, and lightly tapped his chest. Genghis immediately responded by climbing up. As expected, the cat quickly began to knead. It didn't take long before Genghis emitted a series of rumbling, snorting purrs.

"Watch out, he's got you now," said Maureen.

"I know, but it's fine," said Jeff. "Dinner isn't for another half hour. I've been gone so often with work lately, I'm not going to deny Genghis his cuddle time."

"I need cuddle time, too, you know." She said it gently. It wasn't a rebuke.

Jeff stretched his other arm, inviting Maureen to snuggle against him. "Come on over. I'm sure Genghis will graciously accept your pets."

"Oh, such an honor."

Jeff rested his head against his pillow as he waited for his wife to snuggle into position. "Have you noticed that they've been sleeping a lot lately? Not just Genghis. All the cats."

"I did," said Maureen. "I've been keeping a close eye on them, ever since that night where we couldn't get them to wake up."

"Yeah, that was strange." Jeff didn't want to admit how much he panicked that night. There were only so many losses he could take. Losing the cats would have ripped his heart out. He knew he was being irrational. All the cats woke up, and even if they didn't, he would have gotten them to a vet. Everything turned out fine. They were never in any danger.

"Who knows what they were doing?" said Maureen as she carefully scratched Genghis' cheek. "Maybe they were secretly gathering in their dreams, teaching Chairman Meow how to hunt chipmunks and cast spells. He strikes me as a wizard."

Genghis glared at Maureen before nipping her hand.

"Okay, Genghis. Let me know when you want me to pet you again."

Jeff carefully drew his hand along Genghis' fur, making sure it was alright to keep petting the cat. He kind of liked the concept of all the cats meeting in their dreams, hunting spectral chipmunks in a magical world. Maybe after he finished writing the series he was working on, he'd pitch it to his publisher.

ACKNOWLEDGEMENTS

Since this is an oddly autobiographical fantasy novel about cats, I think I probably should acknowledge the cats.

Genghis Khan is the oldest, and he regally holds the position of top cat within the house. I suspect the breeder gave him to us a few weeks earlier than normal for a kitten, but it turned out for the best. I'm certain he is the smartest cat I've ever met. He learned our schedules, down to the minute, and often shadows us throughout the day.

Alexander the Great is the second oldest, and despite topping the scales at well over twenty pounds, he is quite the athlete. Alex enjoys climbing trees, and has even climbed onto the roof of the house. He is every bit the gentle giant I've portrayed in the book. If anything, I suspect I failed to illustrate the depths of his kindness.

Justin Trudeau is a very complicated cat. While the rest of the cats respect the flimsy fence I built around the yard, Justin views it with mild derision. He flaunts his ability to climb it and frequently explores the neighborhood. We make him wear a GPS collar and track him on our phones. Fortunately, he rarely stays out for more than a few hours at a time. I suspect, as he grows older, he'll stay inside more often. He truly loves holding paws with Maureen. It's adorable.

And that brings us to the kitten, Chairman Meow Tse Tung. I started getting ideas for this story after feeding him brisket. He couldn't get enough of it. Whenever I went near the kitchen, he followed me, begging for brisket. As I am a sucker for cats, he was fed often.

Maureen started adding a voice to Chairman Meow. Whenever the kitten succeeded in begging for food, she cheered, "I cast summon brisket!"

And that's how this story came to be.

ABOUT THE AUTHOR

A classical pianist, marginal triathlete, and fledgling chef, Jeff Konkol is permitted to live in the sprawling home of four very large cats. He published his first tabletop RPG, *Of Gods and Men*, in the early 90s and has been running games within that setting ever since. He recently returned to writing with the hope of sharing those stories with a wider audience.

Other Titles by J.R. Konkol

REBIRTH OF THE FALLEN SERIES

Citadel of the Fallen

Gathering of the Fallen

Flight of the Fallen

The Crumbling City

The Sundered City

The Fallen City

Crumbling Alliances – Coming Soon

Note from J.R. Konkol

Word-of-mouth is crucial for any author to succeed. If you enjoyed *The Guardian's Gambit*, please leave a review online—anywhere you are able. Even if it's just a sentence or two. It would make all the difference and would be very much appreciated.

Thanks!
J.R. Konkol